My Name Is
Angel

Anthony Scola

ISBN 978-1-68570-526-8 (paperback)
ISBN 978-1-68570-527-5 (digital)

Christian Faith Publishing
832 Park Avenue
Meadville, PA 16335
www.christianfaithpublishing.com

Printed in the United States of America

Contents

PART 1

Angel and the Pastor

My name is Angel. I spend a lot of time wondering about why I was given that name. Not that I mind my own name, but it is like naming a dog, "Dog," or a human, "Human." On the rare occasion when I must introduce myself, I say, "I'm Angel." And a typical response would be "Oh my, and what's your name?" or they may say, "Is that really your name, or is that what you are?"

More specifically, I am a guardian angel. As far as angels go, I'm not very powerful, but I'm powerful enough. I have a set of average defensive weapons, of average strength. I have a shield, a sword, a scabbard, a weapons belt, and shackles.

I am gifted with very strong wings. I can move at the speed of sound, faster if required. Presently, I'm on a long-term assignment. It's been uneventful. For the last 350 years or so. I've been guarding a building. When I got here, the building was a small place of worship, but it has withstood a number of changes. Today, it is a church with a small graveyard, a very tall steeple, and a bell tower. Inside is a modest worship area, a balcony, and a basement. Oh, yes, and a cellar. The worship area consists of an altar, a pulpit, pews, stained-glass windows. There is also an adjacent parsonage. Its occupants are under my protection. It is presently called the First Covenant Church of Charleston.

This unremarkable building has survived as a public meeting hall, an Anglican church, and a Reformed house of worship. Like

1

Charleston itself, this place has gone through an interesting history. The town and this building were founded by King Charles II of England, around 1670. He established the town to honor his father King Charles I. It has survived the American Revolution, slavery, the Civil War, the emancipation of slaves, and countless other noteworthy events. I've kept this church and its various parishioners safe through time, tempest, and turmoil.

I've been faithful to the Almighty and obedient to the Council. I have been successful in the performance of my job assignment, but I have never had to directly battle the enemy.

Until now.

*****

Pastor Harold T. Washington viewed his new home through tearful eyes. The white steepled 350-year-old church seemed to materialize right out of a history book. The bell tower was at least 50 feet tall. The worship center had a capacity for over a thousand people including the balcony. The pipe organ in the balcony was gorgeous. The elevated pulpit, at stage right, had a staircase leading up to it from the altar area. The choir section at the back of the altar area and the balcony area could accommodate over a hundred choir members. Stage left was occupied by a beautiful black lacquered grand piano. The building had once been an Anglican church. One could see the inlays patching the floor where the communion rail posts were. The front of the altar area had been pushed back with the removal of a wall where the sanctuary, altar, and sacristy were. Presently, it is a Protestant church. The choir section is behind the pulpit. Above the choir area hung a fourteen-foot hand-hewn wooden cross. Under the cross is a Bible verse displayed in golden letters: "2 Cor. 12:9 My Grace is Sufficient for Thee."

Harold deduced, by the looks of the property and the salary offered to him, a young pastor and his wife, that the parishioners had money and that they believed in tithing.

When Harold was interviewed by the elders' search committee some six weeks ago, he didn't think he had a chance to land the position. He was barely over thirty, black, newly married. His wife, Annie, was white. Her parents were Jewish and New Yorkers. He had just earned his doctor of divinity from Alabama Theological Seminary, but as pointed out to him by the elders, he had no practical pastoring experience. His original desire was to teach at the seminary, but that plan hadn't worked out.

The twelve elders, bless their souls, were white, over fifty years old, wealthy Charlestonians. The doctrine of the church is Bible believing, conservative, independent, Presbyterian-ish. Baptism is required for membership, and membership is required for any volunteer serving position. The Bible is held in the highest esteem, in its original language, it is believed to be the literal, inspired, plenary, inerrant word of God.

But Harold noticed that there was a lack of energy in the place. Calling the church stodgy may have been too harsh, but serving the community was done only at arm's length. Wednesday night prayer meetings were ill attended. Youth groups were nonexistent. Worship songs were sung solely from antiquated hymnals. The church staff consisted of a secretary, two janitors, and a volunteer worship leader. The elders rotated the preaching duties on a temporary basis since their previous pastor had recently died. Sunday school was taught one hour and fifteen minutes before worship service by volunteers down in the separate classrooms in the basement. There was no assistant pastor, no youth pastor, no adult education pastor, no visitation program, and no community outreach program. The church had been pretty much a one-man show with a dozen elders, their wives, and about a dozen faithful volunteers.

This was Harold's church now, his home, his ministry, his people. God had laid a burden on his heart to revitalize this place with prayer and the power of the Holy Spirit.

*****

It started during the first Wednesday Night Prayer Meeting. After prayer, Pastor Washington faced the cross at the front of the church. He began to sing the "The Old Rugged Cross," a cappella.

The two dozen or so faithful in attendance joined in on the second verse. They sang it again.

Then there was silence.

Pastor Washington turn to the people and said, "And I love that old cross where the dearest and best for a world of lost sinners was slain... For a world of lost sinners was slain."

He looked around. "For you, for me, for the people of Charleston. All the people. For the five hundred homeless out there, for the thousand more who have no church affiliation, for black people, for white people, for the young, for the elderly, for those in hospitals, for those living alone without anyone to care for them and for those in nursing homes, for the lonely, for the single moms, for the lost dads, for the disenfranchised, for the franchised. And what are we doing about it? Jesus was slain for us all, for them all.

"I read scripture and it tells me the 'haves' need to minister the 'have nots,' the 'provided for' need to minister to the 'unprovided for.' The 'found' need to go out and find the 'lost.' If Jesus did it, we should do it. I am not going to tell you all what to do. I'm going to let the Holy Spirit tell you all what to do. What is He telling you?"

He waited. Focusing his steel gray eyes on every person seated before him, one by one. Saying, "You, you, and you." Finally, he said, "I'm listening."

*****

Angel noticed more activity in the church as of late. The Wednesday morning Bible study ladies began preparing meals for the homeless in the church's basement kitchen. They were calling it Lunch and Such. The church doors were opened at 11:30 a.m., and all were welcome to join Dr. Harold T. Washington for a devotion and a hot meal.

In a month, twenty people filed into the basement cafeteria space for a devotion and lunch. Many lingered past lunchtime for prayer with the pastor and the ladies.

In two months, there were fifty, and by the third month, over a hundred filled the basement and spilled over into the worship center.

The effort became larger than the ladies could handle. More volunteers became involved, and soon some of the cooking duties were offloaded to one of the elders' catering business.

Then things began to escalate. Angel watched as his own workload boom. The Wednesday afternoon regulars began to show up for Sunday service. The balcony began to fill. Within six short months, monitors where placed in the basement, now called the Media Center. Chairs were set up every Sunday morning for the additional attendees.

Before a year was up, everything doubled. Mobile units were set up in the church parking lot as classrooms for Children's and Teen's Ministries were added. An assistant pastor was hired, along with a music and worship pastor. Modern worship songs were added to the standard hymns. There were plans for instituting a Thursday Night High School Ministry. Pastor Washington began teaching advanced Bible studies on Sunday evenings.

Angel couldn't help but wonder if he was able to keep up to all this added activity and still protect all these people without additional help.

*****

On a Friday evening around midnight, almost a year to the day when Pastor H. T. Washington, DDiv, became pastor of the First Covenant Church of Charleston, Angel began to feel uneasy. He circled the building. He searched the parsonage. He flew up to the steeple. He went down to the Worship Center. From there he checked out the lower level. He skirted around the borders of the property. Finally, he scanned the cemetery. Then he saw something or someone move. It wasn't a man or an animal.

He drew his sword, swung his shield forward from between his wings. In a flash, he stood in the center of the church cemetery.

"Who goes there? Show yourself," Angel whispered.

"Angel, it's me" came the reply.

Angel was stunned. At first, he thought he had imagined it. A voice from his past, from his memories, from his heart. "Blue?"

He turned toward the voice. He couldn't believe his eyes. She was one of the most beautiful creatures he had ever known. And she had been his best friend for ages. But she was lost, gone forever. How was it that after all these centuries, she appeared now and not more than ten yards from him?

She shimmered like liquid diamonds. She held her sword in the rest position. Her non-threatening posture gave him time to look into her eyes. They were just as he had remembered: the color of artic ice, but warm and inviting. One could get lost in her eyes.

They hadn't seen each other since the Rebellion. Together, they had been the perfect pair, companions, friends, and sparring partners. She was a warrior angel. He was a guardian angel. She always took the offence. He took the defense. She was stronger. He was faster. She was more cunning. His reactions were quicker. They were evenly matched, except for the distraction she posed: her beauty, her eyes.

"Blue, don't, please." Angel began to shake with worry. "I don't want to hurt you."

Blue smiled. "Angel, you know I beat you 7 out of 10 times. Besides, I didn't come here to fight you."

"Then, why? After all these years, why are you here?" Angel didn't dare let his guard down.

"A favor," she responded.

"A favor? For me or for you?" Angel asked.

"Both, but right now, you have ninety seconds to ready yourself. You have been targeted for destruction."

"Why? Where? Who?" Angel stammered.

"Your pastor has upset the balance, here. It's Minotaur," Blue responded. "Now give me your shackles and make certain he attacks you head on," she responded.

Angel steeled himself as he handed Blue his shackles without question. Angel recalled that Minotaur had one move, to attack head on, so that wouldn't be a problem. Minotaur's strength was unmatched. His hide was impenetrable. He was an undefeatable, mindless, destructive force. If he got by Angel's defense, all would be lost: the church, the pastor, the pastor's wife, the people, Angel himself. Thirty seconds and counting.

The roar came on like a runaway train. Angel positioned himself on the center of the tracks. He evaluated his situation. His speed was useless, his shield anemic, his sword felt like it turned to rubber in his hands, but Angel held his ground.

This may be the end, he thought.

"I'm Angel," he shouted as Minotaur came into sight.

Minotaur mocked him as a low laugh erupted from his throat. "I know."

Just as Angel could see the glowing red eyes below Minotaur's horns, Minotaur stumbled and fell. He rolled toward Angel head over heels. Angel took advantage of the situation and dashed behind Minotaur's body. Angel raised his sword. He brought it down on Minotaur's neck with all his might. In the last millisecond, Blue jumped onto the sword, adding power to its downward thrust. Angel's sword went clean through Minotaur's neck and buried itself into the ground.

Minotaur's head slowly rolled off to the side of his body. Angel had just enough time to see Minotaur's ankles were shackled together. And then Minotaur's corpse and his severed head burst into flames. Minotaur was gone, Blue was gone. Only his shackles remained.

*****

"God doesn't add, He multiplies." Pastor Harold was preaching to a full house, and then some.

The techies at church were now streaming the services for the world to see.

"Mary asked Jesus to provide the last round of wine for a final toast at her neighbor's wedding. Jesus provided 180 gallons of the best wine ever tasted this side of glory. That's 900 bottles of wine.

"God doesn't add, He multiplies.

"Jesus told Peter to throw his nests out on the right side of his boat. Peter had not caught one single scrawny fish the whole night long. But Peter reluctantly obeyed. He netted so many fish that two boats almost sank bringing the catch into shore. A full year's wages.

"God doesn't add, He multiplies.

"The apostles found a boy who had five loaves of bread and two fish, and Jesus multiplied the loaves and fish to feed 5,000 men, not counting woman and children.

"God doesn't add, He multiplies.

"One hundred twenty disciples were in the upper room, waiting for a Comforter to come. Over 3,000 people were saved and baptized that same day.

"God doesn't add, He multiplies.

"Jesus originally selected twelve disciples. From those twelve men of humble means, the Bible tells us that in heaven there will be 'a multitude that no one could count, from every nation, tribe, people and language, standing before the throne and in front of the Lamb. They will be wearing white robes and will be waving palm branches in their hands, praising the King of kings.'

"God doesn't add, He multiplies."

Pastor Washington took in a breath, and the whole congregation exhaled. He slowly looked around at the assembly of the First Covenant Church of Charleston.

"I am very proud of you all. In a good way. The Holy Spirit has done a good thing here, but it's time for Him to multiply. There are 400 churches in Charleston, and hundreds more in South Carolina, and thousands more in the US of A. There is more work to be done. There are homeless that need homes, naked that need clothes, hungry that need food, sick that need healing, prisoners that need visiting, unlovelies that need loving, and the godless that need saving."

He reached in his back pocket and took his wallet. He pulled out a dollar bill and smacked it on the pulpit.

"God…," he prayed, "multiple my dollar, have the people within the sound of my voice, in churches all over Charleston, all over the Carolinas, all over America open their wallets and purses, bank accounts and strong boxes, open their hearts and lay their dollars down. Multiple Your blessings on the world."

Pastor Washington looked around the congregation one more time.

"Who," he continued, "will join me?" He paused for over a minute and ended with a final statement.

"I'm listening."

*****

The Council consisted of seven generals. Each represented a different branch of angels; Guardians, Messengers, Servers, Warriors, Watchers, Worshipers, and of course Archangels. The Almighty assigned the generals to the dais, rotating through all the ranking generals of the Realm. The chairperson was voted into position by the seven members of the Council. They served seven years at which time seven new generals were assigned to the council.

It had been over three hundred years since Angel was called in front of the Council. At which time, he received his present assignment.

Angel stood before the Council once again, waiting for the proceedings to begin. The council members were whispering among themselves for a few minutes before the chairperson called the proceedings to order. The Council Chairman addressed Angel.

"Welcome, Angel, would you please inform the Council in your own words what transpired last evening?"

"Yes, General Eli." Angel did his best to relay the facts.

When Angel completed his report, the council took a few minutes to discuss the matter.

The Council Chairman said, "Thank you, Angel, for your clear and concise report. We have a few follow-up questions. Angel, why do you think Blue decided to warn you about the demon's attack and then ultimately assist in the final blow?"

"Generals, I don't really know. All I can surmise is that the favor she mentioned could be a big one," Angel replied.

"What kind of favor?" the Guardian General asked.

"General, as you know, Blue and I had been close friends since before the Rebellion. I don't believe she would ask me to compromise my own loyalty in any way. But I can't help but feel her own is in question."

"That's a big leap in logic, Angel," the Warrior General commented.

"General, with all due respect, I'm going on a feeling more than logic. She saved my life and the lives of the pastor and his wife. Not to mention the property and everything else you put under my protection," Angel replied. "What she did was no small deed. I'm also concerned she may experience severe repercussions if word of what she did gets out."

"Agreed," the Council responded in unison.

"As for you, Angel," the Chairman General continued, "we believe you performed your duties admirably. And because of your actions, you have demonstrated to us that you are in need of and ready for command. We are promoting you to Guardian First Class. Ten warrior angels will be assigned to you. You will also be issued additional weaponry along with the added strength and knowledge to use these weapons."

To say Angel was surprised by the promotion and added responsibility would be an understatement. He didn't feel worthy of the promotion or capable of commanding warrior angels. He said the only thing that came to his mind.

"Thank you, Council," he said. "To the Almighty be the glory."

"Amen" was their final word.

*****

Pastor Washington's sermon went viral. By the end of the week, over 3.5 million had viewed the entire sermon. By the end of the month, more than 17 million dollars was collected via every digital donation method in existence. Pastor Washington immediately established a charitable trust and installed executors from the ten top churches in Charleston. He would not sit on the board. He would not touch a penny. He assigned one of his most trusted and business savvy elders, Dr. Jim Petersen, to take his place as a trustee.

God had multiplied and then "exponentiated." Harold tried desperately to step out of the limelight. But in so doing, he backed right into the political arena. A groundswell of support was gaining momentum for HTW to run for Congress in the coming election. Harold and his wife, Annie Lynn, hit their knees seeking God's will. Through it all, Pastor Washington never missed a service, a sermon, a prayer meeting. He went on weekly visitations to meet with new church members. He visited the sick, encouraged the distraught, and prayed for healing with hospital patients. He even helped serve food for the Lunch and Such weekly Wednesday meetings. Pastor Washington was right with God.

The local papers picked up on the young pastor, calling him the True Heart of Dixie. Soon the national papers ran articles of their own. He was a welcomed feel-good story from the South.

*****

Angel had no problem deciding what to do with his added help. One angel was assigned to the steeple for lookout. One placed in the interior of the church for the attendees' protection. One walked the cemetery, which seemed to be a favorite point of entry. Four were assigned to the four corners of the property. On a more personal level, one was assigned to Pastor Washington, one to his wife. The final angel was assigned to freelance and travel from station to station at his own discretion or if needed. Angel would survey the hearts and minds of anyone coming near to the property.

Angel now carried a golden bow and a quiver full of arrows, a lance, his sword was replaced with two swords, both fashioned from angel's gold. They were quite literally indestructible. As promised, he was given added strength and the added skills to use his new weaponry. Guardian First Class was more than an honor; it proved to be a necessity. Further attacks were imminent. He would need to sharpen his guardian skills and keep himself on high alert.

Pastor Washington was becoming more active in the public scene. His influence in South Carolina was increasing. Angel considered what it would mean if his pastor went to Washington, DC, as an elected congressman. Could this be why he was being targeted by the enemy? Did the enemy know his pastor would become a statewide celebrity? Was his light shining too brightly to be ignored? Angel knew one thing for certain: he would be tested to his limit. He prayed he could meet the challenge.

*****

"Who authorized Minotaur's attack?" Commander Rasputin asked. His demeanor clearly indicated his intent. He demanded an answer, and if he wasn't satisfied with the answer, heads would roll.

Rasputin was second in command of North America. Like most seconds, he wasn't satisfied with his subordinate role. He strove to be first and hoped he could achieve such a goal by being one step ahead of his superior.

"Sir, we believe he acted on his own authority, sir," Lazar answered, because no one else would speak. Lazar was a high-ranking warrior demon; his area of command was Southeastern USA. The moment he spoke, he regretted it. Somehow, he was now the focus of attention.

The war room was dark and dismal. The tension could be cut with a knife.

"Why would he take such a chance?" the Commander now stared down at Lazar.

For the time being, the Commander was showing remarkable restraint. Normally after a defeat like this, there would be hell to pay.

"Sir, we believe the attack was personal. Minotaur despised Angel ever since the Rebellion. He believed that Angel betrayed his company by not joining them. Minotaur saw this as an opportunity to exact revenge, sir."

Everyone waited for the Commander's reaction to that piece of information.

"Well, while I admire his motives, I cannot agree with his tactics." Rasputin was clearly plotting his next move.

"Before General Dagon gets wind of this, I want you to head up another more organized attack. Lazar, take ten of your most skilled commandos and launch a multi-pronged strike. I want Angel dead. I want the pastor dead. I want his wife dead. And I want that whole church burnt to the ground." Rasputin's eyes were now glowing red hot.

"Sir, yes, sir." Lazar beat his chest in a salute.

"And, Lazar. If you fail, don't bother coming back."

*****

If the Council hadn't assigned an additional ten warrior angels to Angel's detail days earlier, if Angel hadn't stationed the warriors exactly where he had, if Rasputin hadn't ordered a multi-pronged strike instead of a spearhead thrust, if Lazar had sent out a scout before the strike, if Angel didn't have the additional weapons and skills to wield them, things would have turned out a lot differently. But the Council did, Angel did, Rasputin had, Lazar didn't, and Angel did.

The attack was sudden, but the warrior angels were alert and ready. Their fighting skills were superior to that of the demons. Each encounter turned out to be an angel on a demon duel, a one-on-one match-up. The battle was over before Lazar had time to realize what had happened.

Before the attack, Lazar had already decided to destroy Angel personally. Lazar spotted Angel in the church's garden. Angel barely had time to present his shield when Lazar launched a "dark lightning" bolt at him. Angel's shield was obliterated. Angel was knocked back, stunned. Angel was just able to get to one knee when Lazar struck down with his axe, intending to cleave Angel in half. But Angel had both of his new swords crossed over his head, blocking the fatal blow. Neither Angel nor Lazar could release their position without giving advantage to the other.

It was a momentary stalemate. When suddenly, a spear's tip exploded through Lazar's chest. Angel lost his grip on his swords and Lazar's axe came down violently. It was deflected inches to Angel's side, slicing through Angel's right wing. The pain drove Angel to the ground. He felt himself losing consciousness. As he did, he saw flames and Lazar being sent to the pit. He also thought he saw a streak of blue.

PART 2

Angel and the Congressman

"Pastor, it's been two short years, and we're praising God for what you have done to revitalize our church," Jim said. It was their monthly elders board meeting.

Dr. Jim Petersen was the chairman of the elder board. He was a certified family medicine physician and the town's favorite doctor. He was also Pastor Harold's biggest supporter. He was a dedicated follower of Jesus. He came from old money in Charleston. The people of the church considered him wise beyond his years. He often said, "I'm not that wise. I just pray a lot."

"Thank you, Jim, and thanks to all of you here tonight. I want you all to know that Annie and I hold this church close to our hearts. This is not only our church but our home. And the Lord willing, we want to continue ministering here for as long as you'll have us. I have no intention to run for public office or give up my calling. We want to serve the Lord in this place," Pastor Harold assured the elder board.

"Pastor, I believe we haven't made ourselves clear. While we want you to continue to be our senior pastor, we also believe God is calling you to go to DC. You must take this opportunity to influence our government in a way only you can. Important issues are looming over our heads. We, the elder board, have prayed about it and have unanimously agreed that we will support you in any way the Lord leads you. And we believe this is the Lord leading you. This is your home, we are your church, and you are our pastor and hopefully our next US congressman. You are not alone in this. Presently, there are five Christian ministers in the House and two in the Senate. We would like to see one more well-placed Christian help lead our leaders and our country. That person is you."

Harold was flabbergasted and didn't know what to say.

"How long do I have to decide?" Pastor Harold asked.

"Three months, tops." Jim looked Pastor Harold in the eye.

"I know a campaign takes time and energy and money. What's the minimum amount of money needed?" Pastor Harold asked.

"Conservatively speaking, since the incumbent is retiring, about a million dollars." Jim's stare did not waiver.

"Jim, friends, I'll tell you what I think I need to do. I'm going to put out a fleece. If we could raise a million dollars in three months from today, I'll run."

"That's easy, Pastor. The board will contribute half of that today," Richard commented.

Richard Bridgewater was the treasurer of the church. He was a real estate attorney and also came from old money.

"Thanks, Richard, but no. I want to raise the money one dollar at a time. I won't accept more than a one-dollar donation from any one person. We can do that, Richard, can't we?"

Rich thought for a moment and said, "It won't be easy, 'A Washington for Washington.' That's quite a fleece."

"One million is all the people who voted in South Carolina in 2020," Samuel Schumacher said nonplussed. Sam was a CPA and was very concerned about present-day social issues. He was a strong Christian and leaned a little left in his thinking. Samuel's family and their connection to Charleston went back to the 1600s.

"But, Sam, only half of eligible voters voted. That's why it's a fleece. God can manage what man can't imagine. Let's do the internet donation thing. Make it clear that if we don't hit our goal in one hundred days, we will transfer the money to Lunch and Such for South Carolina. Can we do that?" Pastor asked the entire board.

"We can legally and practically do it. We have enough followers. But that's ten thousand dollars a day!" Richard responded.

"All right then, it's decided. A Washington for Washington in one hundred days."

Pastor Harold relaxed and said, "It's in God's hands."

Jim said, "I hope He's listening."

*****

The Seven listened carefully to Angel's report. The attack had escalated the situation to a Level 4.

"We thank the Almighty that no one was lost," the Chairman stated. "And we can see your injury is healing well."

"The enemy has clearly decided your pastor is a threat. And being recently elected to the US House of Congress, we can only assume the situation will continue to escalate. We have the go ahead to protect what is our own."

"Consequently, Angel, we are promoting you to Guardian Commander. A thousand more warrior angels will be assigned to your command. We also believe this has become personal for the enemy. We are strengthening you and your weapons arsenal. We are adding a spear, lightning, a golden shield, demon chains, and a golden lasso. Your speed and skills will be upgraded accordingly," the Chairman concluded.

"Chairman and Generals, if I may?" the Warrior General asked.

"Angel, in your report, you stated that the last thing you saw before you lost consciousness was a streak of blue. And the final blow came from a spear thrust through Lazar's chest from behind him, correct?"

"Yes, General." For a second, Angel saw the "blue streak" in his mind's eye.

"Do you think Blue had anything to do with it?" All seven Generals focused not only on Angel's response but his demeanor.

"I do." Angel lowered his head. He felt he had lost the "hand to hand" battle with Lazar. And if it weren't for Blue, he would not have been standing here now.

"Why? Do you think Blue aided you? Do you think it was the 'favor' thing again?" Warrior General Samson followed up.

"I do." Angel wished he could speak to Blue. He had his own questions to ask her. More personal questions.

"Angel, I am going to warn you. You are treading on dangerous ground. You are aware that reinstatement of a fallen angel is extremely rare. It must be earned. Forgiveness and redemption is not a gift offered to fallen angels like it is for the humans we watch over. The Almighty didn't give His Son to redeem rebellious angels.

"In our realm, one must show complete repentance explaining the reason for one's rebellion and prove one's desire for redemption. Also, one must save a life. One must take a life. And one must give a life."

Angel wasn't certain what that all meant, exactly.

The General continued, "And, Angel, be aware of the possibility for deceit and subterfuge."

Angel knew the Warrior General was particularly sensitive to Blue's recent actions. She was one of his beloved warriors before the Rebellion. Angel believed General Samson never got over the loss of Blue.

"Yes, sir. General sir." Angel felt uneasy, he just wanted to leave the Council Room and fly away.

Angel touched his breast plate and saluted, "May the Almighty be praised."

The entire Council responded, "Amen."

*****

"Good morning, Mister President." Chip Stallworth entered the Oval Office as he had done every Tuesday at 10:30 a.m. for the last two years. Chip was an advisor to the president, his personal friend, and campaign manager.

"Chip." President Joe Kennedy nodded to his friend. President Joe Kennedy was a much-stressed person at the present time. He was used to the pressure and his family was familiar with the rigors of public office. He was the second grandnephew to JFK, and he seemed to have aged ten years since taking office. "Let's get started.

I've got the Korean thing heating up again, and I'm meeting with the joint chiefs at noon."

"It's probably just another effort by North Korea to make you look bad. On a related subject, it's not too soon to look ahead to your re-election," Chip said.

"I'm leaving that up to you, Chip. I trust you." Joe's mind was elsewhere.

"Thanks, Joe. I'd like to take a look at the new congressman from South Carolina, Congressman Washington."

"You mean the Washington for Washington pastor?" Joe looked up.

"Yes. He is strong in Dixie, he's a minority, he appeals to the Christian right and does not alienate the more liberal leaning in the South. He raised 1.5 million in dollars bills for his campaign and won in a landslide victory." Chip paused to let Joe soak it all in.

"Are you thinking running mate, Chip?" Joe turned to look out of the Oval Office window, into the future.

"You know Frank isn't going to be your VP again. His wife just died. He's seventy-five. The demographic is changing. We'll need to carry the South and we'll need a minority or a female to stay relevant." Chip felt he now had Joe's attention.

Chip continued, "Let's get him closer to the White House. Let's pull some strings and get him on the House of Foreign Affairs Committee and see how he does. What have we got to lose?"

Chip had his fingers crossed. It was the right political move. But more than anything, he was enthusiastic about Washington's testimony as a sold-out Christian for the Lord. He sent in his dollar bill even though he lived in Delaware.

*****

The rumble was low and steady. It began to build until everyone took notice. The dark, damp cavern became an unsafe place for any living being.

Rasputin had been summoned to meet with General Dagon. Rasputin met with the General only once before. At that time, the

General literally bit off Rasputin's superior's head for an error in judgment. Hence, Rasputin entered carefully into the General's presence.

"General Dagon." Rasputin didn't dare raise his gaze, from above the ground.

"Rasputin, how did you let this happen? It was a massacre. You lost Lieutenant Lazar and ten soldiers. And you have nothing to show for such an embarrassment. What is your plan to make this right?" General Dagon whispered.

"General, I will personally take care of this. Not one of our enemies will survive," Rasputin promised.

"This has gone beyond you. The pastor is now in DC. He is under the Shadow of Nations' jurisdiction now. He has become responsible for the Congressman. But I'm giving you one more chance to destroy Angel." Dagon backed away, indicating the meeting was over.

Rasputin didn't move. He hoped this meant he survived the meeting.

"Rasputin," Dagon said, "'by one more chance, I mean, your life depends on it.'"

*****

Pastor Washington and Annie Lynn were newbies to these DC soirees. Neither felt comfortable with the political scene and strangers they had nothing in common with. But since God was going to work all this out for good, they would have to embrace the "uncomfortable" at times. The plan was to fly under the radar, have dinner, and gracefully leave.

It wasn't long before they realized, however, that they were the center of attention. This United Nations social gathering had turned into a celebrity dinner. And Harold and Annie were the celebrities.

One by one guests introduced themselves to the Washingtons and asked them the same questions over and over again: "How are you liking DC?" "How's the new job going?" "What inspired Lunch and Such?" "How did you ever handle all those dollar bills?"

All through the evening, Pastor Harold was praying that God's will be done and that God would use them in some positive way. With all that Harold had to do, his job, his sermons, his ministries, and with all that Annie did, they still couldn't help but feel that the evening was a tremendous waste of time. The Spirit had a different thought in mind.

*****

Angel knew that things were going to be different, but he didn't expect it to be this different. He was hardwired as a Guardian. This meant he needed to drive the enemy away from his charge and protect his borders; security and safety were paramount.

But here they were, rubbing shoulders with dangerous people. The city was loaded with the enemy. Thousands of demons going about their daily chores. He assigned ten warriors each, to shadow the pastor and his wife. Tonight, he covered the room and building with another hundred warriors. He scrutinizes every person and demon who came anywhere near the Washingtons.

This wasn't a "Hot War," but it wasn't a "Cold War" either. It was a "Guerilla War." He was thankful that his pastor and his pastor's wife kept their hearts and minds on the Lord. They were in constant prayer to know and to do the Almighty's will. But Angel had to remain vigilant. Things happened so fast that he knew his new abilities could be challenged at any time.

*****

After dinner, the men seemed to gather out on the balconies for some fresh air. Some men lit up cigars and sipped on brandy. Harold did neither.

Annie Lynn took a break and went to the ladies' room area. She sat on a chaise lounge to check her email. A beautiful Asian woman approached her and sat down next to her.

"Excuse me, Mrs. Washington. My name is Eun Jung, my husband is the North Korean ambassador, Sung-Ho, we have been following your journey for years now."

Annie was a little taken aback. She put down her phone to speak to the woman. "Good evening, Mrs. Sung-Ho. I am flattered. This is all so very new to us."

"We are admiring you, no. Please excuse my English, we admire you because you have good for the people," Eun Jung explained.

"Thank you. There is no other reason to be here but to serve our people in the way God desires." Annie always spoke from her heart. She was an open book.

"So my husband would like to speak with your husband. But we are official representatives of the Democratic People's Republic of Korea and we could not easily do so without attracting unwanted attention." Eun Jung's voice got quieter, almost a whisper.

"So I was wondering if you could, umm, fix such a meeting." Eun Jung waited for a response, and so did the "others" who were listening.

*****

Harold returned to the main room looking for Annie Lynn. He spotted her standing with a petite Asian woman and a very dignified-looking man. Annie motioned him over to introduce him to the couple.

"Harold, dear, allow me to introduce to you Mr. and Mrs. Sung-Ho. They, too, are fairly new to their post here in DC. They have some very interesting observations to share with us."

Annie's eyes indicated more than her words. Harold knew he needed to be cautious in his response.

Harold glance at the man's name tag, "Pleased to meet you and your lovely wife, Mr. Ambassador. It seems the ladies have already met and are plotting against us. Why don't you and I go out to the balcony and get acquainted?"

"I would like that very much," the ambassador said.

*****

Angel drew his sword. He steeled himself for an attack. A demon was getting too close to his pastor. Angel signaled his lieutenants to draw their swords and take posts next to Annie Lynn. If this was going to be more than a stand-off, Angel was going to strike the first blow.

Every demon in the room froze. They immediately looked to one particularly stoic-looking demon seated at the head table. He appraised the situation and then signaled the demons in the room. His signal was almost imperceptible; he lowered his eyes and adopted a relaxed position.

The demons' attitude in the room immediately changed. They backed down. Angel and his warriors neither relaxed nor backed down.

*****

After settling in a bit with the ambassador, Harold continued, "I could somewhat relate to your situation. Our own country's history went through a war caused by greed and misunderstanding. One side felt they needed to take the moral high ground at the expense of the other. In response, the other side wanted the freedom to choose their own destiny while taking freedoms away from everyone else. In retrospect, both sides wanted the same thing: peace, security, prosperity. They could have helped each other achieve an equitable solution without economic, moral, or human loss. The lack of intellectual communication led to the bloodiest and most costly war in our history, brother against brother."

"You're speaking of the American Civil War. Were your ancestors slaves?" Mr. Sung-Ho asked.

"To the best of my knowledge, my ancestors came to America as slaves from the West Indies. They were moved to Carolina to harvest rice. They somehow gained their freedom. Some moved north some stayed, and some moved south to Alabama where I am from.

"Our country was built and influenced by a combination of many different countries: England, Spain, France, Portugal, Africa. Much like your own country: China, Iran, America, Japan. But I would add, 'influence' is much different than 'control.' No good comes from one country controlling the destiny of another.

"I believe if you would open dialog with your brothers to the south, you both could enjoy great benefits."

Harold knew the ambassador didn't need a history lesson or a geography lesson. But he also knew there were around 15 million Christians in South Korea alone and that North Korea was in desperate need of their freedoms and the gospel of Christ.

"Congressman Washington, I wonder if you can make that happen. Just Ambassador Soo-hyusk and myself and you." Sung-Ho's sincerity was palpable.

"Ambassador," Harold ensured, "I will make that happen, even if I have to pick you both up in my own car and take you to my Charleston home."

*****

In the next six months, tension on the Korean Peninsula subsided. And an open border between the two governments was a distinct possibility. World markets were already reacting positively. Production of oil, coal, wheat, sugar, and pork belly was increased to provide for the projected new demands from North Korea. But in Pastor Washington's view, the best outcome was that Bibles were shipping to North Korea. They were being delivered by South Korean "salesmen" a.k.a. trained missionaries. They began to travel into various towns throughout the country.

"Joe, this is a wonderful windfall. You are receiving all of the credit for the proposed Korean Peace Accord in the media. There's talk about you being a candidate for a Nobel Peace Prize." Chip was beside himself.

"What about Washington? Is he going to try to take the credit?" the president asked.

"He's really not that kind of person, and besides, it doesn't matter. There's plenty of credit to go around. And don't forget, Joe, you appointed him to the House of Foreign Affairs Committee. It's all good."

President Joe Kennedy nodded in agreement as his attention quickly went elsewhere. Chip was also rejoicing on the inside over an entirely different matter. Congressman Pastor Harold T. Washington was not totally opposed to being considered for the vice presidential candidate in the next election.

*****

Rasputin knew that Angel was now more powerful than ever. He had dispatched Minotaur and Lazar. He had become a Guardian Commander. He commanded a thousand warrior angels.

But Rasputin also knew Angel's weakness. He was a guardian. Guardians don't attack, they don't initiate the battle. Guardians hunker down and protect their charges. Which means Angel was vulnerable to a pre-emptive strike: a full out, full strength, fully sneaky attack that would send Angel into the "forever." The key was to figure out the where and the when. He would make certain there would be no warning and no way to escape.

*****

I was following the jet that was taking the pastor and his wife from DC to their home in South Carolina. I implemented our normal escort; my three lieutenants were along: bow, port, starboard, I took the lead. I had assigned the majority of my warriors between the DC and Charleston residencies. From the plane, I could hear Pastor's and Annie's prayers to the Almighty. Adoration, contrition, thanksgiving, supplication, they follow the same pattern every day. I was thinking about the faithfulness of their faith.

Suddenly, the plane took a nosedive. All three of my lieutenants followed the plane down. I could see it would stabilize, but the plane's dive left me alone and exposed. I was hit, head on, by a powerful projectile. My armor held, but barely. A following volley came from behind. I was hit in each wing. I knew I only had seconds to respond. There were two attackers. As I was driven forward by the impact from behind, I shot two golden arrows at my forward target; he was already nocking another arrow. I hit him once in each knee, but I knew he wasn't finished.

My lieutenants were all over the rear attacker, but the forward attacker had to be mine.

"I am Angel," I yelled.

"I am Rasputin and you are dead," Rasputin responded as he drew his sword and flew forward.

Purely by instinct, I threw my chain. Rasputin wasn't expecting the sudden impact of my chain. His movements were a little clumsy due to both knees being immobilized. My chain hit him head on and wrapped itself around his arm and wings. I had him. I quickly tackled him and was able to slap shackles on his ankles and wrists. He was headed for the pit. I would never see Rasputin again. I was hurt, but I would survive, again. The plane stabilized and landed safely. They attributed the plane's sudden loss of altitude to turbulence. I guess, in a way, it was.

*****

I was settling in at the church steeple looking out over the sea. I was healing, planning, praising the Almighty. When I heard someone approach me from behind. Somehow, I knew this wasn't a threat. I listened for the familiar voice.

"Angel? Are you okay?" Blue asked.

Without turning around, I said, "I'll be fine. Are you here to discuss the 'favor'?" I tried to sound casual and nonchalant, but my heart was racing and I could hardly breathe.

"Would you sponsor me before the Council?" she asked.

I was surprised, but I didn't allow myself to show it. Half of me wanted to embrace her, the other half wanted to draw my sword.

"Have you thought this through? Do you know what you're in for? Are you aware that if your request is denied, you will be sent to the pit?" I asked.

She moved around me, so I could look directly at her. While others transformed into wicked creatures, minotaurs, serpents, dragons, large insect-looking beasts, giants, Blue retained her beauty. Her liquid diamond aura, gossamer wings, stunning blue eyes, belied her strength, cunning, and fierceness. She was an anomaly. Was she a demon or an angel? Was she my enemy or my eternal love?

"I am," she said.

"Blue, the requirements are almost insurmountable. The consequence for failure is the pit. You'll be sacrificing centuries of continued freedom for a small shot at Redemption."

I didn't know where that argument came from, my heart or my mind. I was thinking her safest option was to run. But I wanted her to take the chance and return to what she once was, what we once were. I didn't want her to suffer, ever. I was confused. But when it came to Blue, I was always confused.

"Angel, I know I made a mistake. I should have never followed my company into the Rebellion. It seemed at the time that they were the only beings that cared for me. I couldn't just desert them." Tears were forming in her eyes.

"I cared for you, the Almighty cares for you. Your company doesn't care for you or they would have never let you join the Rebellion. They are evil, selfish creatures whose only purpose is to destroy everything that is good."

This conversation was far worse than any battle I had ever fought. I had been holding back the pain for such a long time. I was in misery.

Blue lowered her head and whispered, "I know."

*****

"The Lord is near." Pastor Washington was concluding his forty-five-minute sermon.

"He is my refuge. The Lord is near. He is my strength and my shield. The Lord is near. I will not be afraid. The Lord is near. I will not be anxious. The Lord is near. He will fight my battles. The Lord is near. He will quiet the storm. The Lord is near. He will meet my every need."

Harold paused. He didn't need a breath, but the congregation did.

"The Lord is near. And I will rejoice in Him. And again, I say, I will rejoice!" Harold's heart was beating with the Holy Spirit's power. "Will you?"

The people were frozen by the intensity of the sermon. No one had ever felt the presence of the Lord as real as they did at that moment.

They were elevated into a heavenly realm listening to the truths Pastor Harold had just shared with them from the scriptures.

After a few seconds, the final question resonated in their hearts. "Will you?"

Pastor Harold would not relent. He stared down his church and finally concluded.

"He's listening."

*****

General Dagon was not pleased. He didn't know who to kill first. He was sitting at a long burnt mahogany conference table. Twelve of his highest ranking commanders were waiting for him to explode.

"We have underestimated the severity of the situation. Angel was a low-level guardian who was assigned to a paltry piece of land with a puny pastor and a pitiful congregation. Thanks to your incompetence, Angel is now a commander with a thousand warriors. He is responsible for two dozen of our demons being sent to the pit. His land and his church have become the focus of national attention. The pastor is now a congressman and may become the next vice president. And thanks to him, we have all but lost control of North Korea!"

General Dagan looked at the commander demons sitting opposite him.

"Shadow of Nations, he is now your responsibility. How do you intend to deal with him? What's your plan?" the General asked.

"Simple, he must be destroyed. He won't stop, he won't turn, he won't fall short, he won't fail. I don't know what his ultimate purpose is, but it won't be realized. He must die."

Shadow's reptilian jade-colored eyes never blinked, his head never looked up, his forked tongue tasted the air in the room, searching for dissenters. There were none.

Shadow concluded, "And I will do it."

"You have my full support," General Dagon said. "Whatever, whoever you need, you've got it."

Shadow looked the General in the eye. "I won't need a thing. If I have to drag him into the pit myself and Angel along with him, I'll do it," Shadow responded.

Dagon knew the Shadow of Nations was the next in line for his position as the General of the North American Command. This was a two-edged sword, with both edges directed at Shadow.

If Shadow failed, his closest competitor would be eliminated. If Shadow succeeded, the General would take the credit and possibly a promotion.

This may not be a disaster after all, he thought.

PART 3

Angel and Blue

"Angel, are you sponsoring this demon?" the Council Chairman asked.

Angel couldn't believe this was happening. Not too long ago, Blue was as good as dead to him; now he was here representing her before the Angel High Council.

"Yes, Chairman, I am."

"And what is her request?" they queried.

"Redemption," Angel stated short and to the point.

"And why should we consider her worthy?" the Warrior General asked.

This was the tipping point. He never thought he would be presenting any case before the council, much less a "Redemption" case for a demon, much less for Blue.

"She, that is, Blue, has demonstrated to me that she is sincere in her desire to repent and to make retribution for her deeds and to fulfill the requirements for Redemption as set forth by the Almighty."

"Would you care to elaborate?" the Warrior General asked.

"Yes, General, on one occasion, Blue warned me before a deadly attack was launched against me by Minotaur. Blue, without thought to her own safety, shackled Minotaur as he charged me. Blue then assisted me in my final blow, beheading Minotaur. On the second occasion, Blue saved me from being decapitated by Lazar by driving a spear through his heart." Angel waited for a response from the Council.

"How do you know that what she did isn't a ploy to gain your trust and infiltrate our forces?" the General followed up.

"As you know, General, Blue and I have a history together. I believe I would know if she weren't being sincere," Angel responded.

The council began to consult with one another in low tones. Angel noticed that there were a number of generals shaking their heads. Finally, the Chairman spoke.

"We would like to hear directly from Blue."

The Chairman turned to Blue and asked, "Demon Blue, we would like you to explain: first, why you rebelled against the Almighty. Second, why, now, after all these centuries are you seeking Redemption. Lastly, why do you think we should grant you Redemption?"

Blue knew what she said now would determine her destiny. If Redemption wasn't granted today, it would be game over. She would be sent to the pit for eternity.

"Chairman, Council, Warrior General, I have sinned against the Almighty and I have let you all down. When the Rebellion started, my entire company was ordered to join. I foolishly followed General Dagon's orders without question. Looking back on that moment, I believed there was some doubt in my heart about the correctness of it all. Something didn't seem right about the direction we were headed, but I chose to obey orders as I was trained to do.

"After the Rebellion was put down and we were cast to earth, I knew I deserved to spend eternity in the pit. I did the only thing I could do, follow my General and succumb to my fate. But I resolved to never do any harm to an angel or a human. Although I have been able to keep my resolve, neither did I defend them against the actions of others. And for that, I am truly sorry.

"When I found out that Minotaur was planning an attack against Angel, I only had minutes to decide what to do. I would not make the wrong choice again, no matter the consequences. Because of my..." Blue had to pause and compose herself before she continued.

"Because of my personal attachment to Angel, I decided to stop the attack in any way possible. You know what happened then and following. From that point, I knew my only choice, the right choice was to seek Redemption. I would no longer exist under the circumstances I had caused for myself. I also began to realize how very terrible my sin was against the Almighty. I want, in any way possible, to show Him how sorry I truly am."

Blue could not go on. She fell to her knees, sobbing. Angel wanted to console her but felt it would discredit his objectivity before the Council.

The Chairman turned to the other generals on the council. They made a few indiscernible comments to each other. The Chairman turned to face Angel and said, "Angel, we will need to take a moment to deliberate. Please wait outside with the petitioner."

Angel lifted Blue by her shoulders and walked her out into the antechamber.

Angel waited for Blue to calm down and said, "Blue, I never thanked you for what you did and for saving the lives of all that were under my protection. I want you to know that if this doesn't go well for you, I will retire my commission. I won't be able to continue without you."

Blue looked up into Angel's tear-filled eyes. She couldn't find the words or the strength to comment. Before long, Angel and Blue were called back into the Council Chamber.

The Chairman looked directly at Angel and then Blue. Angel noticed the Warrior General wouldn't take his eyes off Blue. Finally, the Chairman addressed Blue.

"Blue, our Council is split three for Redemption and three against. So it is left to me to make the final decision. First, I commend you for your openness and honesty regarding your part in the Rebellion. Second, I recognize the courage it took for you to come here and submit yourself to our decision. Finally, I believe you are truly sorry for your participation in the Rebellion, and I believe your repentance is genuine. The three other requirements, as you undoubtedly know, are you must save a life, you must take a life, and you must give a life.

"You have saved Angel's life on two separate occasions, not to mention saving the lives of the pastor and his wife. You have taken the lives of two demons and were responsible for sending them into the pit. You assisted in a major way, beheading Minotaur. And you impaled Lazar as he attempted to kill Angel and company.

"However, the third and final requirement has been called into question. Some of the Council wonders if you are capable of giving a life completely and fully to the Almighty. Considering the fact that you had already turned your back on Him during the Rebellion, some of the Council wonder if irreparable damage hasn't been done to your psyche.

"I also have my doubts." The Chairman seemed conflicted. As he paused, it was clear he hadn't decided what to do. He raised his face heavenward, seemingly for guidance. The chamber went silent. No one moved, no one breathed, no eye blinked.

Then, slowly a beam of light shone through the window at the back of the chamber. It grew in intensity until a golden warmth filled the entire room. Just as slowly, the light dissipated, leaving a calming feeling of peace.

The Chairman clearly affected by what had just taken place spoke. "Blue, there is no precedence established in a case such as this. So in a way, I am free to rule as I see fit. I have decided to postpone my decision until further notice. I'm putting you on the track to Redemption. You are to be placed on probation as a warrior angel. You will have complete access to all the resources afforded a warrior angel. You are commissioned to protect Guardian Commander Angel. You are placed under his command. He will sponsor you through this probation period. You realize that he will be held directly responsible for your actions. You will also be placed under the supervision of your former superior, General Samson." The Chairman's countenance relaxed. "Do you accept these conditions?"

"Yes, Chairman, I do." Blue almost smiled in relief.

"Good. Don't make me regret this. You are dismissed."

The Council closed their notes and stood to leave.

"Thank you," Blue said.

*****

"Mr. President." Pastor Harold had no idea why the president of the United States wanted to see him. But even though his president was now seated behind the famous 1880 Resolute desk, a gift from Queen Victoria, he knew his King was seated on the eternal throne of glory. A fact that calmed Harold greatly.

"Congressman Pastor Washington, it's a pleasure to finally met you face to face."

The president stood up, walked around his desk, and shook the pastor's hand.

"The pleasure is all mine. Please, Mr. President, call me Harold. I'd love to tell the missus we are on a first-name basis."

Pastor Harold shook the president's hand. Joe chuckled, breaking the tension.

"Very well then, Harold, I'd like you to call me Joe. And the gentleman to your right there is Charles Lambert. You can call him Chip. Chip is my longtime friend and trusted advisor."

Chip nodded.

"Pleased to meet you, Chip." Pastor Harold walked over to Chip and shook his hand, looking him in the eye and feeling a longer than normal grip. Harold caught the feeling that Chip was a brother in the Lord. Harold had a gift for such things. He never told anyone. It was like the gift of discernment, only super-charged.

After accepting refreshments, they sat on the two couches in front of the famous desk, in the center of the Oval Office. Harold sat on one couch. Chip and President Kennedy sat on the other.

"Harold, I'd like to get right down to it. At first, I see you as a political boon to my administration, being from Dixie and all. Then add to that, your efforts with the poor, your sermons going viral, your overall nonpartisan popularity with the entire country just can't be ignored. Then you went and implemented a détente with the Koreans. You are clearly cut out of the same cloth as Reverend King

33

himself." The president paused, his demeanor turned more serious as he thought of his grand uncles John and Robert.

"That's politics. But I'd like to ask you to help me in an area that I'm not all that well-versed in, religion." The president took a drink of his coffee and looked at Harold for a moment. He was waiting for a response.

"I'm listening," Harold said.

Chip gave a little chuckle at that. To Joe, it seemed like he missed an insider's joke. He'd have to ask Chip about that later.

"Well, we have been invited to send two religious leaders from the US to the Middle Eastern Religious Conference in Jerusalem. I don't think it's a coincidence that the meeting is during Lent/Passover and one week before Ramadan begins.

"Muslims leaders. Jewish leaders, Protestants leaders, Catholic bishops from all over the world will all be in attendance. I'd like to send you as my representative."

Joe took a breath. He had a few more people in mind, but Harold was his first choice.

"May I ask who the other person would be?" Harold asked.

"We're thinking of Sidney Russel, head counselor of the Mormon Church. He's uniquely American, and he'll probably be running for the Senate next year. In fact, you're both uniquely American," Chip said.

Harold looked at Chip for some sort of help. Harold began to pray for the Lord's guidance. This request had caught him completely by surprise. Being singled out by the president to represent America as a religious leader was totally off his radar.

"How long do I have to decide?" Harold was stalling. He meant, "How long do I have to pray and talk to Annie about it?

"Pastor," Chip said, "we need your answer now. I believe this is going to open the door of opportunity for you and the church in general. The world needs to meet Harold Washington."

Harold turned back to Joe. "Mr. President, I mean, Joe, it would be an honor. As long as I'm back for Easter service at my home church."

Harold didn't know the actual dates of the conference, but he wanted to make it clear from the start that if he had to choose between Easter in the Holy Land and Easter in Charleston, he would choose Charleston.

*****

The Shadow of Nations' plan was set. He would wait until the pastor and Angel were in the Mideast six thousand miles from Charleston. A minor diversionary attack on the pastor would occupy Angel's attention. Then Shadow would seize the right moment to kill the pastor's wife.

Shadow figured the three hundred warrior angels protecting the Charleston property would be a challenge, but they were no match for a full-on attack by his demons. Shadow was looking forward to personally squeezing the life out of dear Annie Lynn.

He would then enjoy watching the pastor suffer over the demise of his beloved wife. It wouldn't take long to unravel what was left of him from there. Angel would be humiliated, lost, and vulnerable.

Serpents possess great patience. The Shadow of Nations was the demonic version of an Anaconda. He would wait and slowly squeeze, and when the time was right, he would crush and devour what was left.

*****

Harold thought the American Colonial Hotel was awe-inspiring. The two-hundred-year-old building reminded Harold of his home in Charleston. The Meet and Greet was very stimulating. He made an immediate connection with Rabbi David Levin. Rabbi Levin was a historian and an archeologist as well as a rabbi. He had doctors' degrees in both scholastic disciplines and was teaching at the Hebrew University of Jerusalem.

"We are currently working under the ancient temple site," Rabbi Levin told Harold.

"That must be very exciting," Harold said. "I suppose you've recovered all there is to find by now."

"On the contrary, we have merely scratched the surface, no pun intended." The rabbi laughed.

The rabbi's manner was very disarming. Not at all what Harold expected.

"And what about you? President Kennedy has you very busy, I hear." The rabbi's knowing look emoted his obvious intelligence.

Harold's thoughts flash through the last year. He said, "At times, I think I'm too busy. My fear is that I may lose focus."

"Really, and what would that be?" Rabbi David sounded genuinely interested.

"My calling is to serve the Lord. But that seems to be pointing me down diverging paths: pastor, teacher, community leader, congressman, peace seeker, oh yes, and husband." Harold paused as he thought about Annie.

"How does your wife feel about your multiple callings?"

"Annie? Well, actually, her parents were missionaries for Jews for Jesus, so she fully supports my commitment to God's work. But she says being married to me is like being locked into the front seat of the world's largest roller coaster." They both laughed.

"Well, my wife says being married to me is like being married to dusty old book she can't put down." Rabbi Levin wiggled his eyebrows. They laughed again.

"Jews for Jesus, you know I met Dr. Moishe Rosen. He was a guest speaker at my university. He was a very kind and a very generous man. He obviously loved a challenge. We spent some time together discussing the relevance of the third temple in both the Old and New Testaments. 'Almost doth he persuadest me.'" Rabbi David gave a sly look to Harold.

"Ah, I see what you did there." Harold moved his pointer finger left and right. They both smiled at the inference.

"What is Annie's maiden name?" the rabbi asked.

"She's a Cohen from New York," Harold answered.

"So you met in New York?" Rabbi David asked.

"Actually, we met here in Jerusalem. We were both on the same tour of the Holy Land on a summer break," Harold reminisced.

"Sounds like you got your money's worth. I'd love to meet her someday. Maybe the next time you take a tour of the Holy Land together, you can give me a call. I can show you Jerusalem from a 'deeper' perspective, underground," Rabbi David offered.

"Sounds great, I might take you up on that," Harold said.

"Children?" the rabbi asked.

"Not yet, hopefully, the Lord willing. We're trying," Harold said.

"Well," the rabbi said, "you can't mail it in." He chuckled. "You have to take time for yourselves."

"True, and how about you? Any future archeologist in the making?" Harold asked.

"Two boys and a princess," Rabbi beamed.

"Mazel tov." Harold toasted with his iced tea.

"Pastor Harold, the meeting tomorrow ends at 2:00 p.m. Would you like to join me at the dig site? I'll warn you though, don't wear your fancy shoes or suit."

Rabbi David seemed sincere in his offer. In fact, Harold felt that not accepting such an invitation would be an insult.

"I'd love to. Ever since *Raiders of the Lost Ark*, I've wanted to see a real dig." Harold beamed.

"You have no idea," the rabbi said.

That evening, Harold felt an urge to pray for Annie. There was a heavy burden on his heart for her safety. Harold certainly wasn't alone in Jerusalem, but he was lonely. Maybe he could attribute his anxious thoughts to that. Harold got on his knees and began to pray for Annie.

*****

Angel never intentionally listened in on the pastor's prayer time with the Almighty, but when the pastor prayed out loud, Angel prayed along.

When the pastor got to his room, he walked over to his bedside, knelt down, and prayed, "Heavenly Father, show me your will and give me the strength and ability to do it. Clear the way. May your glory be praised among these sincere leaders in this Holy Land. And back home, keep Annie safe until I return to her. I pray this in the precious name of my Lord and Savior, Jesus. Amen."

"Amen," Angel whispered. It was a privilege to be guarding such a spiritual man, but a seed of concern was planted in Angel's mind. *Annie,* he thought.

Angel hadn't really spoken to Blue since the Council's hearing. Things were very busy with the Pastor's itinerary. Angel had angels scattered between DC, Charleston, and Jerusalem. He needed to talk to Blue.

"Blue?" he reached out to her, knowing she was in the area.

"Yes, Angel," she answered immediately. She must have been miles away, but she still felt close.

"Where are you?" he asked.

"Jerusalem is teeming with demons," she said. "I'm looking for the dangerous ones. I'm also checking out the dig site where Pastor Harold is scheduled to visit. I'm sensing some demon activity here. Did you need something?"

"Yes. Blue, how long would it take for you to get to Charleston?" Angel thought out loud.

"Six thousand two hundred miles? In a hurry, ten minutes. Is there a problem?" she asked.

"I'm not sure. We've got some good warriors over there, but they're not you. Keep alert. I may need you," Angel said.

"You got it," Blue said.

Blue thought, *Just like old times.*

*****

Rabbi David and Pastor Washington were in a tunnel about five meters below the surface of old Jerusalem. Hunkered down in low light, Rabbi David was in his element.

"Pastor Harold, we are nearly below the original temple site. We are looking at the foundation of the western wall. We are using only small spades and brushes, essentially dentist's tools. We don't want to disturb the surface or bring attention to ourselves down here. We have recently discovered some unusual symbols on an old foundation wall that may hold the key to some very important information."

"May I see them?" Harold asked.

"We can't get to the site from here, but we can look at photos in my office," Rabbi David said.

Just as they decided to head up to Rabbi David's office, a rumbling deep down in the earth began to occur.

*****

I heard the rumble and knew Pastor Harold was in danger. I dashed below the tunnels where the rabbi and pastor were working. I saw three creatures cloaked in black, shifting solid rock. I drew my sword but stopped short for fear of further disturbing the tunnels above.

I called for help. Blue and a dozen warriors appeared at my side.

"Don't do anything drastic," I warned. "Don't use your weapons but stop them," I ordered.

"Blue, what do you think I should do?" I asked.

"This may be a diversion. There may be a coordinated attack at the parish," she said. "You can stay with the pastor. I can go and check back in Charleston."

"Do it now!" Angel ordered.

Blue responded, "Don't worry, I got this," and she was gone.

*****

Annie was just cleaning up her breakfast dishes when she heard a loud crash out on the street. She hoped it was nothing too terrible. She began to pray for the Lord's protection as she ran outside to see if she could help.

At the same moment Annie ran outside, she inadvertently left the protection of the church property. The Shadow of Nations sent a hundred demons down in a "spinning spear" formation. The objective was to create a clear path to Annie. Sacrificing the outer shell of demons was of no concern to the Shadow. In fact, losses to either side were of no concern to him. He just wanted to open a pathway to Annie as soon as possible. It should only take minutes to clear the way. It took six. Shadow straightened his body and dove directly toward Annie from thirty thousand feet. He could almost taste her blood. He could almost hear her bones being crushed in his coils. He stretched his body to increase his speed. He had her dead in his sights.

Blue didn't know how fast she had been going. She only knew she got there. Annie was outside of the property line, but she was safe for the moment. Blue looked up and saw the Shadow diving toward Annie. Blue knew she couldn't stop the Demon Commander head on. She drew her sword and shot her body straight up toward the Shadow of Nations. She didn't think he saw her coming. At the last moment, she shifted her body to his underside and thrust her sword into his throat. Momentum did the rest. Her speed continued to drive her up vertically, his speed rocketed him down. Blue only had to hold on to her sword and keep it steady. She used both hands and all her strength. The demonic serpent was cut open from his throat to tail.

The Shadow didn't know what hit him. As he burst into flames, he thought he saw a faint streak of blue.

The remaining demons were routed. Blue looked around to assess the damage. Many warrior angels had been "retired," more wounded. Annie was safe. She was attending to a woman who had swerved her car to avoid an "animal of some kind," who had suddenly appeared in the road. The woman's car hit the light pole head on, but her air bags had deployed. She was shaken, but she'd be fine.

*****

Most of the speakers at the convention touted peaceful coexistence. In the last seventy-five years, an equilibrium had finally been established in Jerusalem. In this divided city, the Jews, the Muslims, the Roman Catholics, the Arminian Catholics, all laid claim to specific holy sites. Each group was protective of their own property and each laying claim to their own truth. Each, in turn, tolerated the existence of the other. There was a united disunity.

Pastor Harold thought, *If no one view is wrong, how could any view be right?*

He wasn't sure he could perpetuate this illogical lunacy. But it was now his turn to address this esteemed group of religious intellectuals. He felt as if he had been given his own little side show in a big circus, and now, he was asked to stand in the center ring of the Big Top and perform.

He was feeling uncomfortable about the compromised position he was in and about the hypocrisy of the situation. He wished he hadn't accepted this representative role.

"Holy Spirit," he silently prayed, "give me the words that will bring you glory."

He took a deep breath, a sip of water, took another deep breath, and yet another sip of water. He decided to lay his notes aside and let the Spirit lead him.

"My esteemed colleges, we have heard a lot of discussion today about tolerance, respect, unity, about future peace, about coexistence and cooperation and hope. And I applaud the sentiment. But I would like to share with you from my heart, the meaning those words have for me."

Most of the attendees spoke English, but as a matter of decorum, each representative had a translator speaking to them in their own native tongue through headsets. Much like those implemented at the UN. A large portion of the representatives had their headsets unplugged or simply laid on the table in front of them. Some were apathetic, some were tired, most only planned to half listen to the representative from America.

"We are all related to each other through God. God is the creator of all, and the creator of us all," Pastor Harold continued.

ANTHONY SCOLA

The Iranian delegate, Mohammad Rajah, looked up from his notes. He checked his earphones to see if they were properly connected. They were. He was hearing Farsi through his earphones, but he was also hearing a dialect of Persian that was spoken in his hometown of Yazd six hundred kilometers south of Tehran where he now lived. This dialect was spoken mostly by the peasants of the area, not by educated imams, such as himself. This was the language of his childhood, his brothers and sisters, his mother and father. He looked for the source of this additional translation. He couldn't believe his eyes or should he say his ears. His language was being spoken directly to him by the American congressman at the podium.

He noticed others looking up and checking their earphones. Their questioning looks told him they too were hearing this man speaking words in their own heart language.

Pastor Harold continued speaking, "We are related to each other through Adam and Eve, our first parents. We are related to each other through Noah and his sons, the only survivors of the Great Flood. We are related to each other through Abraham our father.

"Now I say our father, because some of us are related to him by blood, through Isaac, his promised son. Some of us are related to Abraham through Ishmael, his first son. And still some of us, like myself, are related to Abraham through faith in God. Because it was by faith, Abraham believed God, and it was credited to him as righteousness. And like Abraham, it is by our faith in God that makes us righteous. It is not by our country, our heritage, our religion, our own personal efforts or the efforts of others that we become righteous in God's sight but by our faith.

"We are all the beneficiaries of God's promises to Abraham. God promised Abraham a land, He promised Abraham a seed, and He promised Abraham a blessing.

"We are standing in the Promised Land today. Whatever piece of this land you claim, it is God's land and He has graciously given it to you.

"The blessing promised to Abraham is summarized in His Holy Scriptures and ultimately revealed the Way, the Truth, and the Life to us by the power of His Spirit.

42

"The seed promised to Abraham was not the birth of Ishmael or Isaac, but the birth of His own precious Son, Jesus Christ. He came into the world through Abraham's seed and by the power of the Holy Spirit. The promised Messiah was born here, lived here, crucified, and buried here. And raised from the dead here."

At this point, Mohammed felt like he should leave. He wasn't going to sit still while this American speaker tried to proselytize him. It was against the rules. It was against all decorum. It was against the Quran. But this "speaking" was a sign of some kind. It meant something. This was clear to him. Mohammed could tell it was clear to the others in the auditorium as well. They were all transfixed.

When Mohammed focused back on the speaker, he was still rolling, hot and heavy.

"Christ is our true Healer, Christ is our Prince of Peace, Christ unifies us all, and Christ is our only Hope."

Mohammed thought back to the days he was at Harvard. He thought about a friend he had made when he was there, Jimmy B. Jimmy was kind, considerate, humble. Jimmy often invited Mohammed to come home with him on the weekends for a break and his mama's cooking. Many nights they stayed awake discussing Jimmy's faith and the peace Jimmy possessed regarding his life and his future. Mohammed wished he had a share in that peace.

"Open your heart, seek His face, and call out to Him. For the Lord God said, 'Call to me and I will answer you and tell you great and unsearchable things you do not know.' And Jesus said, 'Ask and it will be given to you; seek and you will find; knock and the door will be opened to you.'"

It was warm in the auditorium, but Harold wasn't sweating because of the temperature in the room. He was sweating because of the power of the Holy Spirit. He stopped took out his handkerchief and mopped his brow. He looked up, smiled, and in quieter tones, he said, "Ask, seek, knock, call." Harold let those words soak in for a moment. And then he said, "He's listening."

*****

The speech was broadcast worldwide on CNN. Annie could tell Harold was nervous. As he approached the podium, Annie prayed, "Lord, let your name be glorified, and for goodness' sake, calm Harold down."

His preaching was short, bold, truthful, even challenging. And per his usual, it was sincere, and truthful. It was a very convincing gospel message. Annie thought, *I hope he gets out of there alive.*

As she watched the telecast, she noticed the representatives of all the other religions looking a little dazed, maybe confused. They were all checking their headsets. But they were also transfixed on what Harold was saying.

When Harold concluded his short speech, no one moved, no one applauded, no one approached him, and no one thanked him. In fact, he just left the podium. It seemed as if the people stepped aside and allowed him to pass. Harold walked right out of the auditorium.

Then all mayhem broke loose. The CNN hosts were scrambling to find out what just happened.

Annie watched intently as she could hear the host begin to ask questions. "What just happened? Was it a trick of some kind? Was it a technical glitch? Someone speak to me. Where did the pastor go?"

Finally, they got ahold of a CNN correspondent from the floor of the auditorium. She was already speaking, "Look, I am Puerto Rican, I heard Pastor Washington's message in person, and I heard it in Spanish. I've interviewed many others here. They all confirmed that they also heard the message in their own native language. I believe we just experienced a miraculous sign from God."

Apparently, those in the audience heard Harold's speech in their own language without translators, without technological aid, without explanation. Those streaming or watching on cable, like Annie, or viewing recordings of his message only heard his speech in English. The initial effect could not be reproduced. Whether people admitted it or not, Harold had manifested the gift of tongues.

*****

"Can someone explain to me what happened?" President Kennedy asked Chip.

"Well, Joe, the most reliable reports explain that the five hundred or so people actually present heard Pastor Harold's message in their own language without use of translators," Chip explained, scratching his head.

Joe looked at Chip like he was losing his mind. "You mean 'tongues'? Snake handling, healing, dancing around, and falling on the ground, that sort of 'tongues'?"

"Not exactly, Joe. It was just the one man, Pastor Harold whom we sent, delivering his message of peace in his own language, English. However, the message was heard by everyone present in their own native language. About fifty-some languages and dialects." Chip couldn't believe what he was saying.

Chip had occasionally heard reports that God used the gift of tongues to aid foreign missionaries to communicate to the lost in a faraway country as a sign to certify the message being transmitted was from God. But this was like a Pentecost moment. It was public. It was extensive. It was bold. Everyone heard it. No one could deny what had happened, not even the Muslims present. Although mostly everyone was still trying to explain it and put their own twist on it. Some were openly calling on Jesus to be their Lord and Savior.

"Joe, we just need to say something. Like we're looking into this unique incident, but we support Pastor Washington in his peace-keeping efforts."

Chip couldn't help but recall the Sermon on the Mount where Jesus said, "Blessed are the peacemakers for they shall be called the children of God." Was he now being a peacemaker?

"When is the pastor scheduled to return?" Joe asked.

"Well, Easter is in three days. Harold is preaching in his church. We could ask him to join us the following week. It's probably best to let things cool down anyway," Chip said.

But Chip wondered if Congressman Pastor Harold T. Washington, DDiv., was ever going to let things cool down.

*****

"His Majesty must not get wind of any of this. He has too many other important issues to attend to."

General Dagon scanned his commanders at the table, which was now one short.

"These little episodes with the Realm must cease. We need to keep our attention focused on the big picture. Since Angel and his pastor have found their way into Jerusalem, we must do our best to have them leave the way they came, clueless. Commander Caiaphas, you've got twenty-four hours to take care of this."

Caiaphas was hoping to escape this meeting without being noticed. "Yes, General Dagon."

Dagon was heating up. The commanders knew Dagon could easily lose what little temper he had. No one dared remind General Dagon that it was his command to destroy Angel and to kill the pastor that led them to Jerusalem in the first place. They knew he could easily incinerate them all with one blast of his demon flame. No one looked up.

"Where is our little pastor now?" he asked.

Sulfurra kept her head lowered, but answered, "Still in Jerusalem but plans to return to the US in two days, sir."

"Good, let him go. And the excavation?" the General persisted.

"The dig is delayed, due to a tremor." Golem smiled as he responded.

"Good." The General pounded the table. "That Jew mustn't find the writings."

Golem knew that it was too late for that. He had underestimated the Jews' tenacity. They had been a thorn in his side ever since Egypt. The rabbi and his team had already found a portion of the writings. At least they had no idea what to do with them. Golem was safe for now.

"There cannot be another temple. We must prove the enemy's prophecy wrong. I'm meeting with the commission on Black Friday and will report that everything is secure."

Dagon's glowing ruby eyes stared down at his commanders. He had them completely under his control. The usurper, the Shadow of Nation, was gone. Dagon still had no idea how that happened. Angel was six thousand miles away when Shadow was defeated. No warrior angel could have destroyed Shadow like that. Angel must have had help. Dagon needed to find out who it was and destroy them both if he wanted to gain the leadership of the General's committee.

"Leave. Go back to your normal duties and do not fail me again."

*****

The Hebrew University of Jerusalem was founded by Albert Einstein in 1918, thirty years before the establishment of the State of Israel. Its Department of Archeology was founded in 1934 and became the Institute of Archeological Sciences in 1967. HUJ was located only a few miles from the City of David.

Harold felt as if he stepped back in time when he entered the lobby of the main building. Artifacts were on display in the lobby, going back to the times of the pharaohs. There were some stones with writings chiseled into them noted back to 1300 BCE. The entrance area was more of a museum than a lobby to a faculty office building. No wonder a number of guards were discreetly situated at the doors and main desk. The guard at the main desk was friendly but business-like. Harold introduced himself to the guard. The guard recognized Pastor Harold and called up to Rabbi David's office for verification and admittance.

Harold found the office on the third floor down a long hallway. He knocked and was surprised when Rabbi David opened the door himself.

"Rabbi David, hello. I was wondering if you had a few minutes to see me."

"Pastor Harold, welcome. Please come in. I was just thinking about you." Rabbi David gestured to the leather chair opposite his large cherrywood desk. His office was reminiscent of a library. Three walls of bookshelves surrounding a singular window that sported 1950s white aluminum blinds.

The shelves were packed with books that seemed to be sectioned off by topic. They seemed to be in alphabetical order, from ancient archeological reference books to Egyptian hieroglyphics to Hebrew theological books. Harold felts a warm vibe from the whole room. The maroon speckled carpet, the pictures on the desk, the hanging pendent lights said, "Welcome home."

"Would you care for a tea, coffee perhaps? And please, call me David."

"Tea would be nice, black, two sugars. And you can call me Harold."

Rabbi David moved over to a table under the window and poured hot water from an electric kettle into a two charming mugs with Hebrew written on them. He placed loose-leaf tea into two small infusers and let them steep. He put two sugars in one cup and four in the other. Both mugs were brought to David's desk. David sat and sighed.

"Harold, the mug there has a verse inscribed on it in Hebrew, Isaiah 26:3. Do you know it?" David asked as he gestured to the mug steeping in front of Harold.

"Thou will keep him in perfect peace whose mind is stayed upon thee," Harold answered.

"Yes, of course you'd know it." David smiled. "Harold, what you demonstrated to the world yesterday was miraculous. I will not deny that. But the content of your message, instead of giving me peace, has taken peace from me. What you did so effortlessly has shook my personal beliefs to the core. I don't know whether to curse you or thank you," Rabbi David said.

"May I speak frankly?" Harold asked.

"I want nothing less," David said as he stared intently at the pastor.

"David, two thousand years ago the Messiah was born. Holy Scriptures prophesied it. God's son came to earth. Just as prophesied by Isaiah, 'a son would be given.'"

"As a sign, the Messiah had a miraculous birth. He was born to a virgin. Also according to Isaiah's prophecy, 'A virgin would give birth.' He would be eternal yet born in Bethlehem, 'A ruler from ancient times would be born in Bethlehem,' as predicted by the prophet, Micah. From that point, God's plan of salvation for the world would unfold like a scroll. Not ten miles from here, the Messiah was sacrificed on the cross, for the 'iniquity of us all,' Isaiah again. He will come again to rule on the throne of David forever. 'The government of us all will be on His shoulders,' Isaiah. And His 'throne will be established forever,' as promised to King David by Samuel. You see, David, your God has 'plans to prosper you and not to harm you, plans to give you hope and a future,' Jerimiah 29:11."

Harold paused. He carefully removed the infuser from his mug and sipped his tea. He looked into David's eyes. "This truth should bring you peace and freedom. 'The truth will set you free,' David. What are those scriptures telling you?" Harold took another sip.

David sat back in his chair, pulled the mug off his desk, and took a sip of his own.

Harold said, "I'm listening."

Like an archeologist's chisel, Harold's words chipped away at David's heart, revealing a faith in God and His Holy Word.

"Harold, I need to think on these things. My faith in the Lord Almighty is strong, but my knowledge of Him may be incomplete. Ezekiel, Zechariah, and Daniel, all prophesy the temple being active on the Temple Mount when Mashiach or 'one like the son of man' comes. I guess this is one of the things that drives me to pursue our work in the tunnel.

"Harold, I believe God has brought you here for a purpose. I would like to get your opinion on what we have found in the tunnels thus far."

*****

At the Generals' Committee Meeting, Dagon sat with the others waiting for Ambassador Apollyon to arrive. It was Black Friday, the day marking the crucifixion. The day that should have marked their greatest victory. The day when the Creator exposed His son to torture, death, and defeat. No one dared mentioned what everyone knew really happened, Sunday was coming.

Then without warning, a putrid-smelling, dark green fog entered the chamber. It traveled around the black obsidian conference table to the head chair. The chair was covered with red-scaled dragon skin that glistened with gold and rubies. Dagon couldn't help but notice the implication. The chair's covering was very similar to his own skin sans the gold and gems. The fog spiraled onto the chair and began to materialize into a green horned beast. His eyes were like glowing emeralds. His jade horns curled upward to points sharp enough to pierce steel. His body was shaped like a two-legged bull. The beast was naked, bulging with large bulky muscle. And when it spoke, the gravelly sound made everyone shrink back in fear. Apollyon was the Ambassador Lord Commander. He was only answerable to the Demon Lord himself.

"We are in command. We are winning this war. We will over-come the Regime. And in the end, all Jews will die!" His words shook the chamber. Sections of the walls began to crumble.

"General Dagon, what is your report?" Apollyon turned to Dagon. His stare daring Dagon to say something that would dis-please him.

"Ambassador, the pastor is leaving Jerusalem tonight. He is crawling back to his church in South Carolina. He is out of the pic-ture. Angel and his warriors are repositioning themselves away from Jerusalem and the tunnels. The Enemy's focus has been diverted from our activity," Dagon reported, gaining a little confidence.

"And what of this mysterious warrior that took down the Shadow of Nations?" a disturbing bit of moisture began to drip from the side of Apollyon's mouth. Dagon couldn't help but envision him-self being crushed between Apollyon's massive jaws. Dagon had no idea how Apollyon even knew about that defeat.

"Ambassador, I am personally closing in on the coward. We believe he was sent from the Enemy's Council. He is either a General or a liaison direct from the Enemy's throne. To destroy him would be an honor and a resounding statement of power from His Majesty." Dagon paused to dry swallow.

"Agreed. I expect to have this resolved as soon as possible and a final report sent to me before our next meeting." Apollyon didn't wait for a response. "Now, what is the King of the North up to?"

*****

Angel stood with Blue before the Council. He was anxious to report what had transpired in Jerusalem and South Carolina. He was hoping for guidance and any additional information the Council could offer.

"Angel, you asked for this meeting," the Chairman stated.

"Yes, sir. You have our report before you. In short, I am concerned about the meaning of the recent activity in the tunnels under the ancient temple site. We saw three black beasts creating a possible earthquake that could have injured or even killed the pastor and those working on the excavation. Blue and my warriors drove them away, but they seemed to flee too easily and without much of a fight which, as you know, was uncharacteristic.

"I realize the Holy City is not my jurisdiction but since the pastor seems to have taken an interest in the area, I was wondering if I shouldn't take a more proactive role. Additionally, I believe the attack was coordinated with the attempt to kill the pastor's wife and take control of our church site."

Angel had said a mouthful. He realized he might have sounded as if he knew more than the Council. He tried to correct that and continued.

"I know Jerusalem is under control and in excellent hands. I was just wondering if I may be more directly involved in what's going on. Especially since I believe the pastor plans to return there."

Angel stopped speaking, finally.

"And what sort of involvement were you wondering about?" the Chairman asked.

Angel looked to his right and nodded to Blue.

"Chairman, Council, permission to speak," Blue inquired.

"Blue, the floor is yours," the Chairman said. Surprisingly, he added a smile to his response. Blue relaxed, somewhat.

"I have kept a very low profile these last few months. I don't believe my former demon mates or demon superiors know of my recent activities." Blue paused.

Samson, the Warrior General, did not smile, but said, "Go on."

"I am almost certain I know who those black beasts were or at least where they came from. I would like to return to their camp and see if I could find out what they were doing there," Blue said.

"Spying!" the Warrior General interrupted. "Angel, you know subterfuge is not allowed. Lying, even to the enemy, is anathema." The Warrior General's heavy white eyebrow arched upward, and his steel gray eyes seemed to grow larger and darker.

"Yes, Warrior General, of course, sir." Angel quickly intervened. "But what if we were able to accomplish what Blue proposes without lying or being deceitful?"

"You're walking a thin line, Angel." the Chairman warned.

"We intend to get in and gather as much information as possible and get out," Angel answered.

"We?" the Chairman asked.

"Yes, Chairman, sir. I intend to go with Blue. If things get a little sticky, I want to be there to help unstick them," Angel answered.

The Chairman looked at the Warrior General and the two of them began to confer with the rest of the Council.

The Chairman finally said, "Angel, Blue, as usual, when the two of you come here, we are obliged to have further discussion. You may go back to your duties for now. We will notify you of our decision as soon as possible. You are dismissed."

*****

"Are these Egyptian hieroglyphics?" Pastor Harold asked.

Harold was flipping through thirty-nine prints of writings chiseled into the temple's foundation walls. Harold was certain that these writings had an important message to convey and a meaningful purpose.

"I wish they were." Rabbi David looked at the prints and shook his head. "We are able to read Egyptian hieroglyphics since the

Rosetta Stone was discovered. But these writings have very different symbols. We're trying everything possible to crack the code. Right now, we're trying to coordinate these writings with the history of the temple itself."

"So what you need is a past reference to help find meaning to these symbols," Harold thought out loud.

"Yes, we're working on that possibility, but we also think some of these writings may be prophetic," David mused.

"These symbols do look familiar to me, somehow." Harold couldn't quite get ahold of the thought or the picture that flashed in his mind. Holding out the prints, Harold asked, "May I take these with me? I'd like to study them further."

"Please, I had them prepared for you. I have a feeling you are meant to have them." David's sincerity was touching.

"I will make it a priority. I will pray that God reveals some truth that will help us both."

"Harold, will you also pray that God settle this turmoil in my heart over what you shared with me about the Mashiach in scripture and how they relate to Jesus Christ?" David asked.

"I shall," Harold assured David.

That evening, Harold dozed off on the flight to DC. He had visions of a sea, a desert, a flame, an Old Testament high priest, performing a blood sacrifice before the Ark of Covenant.

*****

The rock formations of En Gedi are foreboding. They are located in the Judean desert. The Judean Desert is just south of Bethany where Jesus was baptized. Immediately after His baptism, Jesus was led into this desert by the Holy Spirit for forty days and forty nights. This is where Satan emerged to tempt Jesus in a head-to-head match of wills two thousand years ago.

This area belonged to Satan. Demons were allowed to come and go as sojourners while in Jerusalem. Blue knew Dagon had his own lair in this place. As a high-ranking General, his accommodations were suited to the highest of standards.

Many of the rock formations included caves. Some of the caves led to caverns. One cavern in particular had a tunnel that led deep below the surface.

Blue led Angel into this very tunnel. The temperature of the tunnel was rising as they lowered themselves into the earth. Angel's wings were tucked under a black cloak. His golden hair was covered by a hood. His weapons were in his belt and on his back. They were normally invisible until needed. Angel didn't consider this a disguise but more of a wardrobe change. Blue looked like Blue.

Up ahead, Angel noticed a red glow. As they approached the source of that glow, Angel saw a giant beast sitting in front of an entrance. The beast appeared to be sleeping. On his lap was a huge scimitar. Blue whispered to Angel, "If you have to say anything, grunt."

They came to a halt about five feet from the giant and the entrance.

The giant slid his one eye open and said, "I thought I smelled you, Blue."

Blue smiled and said, "Saber, I see you haven't lost any of your charm."

"Well, things had been a little quiet down here. I guess that's going to change now." The beast closed his eye.

Blue didn't say another word and walked into the camp. Angel followed closely behind.

"The best way to get the information we need is to walk around from group to group," Blue suggested. "Most of these demons here are bored and itching for a fight. They'll say anything, at any time, to anybody. If you have to say anything…"

Angel injected, "I know, grunt."

The first group Blue and Angel walked up to were sitting around a campfire. One of the demons said, "How do we know it exists if we can't find it?"

Another demon answered, "Because if it didn't exist, we wouldn't be looking for it."

"That makes no sense," the first demon responded.

A third demon chimed in, "Look the important thing is, no one can find it."

Still a fourth demon asked, "I got to ask, what are we looking for?"

They all froze, stared at the fourth demon, and they all burst out laughing.

"What did I say?" he added.

Blue signaled Angel to move on. They turned a corner around a huge rock and came face to face with the three demons in black that they had seen below the tunnels at the Temple Mount. Blue saw their expression and knew she had been recognized.

In a flash, Blue sunk her stiletto knife into the first demon's rib cage. Angel grabbed the second, as she tried to escape and thrust his sword through her back. The third lost his head to Blue's sword. In less than ten seconds, the three demons burst into flames and were gone.

Blue quickly looked around to see if anyone had noticed. No one did.

Blue saw a red smoke coming toward her. She motioned for Angel to step away. She moved forward into the smoke. Emanating from the smoke came the command, "Come see me."

*****

The temple was already an abomination. Herod had allowed the Roman soldiers to install ornamentation around its exterior walls. Bronze plagues with the Roman eagle insignia on them and large medallions with Caesar's image hung everywhere. Making images of false gods was breaking a primary commandment, and now those images were hanging on the temple walls.

Marketers and money changers, gentiles at that, were slowly pushing their way into the Court of Israel to gain monetary advantage. Even the proud temple guard was subjugated to the Romans. The Sanhedrin had been emasculated and functioned as a puppet arm of Herod and Caesar's procurator. There had been rumors of an all-out Roman invasion. A complete ransacking of Jerusalem including the temple was a real possibility. It wouldn't be the first time such a thing occurred. The Babylonian king Nebuchadnezzar destroyed King Solomon's temple. Records indicated that if it weren't for the Ghib-bore removing all of the temple's treasures and replacing them with replicas, all would have been lost forever.

The Ghib-bore were the Mighty Men of God. Their singular reason for existence was to protect the Holy Artifacts of Elohim. They were the secret arm of the high priest. They did what he could not. Nothing was outside their reach. They would sacrifice life and limb to carry out their duty.

Since the Holy Veil was torn fifteen years previous, a purple linen curtain was placed in front of the Holy of Holies. But this situation was not tenable. The golden curtain wall had to be repaired. And so secret plans were made to move all the artifacts to safety. Once the repair was complete, they would then decide whether or not it was safe to return everything back to normal.

Six hundred years previous, the entire contents of the temple were secretly moved to Egypt. Now that wasn't a possibility. They had to think farther. The Roman Empire extended to the ends of the earth. They had to come up with a plan and that plan needed to be fool proof.

The high priest called the Ghib-bore to begin the move of the Ark and all the holy artifacts as soon as possible. Additionally, they were to remove all that was in their possession that proved the Christian sect had ever existed in Jerusalem. The plan was to encase the items in disguised chests and move them to a secret city where friendships had already been established.

*****

As promised, Pastor Harold made it back to his church for Easter morning service. He let the choir praise God for twenty minutes, He asked his teaching pastor to speak for twenty minutes. Then he got up and approached the pulpit stairs. He slowly ascended. Thousands were waiting to hear the "Pastor of Peace" preach. He began.

"When a king dies, his kingdom goes into mourning. His loyal subjects wear black, they fly flags at half mast, they burn ships set out to sea, they offer prayers, they author eulogies, and they write songs. Extensive burial ceremonies are planned. Pyramids erected, abbeys, chapels, mausoleums, Taj Mahals built. Statues and paintings of their beloved king are placed throughout his kingdom. A successor is chosen. Armies gather. Political power and borders are confirmed or shifted.

"That's what happens when a king dies. But when the King of kings died, only two men and a handful of women remained to take Him off His cross. But not before His heart was pierced and permission sought to remove His battered body so it would not rot on a cross for days.

"His friends ran from Him. His family deserted Him, and His Father turned away from Him. He was alone. Carrying the sin of the world on His shoulders into death, alone.

"He was hurriedly wrapped in linen, unceremoniously laid in a borrowed tomb. Without kind words said over Him. Without beautiful flowers spread before Him. Without spices wrapped around Him. Without a pillow for His head. He was sealed in a damp crypt. The darkness claiming Him as its own. He was place in a tomb carved out of a mountain. A mountain He created at the beginning of time.

"All was for naught: His miracles, His ministry, His teachings, His disciples, all hope, all dreams, all promises, and all future, lost. Instead of a ceremony on earth, there was a celebration in hell. That celebration went on for three days and three nights. Satan had successfully killed the Messiah and crushed God's plan to reclaim Satan's kingdom on earth, or so it seemed.

"But God had another plan. On Sunday morning, a Sunday like no other, a special Sunday morning, the Sunday between the Passover and the Festival of First Fruits, the Sunday between the slaying of a lamb and the appearing of a lion, the broken King of kings opened His eyes and rose from the dead. Hallelujah!"

Unsolicited, the entire congregation jumped to their feet. A spontaneous praising of the Lord erupted. "Hallelujahs" resounded from the balcony to the auditorium to the lower-level media center, from Charleston to Washington, DC, from the internet to the fisherman's net. The praises of the saints were heard from the Holy Mountain to the pit of hell.

"When a king dies, his story fades into the haze of time. When the King of king dies, He is raised from the dead by the power of the Holy Spirit. And by the same power, He will raise the dead. He died so others can live, and He will return to establish His kingdom forever, on earth, and in heaven.

"Can you hear the angel singing? Can you hear the faithful proclaiming to all the earth? He has risen! He's coming again! Can you hear us in the heaven above the heavens? He is coming again! Can you hear us in hell? He is coming again. The King of kings is coming again!

Pastor Harold took a breath. This time, he needed it. He had tears in his eyes. When he finally composed himself to conclude, "Can you hear us in heaven? Can you hear us in hell?"

The faithful knew what was coming. They began to applaud. They began to cheer.

Pastor Harold finally shouted, "Are you listening?"

*****

Blue entered into Dagon's lair. The walls, floor, and ceiling were hardened lava rock. At the back of the lair, she saw the old sleeping dragon. His tail was wrapped around his body. His head was resting on his front legs. It was blistering hot. Dagon opened his eyes a slit.

"Blue, where have you been?" he asked.

"Here and there," she said. Her mannerism was relaxed and casual. Dagon never saw relaxed and casual when he spoke to any other of his demons. That was probably why he liked Blue.

"Where and where?" Dagon moved his head slightly to face Blue.

"I've been with your enemy," she said.

"And what have you found out from my enemy?" Dagon was interested.

"They have no idea what you're doing." Blue sat down on a large jeweled boulder that was situated in the center of the lair.

"Do they know what we're looking for?" Dagon asked. His eyes narrowed as he focused on her words.

"I don't know what we're looking for," Blue answered honestly.

Dagon laughed. "Blue, you're too much, the Ark, we are looking for the Jews' Ark of the Covenant. We want to destroy it. We want to make certain they can't build their temple again."

"But the Dome is already on the site." Blue wanted Dagon to keep talking.

"Nothing's permanent. Buildings fall. People die. Nations come and go. We must prepare for the worst." Dagon struck a proud pose, raising his head to just below the ceiling. He was playing into Blue's plan.

"Blue, you know a position has opened up on the Committee. The Shadow of Nations was eliminated. You could be the next in line," Dagon explained.

"How did that happen?" Blue tried to look shocked.

"We think it was an emissary from the Realm. I'm personally looking into it," Dagon assured her.

"What would you like me to do?" Blue asked.

"Do what you've been doing and don't get caught," Dagon insisted.

"Believe me, I'll try not to." Blue excused herself and left Dagon's lair. She wondered if Dagon suspected anything yet. She knew he'd find her out eventually.

*****

"Good morning, Mr. President." Chip appeared like clockwork, Tuesday, 10:30.

"Chip," Joe responded, "Good morning."

"First things first, Joe. We've got a meeting scheduled for next Tuesday with Congressman Washington. His live Easter Service was viewed by over twenty million on the internet. That's more people than watch your inauguration," Chip said.

"Don't remind me. Did you figure out what we're going to say to him?" Joe had gotten up from his desk, moved around to the couches, and poured coffee for both of them.

"Well Joe, I don't think anyone will approach him from the opposition. Our real competition is non-political," Chip explained.

"Nothing is non-political. You know that." Joe like to debate everything.

"Yes, you're right of course," Chip countered.

"I just meant we may butt heads with his ministry, his calling. Our pitch isn't going to sway him one way or another. I think, we should make our offer and realize he's going to want time to pray about it and wait until he receives his answer from God," Chip said.

"But isn't that exactly why we want him on our ticket? Pence served under Trump and he was an outspoken Christian," Joe rationalized.

"Pastor Washington is more than outspoken, Joe. He all but single-handedly implemented the Korean Peninsula Peace Accord. He arguably used the miraculous gift of tongues before the world. He proclaimed Jesus Christ as the Prince of Peace in the Mideast. He is in discussion with some pretty important characters in Jerusalem." Chip had become a big fan. He had also viewed all of Pastor Washington's sermons on YouTube.

"Sounds like we should clean up our act before we ask him to join us," Joe kidded.

"Not funny, Joe. He'll be here next Tuesday." Chip was feeling a little guilty about some of the political maneuvering he'd done to get them into the White House.

"Good, let's move on." Joe pushed the conversation out of his mind to make room for other stuff.

*****

Rabbi David knew some facts about the Ghib-bore, but most of the stories about their exploits were unwritten. However, David was beginning to explore the possibility that these Mighty Men of

Valor may have carved coded messages into the old temple wall's foundation.

The Ghib-bore descended from Gideon's original three hundred chosen men. The angel of the Lord instructed Gideon on how to select these men. After they defeated their enemies, Israel lived in peace for forty years. According to tradition, the Ghib-bore became exclusively assigned to protecting the Tabernacle and the Ark of the Covenant. Their singular purpose was to carry out the wishes of the high priest. Under special conditions, the Ghib-bore were allowed to look upon and even touch the holy artifacts of the traveling tabernacle, including the Ark. Their goal was to protect and preserve all that was holy.

David was sitting in his office, trying to identify the connections between these stories and the mysterious carvings. His ultimate objective was to determine if the Ark of the Covenant still existed. And if it existed, to find it.

David's phone rang. "Hello."

"Rabbi David, it's Harold. How are you, my friend?"

The phone connection was good, but the reception had a slight delay.

"I'm good, Harold. What can I do for you?" David asked.

"This may be nothing, but I wanted to let you know of a dream I had on my way back home." Harold explained.

"Harold, if you think it is relevant, then I'm sure it is," David assured.

"It's a bit jumbled, but I dreamt of men fighting over the treasures from the Temple. They traveled over land and sea. There were men trekking across a desert with a loaded caravan. I think the temple carvings your people found relate to the period of time from Moses to Joshua and then from Solomon to Herod," Harold said.

"That's good, Harold. We think we've isolated some symbols to mean 'seas,' 'rivers,' and possibly 'desert,' 'tent,' and 'tabernacle.' We're making headway," David posited.

"I'll continue to study the prints from my end. I will continue to pray for your project and you," Harold said.

"Good, Harold, thank you for your efforts and your prayers." David signed off.

David thought about what Harold told him. He recalled that in ancient times holy men of God were guided by dreams and visited by angels. Could such things happen today? On second thought, had they already?

*****

I was trying to look as normal as possible. That is, as normal as a Guardian Angel First Class could look in a demon camp, hundreds of feet below the desert floor. I was leaning against a stalagmite when Blue spoke to me from the other side, "We need to move out. Follow behind me, but don't make it appear that we're together. They may be following me."

We left through the same gate we entered. A different beast was guarding the way. We spiraled our way up to the desert and headed back to the US.

That's when we realized we were being followed.

"Blue, you see them, right?" We were halfway across the Atlantic.

"We've got six on our tail. Fox and Hound?" she asked.

"I'll be the fox this time," I said, as I instantaneously flew straight up vertically. All six demons chose to chase me. Demons are easily drawn into a chase. They are always ready to prove that they are faster than the next demon. Plus they hadn't determined we were lethal yet. Apparently, their intent was to follow us, not destroy us. We had no such intent.

As the string of demons spread out chasing me from fastest to slowest, Blue came up from behind. She sent the last to the pit in flames with an arrow straight though his heart. Before any of them noticed what happened to "poky," Blue cut the head off of the next in line.

This drew the attention of the fourth in line, who turned to face her.

The first three demons were mine. Without slowing down, I shot two arrows through the head of the first. I threw my spear through the heart of the second and engaged the third in hand-to-hand combat.

I glanced at Blue to see if she needed help. She didn't. Since my spear had skewered my second opponent, we were each left with a single demon to dispatch.

Fortunately for us, the demons following us were not very fast or smart or good fighters.

I drew my twin swords. My opponent, who resembled a giant bat, pulled out a chain mace and a double-bladed axe. Those weapons are strong, heavy, and deadly. But they are more suited to a battlefield melee. My blades are light, fast, and surgical. Fast beats heavy. When I saw the bat demon's eyes followed the movement of my left-handed blade, I cut off his head with my right-handed blade.

"My name is Angel," I said has he burst into flames.

I turned to find Blue. She had her last opponent pinned between her and the ocean. The waves proved to be too much of a distraction for him. It was checkmate in three moves.

"Let's go home," she said.

"We must report to the Council first," I said.

*****

The Council consisted of seven Generals: Chairman Eli, an Archangel; Samson, the Warrior General; Jeremiah, the Chief Messenger; Seraphima, the Worship Leader; Debra, General of the Guardians; Raphael, Head of Service; and Joel, the Watcher General. Blue was most familiar with Samson. He had been her General before the rebellion. He now held the one dissenting vote, keeping her from complete redemption, since the final vote had to be unanimous. She was still on probation for an indefinite trial period. Blue had no problem with General Samson's decision since she knew that she would eventually prove herself to be true. Blue still needed to "give a life" to complete the three requirements for redemption. She wasn't completely sure what that would entail, but she knew she would recognize it when the opportunity presented itself.

Angel and Blue were called into the Council Chamber to report on their information gathering expedition.

"Angel, Blue," the Chairman greeted them, "what do you have to report to the council?"

Blue spoke first, "Generals, we believe the information we acquired is important. We will follow up with a written report as soon as possible. We have discovered the enemy's plan concerning Jerusalem."

"Go on," Samson replied.

"They are searching for the Ark of the Covenant," Blue answered.

"To what end?" Samson inquired.

"They want to destroy it completely so that there can no longer be hope for a third temple in Jerusalem," Blue continued. "In so doing, proving the prophecies to be wrong and prohibiting the King's return."

Debra looked up and asked, "How did you find this out?"

"Commander Dagon told me directly," Blue said.

This got everyone's immediate attention. Speaking directly to a Demon Commander seemed an impossibility.

"How in heaven's name did you do that?" Chairman Eli asked.

"Well, he likes me. Since there's an opening on the Committee, he said he was planning on installing me to the Demon Commanders Committee," Blue said. "I told him I was spending time in the Realm and told him you had no idea what his plans were. I also told him I had no idea what his plans were. That's all true. Then he told me his plans." Blue finished; the Council was dumbfounded.

"Sirs, things didn't go quit that smoothly," Angel interjected. "We had a tail following us from their cavern."

Debra responded to this little piece of information, "And?"

"We eliminated them," Angel answered. "I'm not certain if they had been sent or if they decided to follow us on their own. But I don't believe we could safely go back there again."

"That's well enough," Chairman Eli said. "We now know we must find the Ark ourselves. It is written that there will be sacrifice offered in Jerusalem when the Messiah returns. No one knows when that will be, but we do know we mustn't allow the enemy to destroy the Ark.

"Blue, I'm putting you in charge of the search for the Ark. You can have as many warriors as you need. Be discreet. We don't need any added attention. Angel, we believe the pastor is still in the center of this development. Continue your guard and gather any information that may help us find the Ark. This is not over. I believe it has just begun. Great job by both of you. You are dismissed."

Angel saluted and said, "To the Almighty be the glory."

The Council responded, "Amen."

PART 4

Angel and the Running Mate

Pastor Washington had a lot on his mind. His parish and the ministries were doing extremely well. His election fund managers transferred over a million dollars to Lunch and Such Ministries. The ministry had been spreading all across the US. Pastor Washington's Bible devotions books were being printed and distributed to churches all over America.

Pastor Harold was dealing with the dreams he was having. They seemed to be directed toward translating the temple carvings. He was on the verge of something important.

The work as congressman of South Carolina was less taxing on him than he had originally thought. He had to keep up on house bills, try to understand and secure resources to meet the needs of his state, follow up on special interest groups' demands, and to help wherever the need arose.

He could hardly believe the president wanted to enlist his help again. He had no idea what this meeting was about, but he was willing to do all he could to serve his God and his country.

"Pastor Washington, please come in, sit down. Iced tea?" Chip ushered Pastor Harold into the Oval Office.

"Yes, thank you." Harold tried to get comfortable in his new role as a regular visitor to the Oval Office.

"Be anxious for nothing," he prayed silently. "Lord, please guide me to your will. Give me peace. Help me be a light to the leader of our country. Amen."

"Pastor Washington, we're going to come right to the point. In about ten months, we are going to have to announce whether President Kennedy will run for a second term as president. We'd like to be able to do so and also announce our choice for a running mate. The long and the short of it is, we like that running mate to be you." Chip held his breath. He agonized over this conversation all night. He looked at Harold. Then he looked at Joe.

"Why?" Harold addressed President Kennedy directly.

"Well, I'm not sure I know how to answer that. Politically, you make sense. You're from Dixie, you'll help us carry the Southern states. You're a minority. You'll help us carry the big cities across the US, New York, Chicago, Detroit, Los Angeles. You're an Evangelical Christian with warm ties to Israel, you'll carry the non-Catholic Christian and Jewish votes.

"But, Harold, it's more than political. Chip here is a lifetime friend. We think very much alike. You are..." Joe paused, "a man of God. I really believe we can benefit from your perspective.

"I've been feeling uneasy lately about some of the choices I've made, politically and personally. I'm not a very good Catholic. I've lost touch with my faith. I go to church when I have to. I've listened to your sermons, and they have got me thinking in a more 'eternal' way. I'd like to have you as a friend and as a confidant in the years ahead. Even if you choose not to be my vice president."

Harold was deeply moved by Joe's candor. He felt drawn to the man. Harold also got the sense that Chip was a believer, though he hadn't spoken with Chip on that level yet.

"Mr. President," Harold saw Joe's reaction to the "Mr. President" thing. "Sorry, Joe. Your words are beyond kind. I would be honored to be your friend. Your evaluation of the political situation is beyond my expertise. I need to pray about this opportunity. Before I could even consider your offer, I'd have to get the approval from my Lord, my wife, and my church, in that order. Even then, I'm not sure you know what you'd be getting yourself into."

"We think we do," Chip said. "Pastor Harold, can I ask you to pray for us right now?"

*****

Ojiah ben Gideon was a direct descendant of Gideon. He was also the Chief Commander of the Ghib-bore. He knew, as he left his home in Jerusalem, that he may never be able to return. At thirty-two years old, he had never married yet he led his extended family through the current hardships of Roman occupation. The high priest Caiaphas was adamant about removing the Ark and the holy artifacts from the temple and replacing them with exact reproductions as had been done centuries before. Caiaphas also had an ongoing collection of items that he had confiscated from the Jesus followers. They were being persecuted. Some even put to death. Caiaphas was determined to eradicate this cult and remove all evidence of its existence, physical and otherwise.

The plan for Ojiah was to sail from Tyre to Carthage to New Carthage. There they had a community of faithful merchants who would house them until it was safe to return to Jerusalem. Their plan, their route, and their prescribed locations were chiseled out in the foundation stones of the temple. This way, the location of the cargo could be documented regardless of any circumstance that would arise.

Ojiah decided to further record their route as they journeyed on. Leaving multiple records of their whereabouts and documenting their route from beginning to end and each stop along the way.

As a final precaution, they used a coded language developed by their ancestors in Egypt, incorporating Egyptian symbols and ancient Hebrew. Only the high priest and the Ghib-bore knew of the code and of its existence.

He had ten men in his group with ten more disguised travelers following close behind. Each port of call and way station was pre-arranged. They and their cargo were well protected. They were on a holy mission protected by Elohim and his angels. His company of men would stay with their precious cargo for as long as necessary. They would adapt, assimilate, and protect until called to return.

Gabriel was the archangel responsible for the protection of the cargo. He was one of the twelve. They were the greatest angels in the Almighty's army. Michael the archangel was assigned to protect the Messianic bloodline from the garden to the Kingdom. Gabriel was assigned to the protection and the success of the Ghib-bore. Only Michael and Gabriel knew of their mission and held that knowledge safely until it was to be revealed.

*****

Blue asked Angel to meet her in their "secret place" at sundown. Angel knew that only something extremely important would have drawn her away from her new assignment. The hidden mountain in the Andes was secluded, unreachable by man, over twenty thousand feet high. The air was cold and crisp, and from its peak, an angel could see the panorama of half of the world.

It only took minutes to get there, but the place seemed worlds away. Angel loved the time he spent there with Blue in the past. It had been centuries since they last met in their secret place. They had pledged "forever" together, there. He hadn't been back since.

Blue was waiting for him. "Do you remember the last time we met here?"

"I do," Angel said.

"Me too, and I meant every word. I need to apologize to you for leaving. It's all a blur to me now, but I was under a strong influence from Dagon. I have no excuse. I'm sorry. Can you ever forgive me?"

"I do," Angel said.

"I feel like I've ruined the most important thing in my life. No one could go through what I put you through and still love me. I can't see how things can go back to the way they were between us."

"I do," Angel said. He took Blue in his arms and did something he had never done with any other creature, human, or angel. He wrapped his wings around her. When angels embraced in this way, there is an intimacy that surpasses any kind of human connection.

Their beings meld: minds, hearts, and spirits. They became true soul mates.

They stayed together all night. At sunrise, Blue thought out loud, "Don't you think it's strange that no one knows where the Ark of the Covenant is? I mean we have Watchers, Archangels, Guardians, someone had to have seen what happened to the Ark. Not even the demons know and they're everywhere. Not to mention the fact that the Almighty knows. He could reveal its location at any time."

"I guess it's not time. I know what I'm commanded to do. You know what you're commanded to do. Things always have a purpose, and that purpose is always meant for good. Just keep looking," Angel encouraged.

"Oh, I will. And I will find it. And I will find out who's hiding it and why."

Blue was encouraged by Angel's understanding and commitment to her. She had the freedom to be herself again, come what may.

Angel felt Blue was about to leave. He touched her shoulder. She turned around and looked intently into his golden eyes.

"Yes?" she said.

"You will always be my Running Mate."

She smiled, and with tears in her eyes, she said, "And you will always be my angel."

He smiled as she flew away.

*****

Demons feel like they're in a constant state of falling. Like rocks feel gravity, demons are being pulled down to the inevitable destination of loss. This feeling, more than any other influence drives their desire to destroy anything and everything in their path, even each other.

Gog, the King of the North, was responsible for the destruction of more Jews than any other factor in history. Babylon, Rome, Spain, Germany, Russia, Iran, and all of the countries of the Mid-East were pawns in his hands. Twelve million Jews in total, killed. Yet the chosen people of God survived and thrived. They re-established their nation, possessed Jerusalem, poised themselves to build a temple. But the greatest defeat of all for the King of the North was the birth and resurrection of the King of kings.

Gog had one goal now, to block the return of Israel's Anointed One. If he could destroy the Jews, destroy Jerusalem, stop the building of their temple, then all hope would not be lost. He alone would rise to power above Dagon, the kings of the south, east, and west, all the commanders and generals and even Apollyon. The Demon Lord would have no choice but to install him as his second in command. He would become greater than the Ambassador. Without the return of the King of kings to Jerusalem, their kingdom on earth would reign forever.

"We need a war," Gog addressed his strategic committee. "We need the temple site destroyed, Jerusalem ruined, and the Jews dead. How does this esteemed committee propose we do that?"

"Your Lordship, we always have terrorists. They could start a bombing spree. The trigger-happy Jews are sure to respond," Grisly proposed.

"And world opinion would support the Jews and grant them whatever they demanded. It would be a disaster," Gog dismissed the suggestion with a wave of his claw.

"Why don't we just take matters into our own hands and crush them all, Jews, Christians, Muslims, the whole thing?" Grizella asked.

"You think I haven't tried? The Restrainer won't allow it."

Frustration began to turn his black bear-like fur red, not ever a good sign.

Magog sat in silence. He waited for the fools on the committee to humiliate themselves. He finally said, "Why do we have to do anything?"

All eyes turned to Magog. He was the most hated and the most feared demon in the North, except for the king himself.

"Magog, nice of you to join in on the conversation. Please elaborate," his king said.

"We know the Jews must build their temple on Mount Moriah. This spot is taken. Let's stir up both side of the border to fight over the location. The Jew want the Dome down. The Muslims want it protected. We could spread the rumor that the Jews are ready to move against the Dome. We can even suggest they found the Ark of the Covenant." Magog looked around the table. "Then we bomb the Dome. War would be the only option, and it would be justified by the world."

Everyone looked at the king to gage his response. Gog stood to his feet. He dwarfed them all by his power and his mere presence.

He then said, "Excellent!"

*****

"Dear Lord, I want only your will to be done in my life. Like Moses, I don't seek power. Like Gideon, I don't seek a battle. Like David, I don't seek a throne. Like Jesus, I don't seek what the world has to offer. If you want me to be a preacher, I want no more. If you want me to be vice president, I seek no less. Forgive any evil way in me. And lead your humble servant to the place you desire. Amen."

Harold was on his knees holding Annie's hand.

"Amen," she said.

Unheard by either of them, Angel said, "Amen."

I'm going to need more help, Angel thought.

He called his Warrior Centurions, ten in all, to a staff meeting.

"Captains, I need each you and your warriors to cover one of the following; the parish, DC, Jerusalem, the tunnels, Annie, the elders, Rabbi David, and the pastor, Blue, and me. Watch for the enemy. They are sure to mount an attack on one or all of those fronts. I haven't figured out what they're up to yet. But I don't want to be caught on the wrong side of the country or the wrong side of the ocean for that matter.

"This may not only be a spiritual attack. We should be looking for physical attacks as well. The enemy has many agents, trust no one. The pastor is probably the primary target. We know all things work together for good, but I need this thing to be safe. So far, we have seen spiritual attacks, physical attacks, car crashes, airplane crash attempt, earthquakes, and tunnel cave-ins. I expect things to get even worse and soon. Be prepared, be ready, and be safe. You are dismissed."

He called Blue to the side, "How's the search going?"

"Slowly," she said. "But I have a lead. Have you heard of the Ghib-bore?"

*****

Dagon knew Apollyon expected an answer to the question, "Who destroyed the Shadow of Nations?"

Although someone had done Dagon a service by eliminating the Shadow of Nations, he knew he had to find out who destroyed this powerful demon. He was out of ideas and decided to take a direct approach. He assigned twelve squads of twelve demons to attack the pastor and his wife. Dagon's plan was to create havoc and draw out this unknown enemy.

The attack was planned for a Tuesday, at midnight. This way no one would be praying, the pastor would be alone, his wife would be sleeping, and the guardian angels would be relaxed and off their game.

"Sorrow, worry, anxiety, and tears come at night," Dagon said out loud. He looked at Golem and his twelve squad leaders and said, "Shake his faith, fill him with doubt and fear. Push him to the edge of the hopeless pit of despair. Do your worst."

"Can we attack his body?" Golem asked.

"His body is protected by the Restrainer, but his mind is vulnerable. More damage can be done by one wayward thought than a thousand arrows," Dagon responded. "Now, go!"

*****

It was late Tuesday night; Harold was home working on his Wednesday Night Prayer Meeting devotion. Annie was outlining a monthly "Women of Worth" meeting's agenda. They were planning to turn in early after they finished a late-night dessert. A knock came at the door.

Pastor Harold looked up. "What on earth?'

Annie said, "This can't be good. Dear Lord, help us."

Pastor opened the door and couldn't believe his eyes. Three of the church elders stood on his front stoop.

"Jim, Richard, Sam, please come in." Harold stepped aside and gestured them into the living room. "Annie had just put on a kettle of hot water for tea, can we offer you some?"

"Yes, Pastor, that would be nice, thank you," they each said.

Jim spoke first, "Pastor, I know you might find this hard to believe, but I had an uneasy feeling that you needed our immediate help. I was watching the Evening News, and I heard a voice that didn't come from the TV say, 'Pastor needs your help. Now, go!'"

Jim looked around, at Richard and Sam, "So here we are."

"Okay, Jim. Clearly, the Spirit is leading you," Harold said. "Thank you for obeying His prompting. What is He prompting you to do now?"

Annie came in from the kitchen with a pot of hot water and herbal tea and cookies.

"Wow, that was fast," Sam said.

Annie chuckled. "It wasn't the Spirit's leading, Sam. We already had the pot on."

"Well, thank you, Annie. Please join us," Jim said. "Pastor, can we pray through the attributes and character of God? Your sermon on His power, knowledge, and presence was so comforting. Along with the fact that He is merciful, loving, and our fount of peace."

"That sounds great. Jim, you pray," Pastor Harold said. "I'm listening."

And so, the five of them started to pray. Before long, they opened their Bibles and began to share their favorite verses with one another. An hour later, they began to sing hymns. They were mindful of the nearness of God. They were thankful for His countless blessings. Finally, they prayed the Lord's Prayer out loud.

"And lead us not into temptation but deliver us from evil.

For Thine is the kingdom, and the power, and the glory, forever. Amen."

*****

Like moths to a flame, their time of prayer, of Bible reading, and singing hymns attracted the attention of every angel for miles around. This attraction added hundreds of angels to the four hundred warrior angels who were already assigned to the parish, Harold, Annie, and the elders.

Angel and his warriors had just returned from patrol and descended upon the scene. Angel's presence changed the entire mood of the angelic force. Angel drew his swords. This served as a signal for every angel present to go on battle alert. Angel checked his defenses and slowly turned his gaze to the north.

Golem approached the pastor's residence from the north. He was in command of the attack force that would destroy the enemy's guard and the pastor. At midnight, he sent in the first three squads. From ten miles away, Golem could see his demons in formation for the first strike. He smiled to himself. *This is going to assure my promotion,* he thought.

Lights of flame lit the sky. Golem realized that only demons burst into flame when sent to the pit. Somehow, the element of surprise had failed. He had to do something and quick. He lifted his war hammer in the air and shouted at the top of his voice. He led a full-on charge with his remaining squads. Angel and his warriors met them head on.

Golem blasted Angel with dark lightning. This time, Angel was ready for it and blocked the dark force with his golden shield. He responded with a golden lightning strike of his own. Golem was startled but not deterred. Hand-to-hand combat would be just fine with him.

"Who killed the Shadow of Nations?" Golem yelled, as he raised his hammer for a deadly strike.

"Blue," Angel answered.

Golem was stunned by the mentioning of her name. In the fraction of a second it took Golem to process this shocking information, two golden arrows penetrated his heart.

"My name is Angel," Golem heard as he joined his army in the pit that burns forever.

*****

At Fort Masada, the high priest gave final orders to his son. He was instructed to escape to Carthage and find the Ghib-bore.

Ben Jordan was the rightful heir of the high priest. Although now that the temple was destroyed, sacrifices for the purposes of worship, thanksgiving, forgiveness for sin, and the blessing of Israel had to cease. Even so, the line of Aaron, through the tribe of Levi, had to be preserved for posterity.

Ben Jordan found himself in a new role to fulfill. His primary duty was to secure the treasures of the temple and the records of their history until Elohim called His people back to the Promised Land. He must give his all to do whatever was required. Along with the Ghib-bore, he would make it so.

Ben Jordan found Ojiah and his son at New Carthage in Iberia across the Mediterranean. It was a bittersweet reunion. The Jewish community of merchants had grown there, but they could never really be safe.

Ben Jordan settled there and raised a family. After thirty years, however, he found himself in the same position as his father. This time, it wasn't the Romans threatening them. It was Christianity. He saw Christianity growing stronger in the region and along with that growth came an increased prejudice against the Jews. They would be pushed out of their homes in less than a generation. Meeting with Jaier, Ojiah's son, and his own son Aaron, Ben-Jordan had to make an extremely difficult decision.

"We must move the treasure," he said. "Things may seem comfortable now, but the times are changing."

Jaier said, "If necessary, we can be ready to go in three months."

"My friend, it must be different this time. We must be discreet. We must be deceptive. I would like you to take a trial shipment north. Make certain it is packaged in the same way as you would the treasure. If your journey is successful, prepare a place and come back for the real thing." Ben Jordan continued, "Then you must plan to live not as Jews, but as Gentiles. You must blend in for the sake of Elohim."

"I cannot! It would be blasphemy," Jaier protested.

"My friend, for us, in time of war, the laws and traditions of our forefathers must take second place to our duty," Ben Jordan explained.

"You are to remain faithful to Elohim by remaining faithful to your calling. And remember, the Ghib-bore are protected by Gabriel the archangel. I will chisel the story of your journey into the foundation walls of our meeting place myself."

Jaier stood and embraced the old man. He knew he may never see him again. "May Elohim protect us both" and left.

*****

President Kennedy asked Pastor Harold to fly to Jerusalem and try to settle things down between the Israelis and the Muslims over a recent rumor. The internet was ablaze with warnings to the Muslims that the Jews intended to take possession of their Temple Mount, dismantle the Dome of the Rock, and build their own long-desired temple.

*****

The Dome was originally built as a memorial shrine to Muhammad in AD 692. Its location was selected as an insult to the Jews and an affront to the Jewish god. It was located on the very spot known as Mount Moriah. It was the singular spot where Abraham offered up Isaac and where Solomon's temple was built and Herod's temple after that. The Holy of Holies was located where God Himself had willed it.

In AD 1015, the building collapsed only to be rebuilt in AD 1023. The crusaders took control of Jerusalem in AD 1099 and converted the Dome into a Catholic church. It remained a Catholic church until AD 1187, when the Muslims took possession of Jerusalem again and turned the church back into a shrine.

At that time, six hundred years after the supposed event, the Muslims declared that the rock was the very place Muhammed physically ascended up into heaven. It became the third most sacred place in Islam after Ka'ba in Mecca an Al-Masjid in Medina.

To Harold, this spot was the most important place on earth. He had long studied the prophecies of the Bible. He believed that before Jesus returned to earth as the conquering King of kings, the third temple needed to be built, the sacrificial system of the Old Testament would be reestablished by orthodox Jews, the antichrist would defile the temple and break a peace covenant with the Jews.

Harold knew that nothing he did or didn't do could affect God's timing on any of this. And that the day of Jesus's return was only known by the Father in heaven. But he strongly felt that his duty was to daily follow the path laid before him. So in obedience to God and per the request of the president of the United States, he flew to Jerusalem.

A meeting was set up with Harold and multiple representatives from the surrounding Muslim countries and Israel's assistant to the minister of defense. When Pastor Harold arrived in Jerusalem, he soon realized that he was regarded as a celebrity.

Before he got to the reception desk at the American Colonial Hotel, he was approached by a news reporter and a camera crew.

The reporter pushed a microphone in his face and asked, "Congressman Washington, what is your main message to the world regarding the Temple Mount?"

"Friend, what is your name?" Pastor Harold asked.

Taken aback somewhat, the reporter answered, "Hakim."

"Hakim, I just want everyone to know that people are more important than places, and the peace from God and peace with each other is more important than religious traditions and political posturing."

Harold looked directly into the camera and said, "Friends, I'd like to know if you agree with me. Do you think that another war and the destruction it would bring is more important than what building is sitting on top of the Temple Mount?" Harold paused and looked at the crowd that was amassing in the lobby. A smile broke through his tired face and said, "I'm listening."

*****

A rally was organized by the political activists in the city. They carried signs that were written in Arabic, Hebrew, and English that said, "People, more important the Places," and "Peace, more important than Politics." The crowd surged to over one million people in the streets. The attitude of the crowd was unprecedented. It seemed like a positive force descended upon the city, and for the moment, peace and goodwill would prevail.

"This could not have been accomplished without prayer," Eli said.

"The Lord is good," Seraphima answered. "Let's enjoy it while it lasts."

The next day's meeting had a clear direction. The diplomats truly wanted to resolve the issue quickly. Pastor Harold had said all that needed to be said. Israel wanted to appear to be a firm but peaceful steward of the land. The Muslims wanted to emerge with worldwide assurances that their sacred site was secure. It was a win-win.

Hakim, with camera crew in tow, managed to get to his new friend just before he left for the airport.

"Reverend Washington," Hakim said, "do you have any final statement to share with the world?"

"Good morning, Hakim. Yes, I would like to thank all the hardworking diplomats, the governments they represent, our host, and the people of Jerusalem for their open and honest participation in the resolution of this misunderstanding."

"A Memorandum of Understanding will be made public today that 'No Israeli, no agent of Israel, no plan of Israel will condone or instigate any action against the existence of the Dome of the Rock.'

"However, Hakim, that being said, I believe that if God Almighty wants the Dome down, no power in heaven or on earth can keep it standing, and if God wants the Dome to stand, no force in heaven or on earth can tear it down. He makes the ultimate decisions."

Harold said his goodbyes and got into his cab. Headed for the airport, Harold studied the Holy City as his flew over. Harold prayed a prayer of thanks to His Lord and Savior. He was pleased that he got the chance to make the public statement that put things in the proper perspective. He felt this trip was a "win, win, win."

*****

Wherever Blue turned, she ran into a brick wall. She was perplexed that not one Watching angel could account for the disappearance of the temple treasure. Knowing that Dagon was also looking for the treasure ruled out any demon involvement in hiding the Ark. There remained only one explanation. Knowledge of the relocation of the temple treasure was being protected by an angel greater than all of them.

Blue suspected an Archangel was involved. Eli, the Archangel and Chairman of the council, wasn't aware of the treasure's whereabouts. So if it wasn't the head archangel on the Council, he or she had to be an Archangel serving the Lord Almighty directly. This realization represented more than a brick wall. It was an impenetrable solid gold wall.

Since Blue was still working within her assigned duty, she continued to pursue the location of the Ark and the treasures that accompanied it. But this time, she decided she would find out what the humans knew. She disguised herself as an independent research scientist offering to work with Rabbi David Levin. She told Dr. Levin that her plans were to one day write a book of her adventures.

David assumed that Sarah Silverstein, aka Blue, was as a cryptanalyst sent by the government. To Rabbi Levin, Sarah was an intelligent, mysterious, beautiful woman. She did her best to hide her beauty with shabby clothing, a Stetson fedora, and sunglasses, but they couldn't hide her intelligence. Rabbi David suspected Sarah was a Mossad agent. He didn't mind her involvement. They were on the same side and wanted the same thing, the Ark. David welcomed her help.

Blue gained access to the dig sites. When she finally saw the carvings, she had a strange feeling that she had seen similar writings once before. Try as she might, she couldn't remember where or when. This in itself was unusual because Blue never forgot anything.

However, Blue was quick to uncover the meaning of the writings. She kept that fact to herself. The writings told the history of the Ark. Its creation and its contents, its movements through the desert, its capture, its victories, its glory. The writings documented the relocation of the Ark to Africa during the Babylonian captivity and its eventual return for the building of the second temple. But that is where the information stopped, except for a final mention of the Ghib-bore and a planned move to Carthage. The movers and the guardians of the Ark were descendants of the three hundred Mighty Men of Valor call the Ghib-bore. They were faithful soldiers who served Gideon. Tradition held that Gabriel was the archangel who appeared to Gideon and directed his actions.

At this point, Blue knew she needed to find out more about the Ghib-bore. She sent the one hundred angels that were under her command to scour libraries, museums, and anywhere else historic records could be found. They were to search ancient Hebrew marketplaces, worship centers, rabbis' dwellings, any place the Ghib-bore may have left a clue as to their activity and the Ark's location. They listened in on conversations. They disguised themselves as students, professors, librarians, and even as illegal aliens and derelicts. If a clue existed, they would find it.

*****

In Iberia, pressure from invading Muslims and aggression from crusader mobs made the relocation of the Ark and its treasure necessary. The surviving Ghib-bore consisted of ten men and their families. They made contact with friendlies in Brittany. Although some of their people there had converted to Christianity, they were still trustworthy and dedicated to the preservation and protection of the Ark.

Jaier ben Ojiah realized his choices were limited. He knew they were protected by the archangel Gabriel, as they had committed themselves to this holy mission. He had just dreamed that sand was running out of an hourglass. That next morning, he decided to move north.

"Salvador, we're moving. Can you finalize our records? Make certain the carving can't be found unless directed by heaven," Jaier said.

"It will take at least two weeks to complete," Salvador said.

"Try to push it to one," Jaier stressed. "We may have to leave sooner."

They left in five days. Two days before their synagogue and homes were burnt to the ground by Muslims.

*****

There are seven Districts of Evil or Theaters of Operation on earth: the North (of Jerusalem) including Russia, the South including Egypt, the East including China, the West including Europe, North America, South America, and the Pacific including India and Japan. Apollyon was the Ambassador of the Demon Lord who ruled over all the earth.

Gog was the King of the North. Dagon was the General of North America. They did not have a working relationship with each other. In fact, none of the leaders of the individual districts had a working relationship with the other. They were all driven by greed, self-interest, and an insatiable desire for power. They all agreed, however, that the Son of Man must not return to earth. They were also in agreement that the best way to accomplish that goal was to kill Jews and destroy the Church.

The Kingdom of Darkness had one enemy on earth, the Church. The Church's power was the Indwelling One, the Restrainer of evil. The Church accessed the power of the Holy Spirit through prayer, Bible study and fellowship with one another. The Church had grown at a steady rate since Pentecost through various ministries across time and around the world. But during the last century, the Church began to weaken.

Most of the Rebellion's success was accomplish by infiltrating the Church's membership and destroying it from within. False preaching and false doctrine was working its evil magic and the Seven Deadly Sins accomplished the rest.

Evil was gaining momentum. The Church's presence had reached every corner of the world, but it was losing influence with the current generation. Science or more accurately, science without the recognition of a Creator, became the new religion. The sanctity of life was replaced by the convenience of life. Moral absolutes were ridiculed and overtaken by moral relativism. Like gravity pulling on a ball rolling downhill, man's fallen nature pulled him down toward sin and away from God.

In 1870, Dwight Lyman Moody said, "The world has yet to see what God will do with a man fully consecrated to Him." Pastor Washington was the Moody of his century. In a world so interconnected and instantaneous, Pastor Washington's impact was complete and immediate. The darker the night, the brighter the morning. Pastor Harold T. Washington provided that light. He wasn't the light but a reflection of it. He never set out to be that person, most men of God never do. He merely desired to please his Lord and wanted to know and do His good pleasure. So when a man of God rises up to do the work of God, all heaven and hell take notice.

Hell took notice.

*****

Apollyon ordered Gog and Dagon to a meeting at Mount Kailash in the Tibetan mountain range. Since the flood, Apollyon controlled this sacred mountain range. Mount Kailash was an insurmountable peak for demons as well as humans, unless one was summoned. The cavern just under its peak was large enough to accommodate an army of demons. Apollyon's army is named Demon's Teeth. It is a million demons strong. It is the largest standing army in the Rebellion. They camped under the peak, but they were ready to mobilize at a moment's notice.

The Realm had twice as many warriors as the Rebellion. So the strategy of the Rebellion was to engage, battle, win, and run before the Realm could respond. Its goal is to weaken the enemy until they could no longer be effective. Be swifter, more cunning, deadlier.

Although he wouldn't admit it to anyone, Dagon was worried. He had never been to Mount Kailash, the story was that few were ever summonsed there and fewer still ever returned. And now, here he was. The camp was enormous. He couldn't see the end of the troupes amassed there. He had clawed his way to the top and was successful because he deceived, defeated, and destroyed every competitor. He became the General of North America, and he had earned it. But this could be his end. Had he just clawed his way into the beast's lair to be devoured?

Gog was a fearless bear. He conquered his rivals until none remained. He had not only taken his kingdom by force but aspired to have more. He secretly set his sights on the ambassadorship. He would wait for the right opportunity and take it from Apollyon. If he had to take control of the other districts first, he would do so, one by one. North America was weak. The Christian influence there and its sympathetic ties to the Jews made this district vulnerable. Dagon was losing his grip.

Apollyon had called the two leaders to his private quarters. The doors were sealed. If there was to be a battle, it would be two against one. But Apollyon had the advantage. He was more of an entity than a creature. He moved like smoke and could choke the life from his enemy without even fully materializing. When he did materialize, one wished he hadn't. He was a beast. There was none like him. He was twice the size of Dagon. His horns were as sharp as green ice. His teeth matched the stalagmites and stalactites of his inner mountain. His bite was inescapable and deadly. He had six arms and his claws were poisonous. He laughed at any challenger. He would strip his opponent of his outer shell and expose his naked spirit before crushing it.

The General and the King were ushered into Apollyon's private office. They were told to sit on the two chairs opposite Apollyon's desk. Suddenly, the door to the office locked, sealing them in. A green smoke entered the room. It traveled through the air and into the lungs of the General and the King. They each felt violated as Apollyon searched their minds. The smoke settled in the throne like chair behind his massive desk of obsidian. His chair was covered in red bejeweled dragon hide. Between the desk and the two chairs facing the desk where his guests sat was a giant black bear skin rug. The message wasn't lost on either of them.

Apollyon spoke to their minds without verbalizing a sound. "We must find out who is behind this new movement of the enemy. Dagon, your pastor is in the thick of it. Gog, this pastor has shifted his attention toward Jerusalem and the temple site. It's time for you two to put your petty differences aside and work together. Put an end to this once and for all."

"Yes, Ambassador," the general and king responded in unison.

"If a higher power is at work here, you must bring it out in the open and let me know. If it is something else, you must identify it, find it, and destroy it. Do I make myself clear?"

"Yes, Ambassador," they answered again.

"This will be done, or you will be replaced. Do I make myself clear?" Apollyon said as he began to dematerialize.

"Yes, Ambassador."

Apollyon began to dissolve into green smoke and was gone. Neither Dagon nor Gog hesitated to leave.

*****

Pastor Harold was back home in his pulpit. The church was filled to capacity. It was Pentecost Sunday. Thousands, if not hundreds of thousands, were viewing the service live. The local TV station was carrying the service and the church was streaming it worldwide.

Pastor Harold continued his sermon. "I think that the saddest end to my life would be to feel the shame of what I should have done but found excuses not to do it. Or to regret what I could have done but never considered it. Or to carry the remorse of what I would have done if only I got around to it." Pastor Harold looked up from his notes and spoke directly to the people.

"When Jesus asked the rich young ruler to sell all he had and follow Him, the rich young ruler walked from it. When Jesus told Nicodemus to be born again, Nicodemus debated it. When Jesus told Peter Satan was after him, Peter denied it.

"What is God telling you to do today? What does He want you to become today? Why aren't you obeying it? Doing it? Becoming it? Now.

"Now is the acceptable time. Now is the day of salvation."

He took off his reading glasses, bowed his head, spread his arms, and began to pray. "Lord God Almighty, bless us today. Send your Holy Spirit to guide us, teach us, show us the way. Let the precious blood of Jesus wash over us and cleanse us from our sin and make us pure and acceptable in your sight. Let your glory come down on us, I pray."

As Pastor Harold prayed a rumble began to run through the church. It wasn't a threatening thing but a powerful thing. Even though the church was air conditioned and the windows were shut tight, a warm gentle breeze began to blow throughout the building. Not in a threatening way, but it seemed to embrace all those present. People began to stand and pray. Not a fearful prayer but a glorified, worshipful prayer. And then a light shone all around. Not a light that reflect itself off objects and people like an earthly light. But a light that glowed with goodness, a holy light, brilliant but not bright. A light that contained all the colors of a rainbow, an independent light from above.

Pastor Harold began to sing.

> There's a sweet, sweet spirit in this place
> And I know that it's the spirit of the Lord
> There are sweet expressions on each face
> And I know that it's the presence of the Lord.

The church choir joined in. Then the organ and piano began to accompany them. Then the people spontaneously began to sing.

> Sweet Holy Spirit
> Sweet heavenly dove
> Stay right here with us
> Filling us with your love.

This wasn't a hymn the congregation normally sang, but everyone seemed to know the words.

> And for this blessing
> We lift our hands in praises
> Without a doubt we know
> That we have been revived
> When we shall leave this place.

The elders felt led to head to the front of the church. They began to beckon those who wanted to receive Jesus Christ as Lord and Savior to come forward. The aisle began to fill with people, hundreds of people. People crying, people praying, people singing, people seeking, people confessing sin, they all came. When Pastor Harold saw the tremendous response, he signaled the elders' wives and Annie to help with the ladies.

Pastor Harold turned toward the cross at the front of the church and began to sing.

> So, I'll cherish the old rugged cross,
> Till my trophies at last I lay down;
> I will cling to the old rugged cross,
> And exchange it someday for a crown.

And the people continued their worship. At the end of the last verse, a peace filled the church. Pastor Harold prayed. "Lord, thank you for manifesting your presence to us. Thank you for revealing your shekinah glory. Thank you for letting us know… You are listening."

*****

People are generally unimpressed by what they see on their screens. They are desensitized to tragedy, unmoved by natural phenomena, jaded by CGI. They watch aliens, dinosaurs, vampires, zombies, and talking animals, daily. From births to beheadings, living and dying, it is all nothing but flashing lights and background noise. But what they saw on Pentecost Sunday was different. Not all the witnesses were believers. Some were seekers. Some were naysayers. Some were downright hostiles. But no one could deny that what happened was real.

Christians couldn't help but make the comparison between the first Pentecost and this Pentecost. Evidence of the Holy Spirit's presence was undeniable. The rumbling, the wind, the light, the gospel message delivered by a New Age Peter had culminated with the shekinah glory of the Old Testament coming down from heaven. Pastor Harold preached to the Gentiles about Jesus Christ, while embracing Old Testament truths. And God affirmed Harold by filling the church with His glory and over two hundred people receiving Jesus as Lord and Savior.

Angels watched in wonder. The Almighty hadn't made an appearance like this in ages. Angel remained on high alert, but he knew a power greater than his was in control. Blue reported that not a demon was present for hundreds of miles. The Restrainer had made it so.

Demons were infuriated. They had been driven out of the area by the Almighty. This was a bold move that signaled a change was coming. Dagon was inconsolable. The church was in his domain. He would have the last say before this was over. He wouldn't need Gog's help. He would take matters into his own claws and soon.

"What do you want me to do?" Blue asked Angel.

"You know I can only defend what is mine to guard. I want you to take the fight to Dagon before he attacks the pastor. Use every warrior we have and take him down," Angel commanded. "And, Blue, be careful. I can't lose you again."

Blue smiled and said, "You won't."

*****

"Joe, we need him. He is the most genuine person DC has ever seen, America has ever seen!" Chip stressed.

It was Tuesday, 10:30 a.m., in the Oval Office. "Look, even unbelievers recognize his honesty and we can't deny his effectiveness as a politician. He has succeeded in every task we've given him, exceeded."

"Calm down, Chip. You're going to have a stroke." President Joe Kennedy raised his hands in submission. "I already asked him to join us for lunch next week. I watched the service last Sunday."

"And?" Chip asked.

"Quite frankly, I'm speechless. I don't know what to think or even what to say about it." Joe's honesty with his close friends was his best characteristic.

"America has seen great spiritual leaders: Warfield, Billy Sunday, Moody, Graham, King, and now Washington. If he doesn't choose to be our vice president, at the very least, we need him to advise us. He is a blessed man of God."

Chip was now shaking his head. He couldn't believe God had brought this pastor into their lives at this time without having a higher purpose.

"I think I'd like to meet with him alone next week before lunch. I want to look him in the eye and have a heart to heart with the man," Joe mused out loud.

"Great idea. I'm confident once you sit down with the man, you'll make the right choice." Chip looked down at his notes for the coming week, shuffled through some pages, and said, "Shall we move on?"

*****

Dagon's spies listened in on all the Oval Office meetings. The pastor was going to be in DC the following Tuesday, which meant Angel would be guarding him. Angel would be away from his fortress in Charleston. Dagon planned to take this opportunity to attack Angel. Dagon decided that the best way to resolve the "pastor situation" was to cut off the spiritual head guarding him. Angel would be at his most vulnerable in DC. If someone came to Angel's aid, Dagon would be ready with a deadly counterattack.

Sulfurra and Whiplash would head up the initial attacks. They were Dagon's most reliable warriors. They were vying for the position on the council that the Shadow of Nations left behind. Dagon would use their rivalry to his advantage. He would watch their battle and wait with a thousand demon warriors.

When a demon was defeated in battle, he or she would burst into flames and ash. His spirit would be sent to the pit for eternity. When an angel was defeated in battle, he or she would burst into a bright light and be transported into the Almighty's presence. He or she would be celebrated as a hero and would enter into the king's presence for eternity.

Sulfurra would attack first. Her poisonous breath could paralyze a victim, leaving him to suffer indescribable torment. If Sulfurra succeeded, Dagon would take the credit. If she failed, the door would be opened for Whiplash to stage a second attack. Whiplash had eight arms. Each could tear an angel in half or just as easily snap off their head. If Whiplash succeeded, again Dagon would take the credit. If he failed, Angel would most probably be wounded or worn. Dagon would be ready to overwhelm Angel and put an end to him once and for all. There was one more possibility, if it appeared that the Restrainer was protecting Angel and his pastor, Dagon would retreat and report to Apollyon as ordered. It was the first time in a long time that Dagon was excited. He could almost taste victory.

*****

In 1600, in most of Europe, the negative attitude toward the Jews was intensifying. Life was becoming more difficult. Satan and his henchmen were relentless in their efforts to destroy God's chosen people. Over the centuries, less than half of the Ghib-bore had survived.

Some of the Ghib-bore became followers of Jesus Christ the "Mashiach," God's anointed one. They didn't consider themselves "Christians." They considered themselves the true heirs of God's promise given to the Jews through Abraham, completed Jews.

Scripturally, they recognized that Isaiah 9:6 referred to Jesus: "Unto us a child is born, to us a son is given, and the government will be on his shoulders. And he will be called Wonderful Counselor, Mighty God, Everlasting Father, Prince of Peace." They also recognized that Jesus died for the lost sheep of Israel and that the Jews would pass on that blessing to the entire world. Isaiah 53 convinced them that the Almighty Father had this redemptive plan for the future of the world. Isaiah 56 predicts the existence of a third temple when it becomes the house of prayer for all the people of the world. The Ark of the Covenant also makes its glorious appearance for all eternity in God's temple, Revelation 11:19.

They believed literally that King David's throne would last forever. "Your house and your kingdom shall endure before Me forever; your throne shall be established forever. In accordance with all these words and all this vision, so Nathan spoke to David" (2 Samuel 7:16–17).

Regardless of their belief in Christ, however, they were faithful to their mission. God had blessed the Ghib-bore for keeping their promise. And Gabriel the archangel protected them. And so, the Ghib-bore survived. And so, they kept the Ark and its treasures safe.

In spite of what was happening throughout Europe, England had become more tolerant of the Jews. They had broken ties with Rome and established their own church. Some in England believed that the rightful throne of King David of Israel had genuinely found its way to the throne of England. And that the king of England was also the king of ancient Israel and the head of the Christian church.

By 1600, the Ghib-bore consisted of over a hundred families in France and Spain. However, only the key members of their communities knew of their actual mission and the whereabouts of the treasures that were in their keeping. The others considered their tight-knit communities a blessing from God and a protection from outsiders.

The Ghib-bore leader was David ben Gurion. He was a clear-thinking businessman. He was the eldest son in the continuous line of eldest sons tracing all the way back to Gideon, God's Mighty Man of Valor. David never lost sight of the primary objective: keep the Ark and its treasures and its secrets safe. Their mission was to be prepared to return to the rebuilt temple when called back to Jerusalem by God.

David had lived his whole life in Brittany. He and the ruling council decided that it was time to once again relocate. This time, for safety's sake, the move would be discreet. He would only send an elite core of the Ghib-bore and their families. He also decided to send the Mashiach believers. They would fit easily into English society. They could pass as Gentile Christians and would not have to be confined to the Ghetto. Since 1555, the Jews were singled out in Spain and other parts of Europe. They were forced to live in assigned areas of large cities.

"How long do you think we will be gone?" Francis asked David.

"I'm not going to lie to you. I just don't know. In fact, the rest of us may join you in London within the next few years," David answered. "Have you made the proper preparations?"

"Yes, Warwick Castle is ready for a new noble family to take up residence. We've paid tribute to King Charles II, and he has seen fit to grant us nobility. We can easily present ourselves as English nobility returning from Brittany. We have the finances and enough skilled people to influence the locals positively in our favor," Francis explained. "As long as we keep our true identity and purpose secret, we'll be fine."

"Good," David said. "I want you to take Benjamin with you. I want you to prepare him for leadership. Should something happen to us here, you will have the next commander with you."

"Are you certain?" Francis was a little surprised that David would entrust his eldest son to him.

"He is eighteen years old. He is ready. I've been training him for this his entire life. Besides, we are only seven days travel to London. It's not like you're traveling to the New World. We will document your relocation on the monument stones throughout Carnac. Now go in peace and may the Almighty protect you always." David embraced Francis as the two old friends parted, once and for all.

*****

Rabbi David with Sarah Silverstein's help was now certain the Ark was removed from Jerusalem in AD 66. The temple carvings indicated that Caiaphas the high priest was convinced that the temple would be plundered by the Romans and all would be lost. David wondered if Caiaphas had taken Jesus's prophecy to heart. Pastor Harold had quoted Jesus's words to him when they surveyed the dig together. Jesus said, "Truly I tell you, not one stone here will be left on another: everyone will be thrown down."

David hadn't determined who relocated the Ark or to where. He wondered if Pastor Harold could shed light on these missing pieces to the puzzle. He decided it was time to place a call to his friend.

"So, Pastor Harold, what signs and wonders have you performed today?" Rabbi David chuckled.

"Sadly, none." Harold laughed. "But the day's not over."

Harold turned the conversation on a dime, "How is the dig coming? Tell me, what have you found?"

"I believe the Mossad sent us a special agent to work the dig. She was posing as a researcher interested in writing a book. But she has incredible skills and an unbelievable ability to crack code. Within a week, she pretty much cracked the code singlehandedly." David could barely keep his excitement contained.

"The Lord moves in mysterious ways. Where is she now?" Harold asked.

"Gone. She gave us the push we needed and left without a word."

Harold could hear the disappointment in David's voice.

"Maybe it's for the best," Harold said.

"How so?" David wondered out loud.

"David, I've been having dreams again. I think the appearance of the Ark will bring danger to the world. In fact, I believe it's being hidden from the world until the End-Times." Now Harold was thinking out loud.

"But maybe we are the ones God will use to reveal the truth to the world. Maybe God will use us to help the world believe in Him again," David never said these thoughts out loud before. In fact, he never had these thoughts until now. Pastor Harold had a knack for bringing his deepest thoughts out into the light.

"Maybe. All I can add is that I had a dream about Masada. The high priest in charge sent his son to find the Ark and ensure its safety. No doubt, you've got some top-secret information about your high priest lineage and their locations throughout history." Harold waited for a response.

"No doubt," David said.

"Follow the priest. You'll find the Ark," Harold said.

"Thus, saith Pastor Harold?" David kidded.

"You betcha," Harold responded.

"I'll take your words under advisement and, Harold, thanks." David ended the call.

It took David a moment to digest what they had just discussed. Was God working through him? Was Sarah's help from the Lord? Were the End-Times, as Pastor Harold put it, near? How did Masada enter the conversation? How did Harold know about the fastidious records that kept track of the high priest from Aaron to the present day? Was Jesus the Messiah?

*****

Angel left Blue to watch over the church. There weren't demons within hundreds of miles of the area. But Angel knew things could change in minutes. He was following the pastor to DC. Angel was certain Pastor Harold was going to be asked to be the vice presidential running mate for President Kennedy.

Angel had his escort of one hundred warriors and one hundred more were already assigned to DC. But the area was in stasis. There were thousands of demons in DC, but very few posed a threat to the pastor. They had their own assignments. They were controlling senators, congressmen, special interest groups, multiple committees, and the media. Angel did not see or feel any threat to the pastor.

He instructed his warriors to stay close to the pastor and stationed the DC guardians around the White House. Judging everything secure, Angel rose above the Capitol to study the horizon and look for any possible threats.

"It appears safe for the time being," Angel said to no one in particular. *I wonder how Blue is doing.* He called out to her, "Blue, how are things at the church?"

A feminine voice came from behind him, "Angel?"

He turned expecting to see Blue. It wasn't. A yellow gas surrounded him. He tried not to breathe, but the shock caused the opposite effect. He sucked in the poison. Angel lost control of his facilities. He plummeted to earth. Sulfurra followed him down. She moved behind him and grabbed Angel's wings. She then drove her sword through his wings and anchored Angel to the ground. He screamed out in pain.

"So, Angel, I've heard a lot about you. Want to have some fun?" She produced a pair of shackles and bound his hands and feet.

Angel had regained his composure, but he knew he was in mortal danger. *Blue, I need you,* he thought.

Sulfurra unsheathed a long sapphire-handled knife and stabbed Angel in both legs. She smiled as she did. Angel screamed out in pain. Golden liquid began to run from Angel's wounds. Sulfurra was beyond ecstatic. After this victory, she could not be denied her rightful place at the Generals' table.

"Tell me, Angel, before I send you to your Maker, who's been aiding you in your little campaign of destruction?"

"Whiplash," Angel said as he lost consciousness.

"That's ridiculous," Sulfurra scoffed.

A tentacle wrapped itself around Sulfurra's throat, keeping her from releasing her poison. A second tentacle wrapped itself around her body, pinning her arms back to her wings.

Whiplash turned Sulfurra around to look her in the eyes and said, "You think you're smarter than me? You think you're stronger than me? You think you're more deadly than me?" Whiplash smiled a humorless smile and said, "Think again." He ripped her head off her body. She burst into flames.

Turning to Angel, Whiplash slapped him. He demanded Angel open his eyes. He wrapped his tentacle around Angel's throat and squeezed. "Who's been protecting you? Is it an archangel? Is it the Restrainer?"

Angel came back from a deep place in his mind, looked into Whiplash's eyes, and said, "Blue."

In a frozen blue flash of ice, the tentacle holding Angel by the throat was amputated. Then in a second flash, his other tentacles hit the ground. Before Whiplash could react, Blue had driven an ice lance through the back of Whiplash's head into his heart. Whiplash burst into flames and was gone.

Blue heard a roaring behind her and saw a red dragon streaking their way. It was Dagon accompanied by at least a thousand demons. She knew this was the end. There was no way she could leave Angel and no way she could stay and survive. Without hesitation, she decided to protect Angel with her dying breath.

Blue ascended above the Capitol and yelled, "Come get me first, you disgusting beast."

Dagon roared back, "Traitor, I will destroy you in one bite."

Dagon propelled his way toward Blue. He opened his enormous mouth filled with a thousand of crushing teeth. Blue prepared to be taken. She amped up her inner power and prepared to release it at the right moment. She knew it would be her end, but the explosion would kill Dagon and save Angel.

Louder than thunder and quicker than a lightning bolt, a golden sword swung through the air and into Dagon's opened maw. The strike went through the dragon's skull and severed the top of his head. Dagon burst into flames. A thousand warrior angels fell onto a thousand demons. The battle was over in minutes. Both sides sustained losses. But in the end, without a leader, the demons were routed.

Blue was stunned. She fell to the ground next to Angel. He hadn't left her yet. She gently pulled Sulfurra's sword from his wings. She quickly froze his wounded legs to stop any further loss of golden blood. She held his head and whispered, "Don't leave me."

A shadow appeared next to her. She looked up and was struck speechless. It was General Samson. Blue managed to ask, "It was you? How did you know? Can you help Angel?"

Three healing angels had already taken Angel away into their care. "I'm sorry I didn't arrive soon enough to help Angel. But I've been following you and observing you throughout your probation. You were my top warrior in the past, and it turns out, you still are. I never wanted to lose you. What you just did completed your Redemption."

Blue just stared at General Samson with tear-filled eyes.

One of the healing angels returned to report. "General Sir, Angel will survive. His wounds are already healing."

"Thank the Almighty," General Samson replied. "And thank you for your efforts, soldier."

Sampson turned back to Blue and said, "As I was saying. Blue, you saved a life, you took a life, and now you gave a life. You were willing to give your own life to save Angel's. You are a worthy warrior angel. I'm proud and quite frankly pleased to have you back. We still need to make this official. But since I was the last remaining no vote, I'm sure your probation will be lifted."

*****

Harold was surprised to find he was being ushered up to the sun deck at the White House. The president was there waiting for him, drinking coffee at a table.

"Pastor Harold, please sit down. Would you like some coffee?" The president got up and shook Harold's hand.

"Yes, thank you." Harold sat down across from the president. "Please call me Harold, Mr. President."

"Fine, but you must call me Joe." The president poured Harold coffee from the carafe on the table. "Harold, I wanted to meet with you alone, except for the half-dozen Secret Service agents not staring at us from behind sunglasses. I wanted to ask you, just between you and me, are you for real?" Joe asked.

Harold chuckled, felt his belly, and said, "Well, Joe, I think so."

"What I mean is I've never met anyone who didn't have an ulterior motive. You seem to not. You help people for people's sake. You preach sermons to teach and to edify others. You don't ask for money, power, prestige, or recognition. Any success you have you deflect the praise and attention away from yourself and shine the light on others or God. You reluctantly became a member of Congress. You wholeheartedly carried out our toughest assignments. You never asked for anything in return. Finally, I've offered you a shot at the vice presidency, and instead of jumping at the opportunity of a lifetime, you hesitate and ask for more time to decide. What you do isn't normal. If it isn't normal, what is it?" Joe felt like he got a load off his chest even though he didn't plan to say what he just said.

"Well, first, thank you for your kind words, I think. Second, I don't choose to behave one way or another. I choose to obey my Lord. Colossians 3:23 says, 'And whatsoever ye do, do *it* heartily, as to the Lord, and not as unto men.' Third, the most difficult thing in my life is to determine what my Lord wants me to do. When given the choice, I try to choose how Jesus would choose. If I don't have a choice, I ask God to show me the way and to grant me the wisdom, strength, and the fortitude to carry out my duty. So I guess, for me, it's Jesus first, others second, yourself last. That's how a Christian achieves real JOY in his life." Harold thought he said enough without getting too preachy.

"And what has your Lord told you about the vice presidency?" Joe asked. He genuinely liked Harold. He was already thinking about asking him to be his personal advisor.

"Joe, Jesus is not only 'my' Lord. He is 'your' Lord too. In fact, one day in the near future, the Bible says 'that at the name of Jesus every knee shall bow, of those in heaven, and of those on earth, and of those under the earth, and that every tongue will confess that Jesus Christ is Lord.'" Harold took a sip off his coffee.

"Okay, allow me to rephrase that, what has 'the' Lord told you to do about the vice presidency?" Joe acknowledged Harold's point.

"Nothing yet." Harold saw the disappointment on Joe's face. He continued, "Which either means it's a neutral choice: 'Ford or Chevy,' 'with cheese or without cheese.' Or it could mean to wait. Let me ask you. How long can I wait?"

"Technically, up to the convention. About three months before the election. That would be eighteen months from now. Which put us in September of next year. Ideally, we'd like to know sooner," Joe said.

"At this point, I feel I need a sign from the Lord to decide. Can I wait until the convention and ask for a unanimous consensus?" Harold asked.

"Well, that would be more than a sign, that would be a miracle." Joe quipped. "Of course, I would like to announce sooner since it's becoming common knowledge that Frank Silvester will be retiring after this term. But I don't want it to appear as if I'm pushing a seventy-five-year-old man out of office." Joe paused for thought. "Would you do this? Would you be my personal advisor? Can I rely on your wisdom and your personal relationship to the Almighty to guide me through these next eighteen months? Whether you choose to be my vice president or not. Will you stand by my side personally? In so doing, maybe the Lord will give you clarity as to your political career and He will give me a fresh perspective on true spiritual living."

Harold said a quick prayer, then said, "Joe, I'll do this. I'll be your pastor. I'll love you, care for you, guide you, and pray for you. If you need me, you can call me. We can schedule regular meetings and discuss whatever you want. All I need you to do is two things. First is to read your Bible every day."

"I can do that. What's the second?" Joe asked.

"Second," Harold said, "pray for wisdom. The Bible says if any of you lack wisdom, let him ask for it from God, who gives to all men liberally and will not withhold it. Do we have a deal?"

Joe smiled, shook his head, and said, "Now I see what the world's been dealing with. You drive a hard bargain. We have a deal, Pastor." Joe offered his hand.

*****

"You disobeyed my direct orders. What last words would you like to say?" The voice of Apollyon came from a swilling green gas cloud. The six remaining rulers of the Seven Districts sat helplessly at the conference table. Five of which kept their heads bowed, their eyes down and their mouths shut.

Gog knew he had only one chance to speak. "Dagon was insubordinate, not me. He never informed me of his plans to attack alone. He staged the attack in his own district. I had no knowledge of the attack until I was informed of its failure by you. Dagon and I were working on a plan to get Angel to come to En Gedi where we are the most powerful and he is at his weakest."

"Enough! You sniveling fool," Apollyon yelled. The cavern shook. Apollyon's face, horns, and teeth appeared in the midst of the green cloud of doom. "If I hadn't invested so much time in you, you would be gone by now. I want you to personally destroy Angel and bring me his wings. I don't care how you do it."

Gog responded quickly, "Yes, Ambassador."

"I am assigning Mammon to take over the North American District. He is now responsible for the pastor and whoever or whatever is going on there. You will all give him your full cooperation. Am I making myself clear?" Apollyon sent a portion of the green cloud to face each ruler present. The threat was clear if nothing else.

"Yes, Ambassador," the generals and kings responded instantly and in sync.

Apollyon sat back in his chair, pressed three sets of claws together, and asked, "Did any of Dagon's surviving demons see who came to Angel's aid? Surely he didn't destroy three of my best demon warriors without help." Apollyon now fully materialized at the head of the table.

The King of the East, Jinn Sing spoke up, "We have reports that a lightning sword severed Dagon's head. Also, those who saw the deed said Angel did not wield the sword. And that General Dagon was attacking a bright light, a bright blue light when it happened."

"Did you say blue?" Apollyon asked.

"Yes, Ambassador," Jinn Sing repeated, "blue."

*****

Rabbi David went to the office of Chief Rabbi Kohen. Rabbi Kohen was the director of the Third Temple Institute. Among its various functions, the institute was harvesting stones from the Dead Sea area. According to Holy Scripture, stones used for the three altars in the temple needed to be uncut and formed by God alone. These stones could not be struck by human tools since that would render the stones unclean. These stones needed to fit together perfectly in their natural state.

The institute was also fashioning implements and vestments for the Kohanim or priests and Levites in accordance with Holy Scriptures and tradition. Many other preparations were in process for the operation of the third temple. In fact, the rumor was that red heifers were being raised in a secret location for sacrifice. The Kohanim and Levites were also being trained at the institute for the daily operations of the temple and the performance of those sacrifices.

Considering all of this, David was convinced that Rabbi Kohen had a list tracking the lineage of the qualified high priest. David hoped he could convince Rabbi Kohen to admit to its existence and to share some of the information with him.

"Rabbi Kohen, I am sure you know we are hard at work trying to unearth the Temple Mount and verify its proper location. We are looking for clues to aid us. The Muslims have spent centuries trying to destroy all evidence of the temple's existence, but they have not succeeded."

"Yes, Rabbi, you are doing Elohim's work. We too are preparing for the day when we can worship at the temple again. How may I help you?" Rabbi Kohen asked. He was a man in his early eighties but looked like he was ready for any challenge coming his way.

"Well, we have reason to believe that the Ark of the Covenant is still in existence. And that God has protected it for such a day." David watched for a reaction in Rabbi Kohen's demeanor.

"From your mouth to God's ears, Rabbi." Rabbi Kohen seemed to shift gears from politeness to interest.

"Indeed, we also believe we have found a way to locate it." David presented the bait. He now needed to set the hook.

"We believe the Ark and the qualified high priest have been tracking each other since one is useless without the other." David paused. Rabbi Kohen gestured to continue. "And if we had a record of the high priests' movements through the centuries, we may be able to locate the Ark."

"And you believe we possess such a record and that we would want to share it with you?" Rabbi Kohen completed David's thought. "Rabbi David, if such a list existed, it would have to be well protected. The record of such a genealogy tracking the high priests through our history, documenting the line of Aaron to a person and location today would be very dangerous for the heir and for the future of our people." Rabbi Kohen leaned back in his leather armchair and waited for a response.

"Rabbi, we can use any information you can safely share with us. We aren't looking to expose the identity or the whereabouts of the high priest today. We just need to be pointed in the right direction. We know, for instance, that Masada was the last place the high priest Caiaphas appeared. We could assume his eldest son was sent away with the Ark. But we are yet to verify this." David figured he had one last card to play to get Rabbi Kohen to open up. "We have also broken the code used by the priests to document such movements."

"The Kabbalah Qadosh! This is a mystery to all but a handful of the chosen Hebrews. How did you uncover such a thing?" Rabbi Kohen was noticeably shook.

"We had help. And now we need yours."

*****

102

"We cannot be in two places at one time. That goes for our minds, souls, and spirits as well as our bodies." Pastor Harold was halfway through his sermon. He was preaching to FCC of Charleston, his home church, but he was also addressing millions more on this particular Sunday morning. "We cannot have faith in God and doubt His presence and His power. We cannot have Jesus as our Lord and follow the world. 'No one can serve two masters; for either he will hate the one and love the other, or else he will be loyal to the one and despise the other. You cannot serve God and mammon.'

"We cannot be committed Christians and behave like committed demons. We cannot walk on water and sink beneath the stormy waves. We cannot layup treasures in heaven and seek immediate gratification in this life. James tells us not to think we will receive anything from the Lord if we are double-minded men and women.

"Love God and hate the world. Pray for your enemies and be kind to those who despitefully use you. Seek good for others at your own expense. Walk worthy of the calling to which you were called. These are all directives given to us by the Holy Spirit in His holy word. Are you obeying them? Or are you being double minded? Are you playing the hypocrite? Talking one way and living another. Angels are watching. The Holy Spirit is either being obeyed or He is being grieved. Jesus is calling.

"Are you listening?"

Pastor Harold had a lot more to say. His sermon was slotted for forty minutes. It had only been speaking for twenty-five minutes, but he felt led to stop and pray for his congregation. He came down the stairs of his pulpit and knelt before the people.

"Heavenly Father, forgive us our trespasses. Give us strength. Heal our land. Save our people. Draw near to us as we draw near to you. We ask so that we may receive. We seek so that we may find. We knock so that the door may be open. Come Holy Spirit. Come sweet heavenly dove. Stay right here with us. Fill us with your love."

Then the inexplicable happened. People began to stir in their pews. They slowly moved into the aisles. Gradually, cries of wonder, praise, and gladness began to build throughout the auditorium. People were being healed. From the deaf to the paralyzed. From the broken boned to the broken hearted. Irregular heartbeats became regular, cancer was no more, anxieties became joys, the hopeless became hopeful. Tears of joy began to flow. Songs of praise began to be sung.

Pastor Harold continued to pray as tears were streaming down his face. Annie was shocked by this miraculous turn of events. But then something happened to Annie. After five years of nothing but frustration, Annie felt a stirring deep in her body. She looked up and saw Harold looking at her. They both knew their countless prayers had been answered. Annie was pregnant.

God was listening.

PART 5

Angel and the Colonel

Blue was at her special place in the Andes. She was grateful to the Almighty for giving her the opportunity to earn redemption. *The Almighty is good and merciful,* she thought. She was aware that it all almost came to a crushing end. She could hardly believe General Samson was watching out for her. She was awed by his concern and humility. He was one of the mightiest Warrior angels in creation, and he chose to spend his time and attention to ensure her safety. But she was also worried about Angel. He had been wounded badly. Her prayer was that he would heal completely.

"Blue." His soft sweet voice vibrated warmly through her being. She felt he was near.

"I'm here," she thought.

"May I join you?" He was her gentle, mighty, golden Angel.

"Of course." She turned to the North to meet his gaze. "How are you?"

"Healed, with a few added scars." He turned to display his wings.

She smiled sadly. "I'm sorry I didn't get there sooner."

"You got there soon enough. I was careless. I should have never allowed Sulfurra to sneak up on me like that." Angel shook his head.

"We beat them this time, but it's far from over. Dagon will be replaced. Others will come for us," Blue warned.

"And we'll be ready," Angel added. "I didn't have an opportunity to congratulate you on your new commission, Warrior Colonel Blue."

He took her hands and pulled her into his arms under his overshadowing wings and held her for an eternal second. She brushed his hood back off his head, grabbed both sides of his golden locks, and drew him near for a kiss.

Angel wished this moment would last forever. He looked deeply into her eyes. He never expected her cool presence, her powerful spirit, her inner strength could also be so gentle and beautiful. After a while, Angel said, "I've got something for you." He motioned to the northern sky. A bow appeared. While this bow was similar to the promise rainbow given to Noah, there was one major difference. Instead of seven distinct colors ranging from red to violet, Angel's bow consisted of seven shades of blue.

Blue was stunned. She named the colors as she pointed to each, "Baby Blue, Maya, Carolina, Cornflower, Azure, Navy, Royal, it's amazing. How did you do this?"

"Simple," Angel said, "I took every thought I have of you and colored the sky."

"Thank you, it's lovely," she said and kissed him again.

"Although I would like to stay here forever, I've come for another reason," Angel announced.

Blue gathered herself and responded, "Okay, shoot."

"The Council wants to discuss our next assignment." Angel waited.

"When?" Blue asked.

"Well, now." Angel shrugged.

Blue took his hand, nodded, and said, "Let's go."

*****

To say the Jews were not truly accepted wherever they settled would be an understatement. In spite of this truth, however, in 1600, many Jews thrived and became wealthy in the Netherlands. They were merchants and brokers situated in the center of a primary food production hub. The Netherlands provided food throughout all of Europe. The Jews also offered banking and financing to farmers and other purveyors of this fertile region.

One of Amsterdam's wealthiest family was led by Rabbi Menasseh ben Israel. Unknown to the Jewish community and most of his family, Rabbi Israel was also the qualified high priest of Judaism. He kept in contact with the Ghib-bore. He knew that the Ghib-bore had moved the treasures of the temple to Warwick Castle just outside of London.

In 1650, Rabbi Israel went to England to make a case with the crown to establish a Jewish settlement in London. Along with the financial pressures from the Spanish War and the continuing hostilities with France, King Charles II acquiesced. The gold tribute and the wealth offered by Rabbi Israel to the crown helped in the king's decision.

Once again, only the third time since the destruction of Jerusalem had the high priest and the Ark of the Covenant been reunited in the same location. But this reunion was short lived. The Kraken followed the Rabbi to England from the Netherlands. He did not want the Jews to expand their influence into England.

This high-level demon was King of the West and lord over the Netherlands. He had isolated most of the Jews to Amsterdam. The Kraken planned to use the hate and the selfish ambitions of the gentiles to destroy the Jews.

He directed and influenced the gentiles to move against the Jews. Portraying them as cultural and religious invaders and Christ Killers. He planned to have the Jews' property confiscated and wealth stolen. Kraken's final solution was to wipe the Jews from the face of the earth.

However, Rabbi Israel's true identity as high priest was hidden from the Kraken and the rest of the demon realm. Archangel Gabriel had the power and the intelligence to thwart every effort the demon realm made to discover the high priest's existence and the whereabouts of the Ark and its treasures. Gabriel knew, however, that it was just a matter of time until the Kraken would discover the truth. Something had to be done.

Gabriel appeared to Francis in a dream and warned him that he would have to move again. Francis knew that the Ghib-bore was under the protection of Gabriel, but he had never been approached by this mighty angel.

"You must leave," Gabriel told Francis in a dream.

"Where can we go? We are at the end of ourselves," Francis said.

"Follow the sun. I, the 'hero of God,' will be with you," Gabriel said as he vanished into a cloud.

Francis realized they had to prepare. It would take years to make the move safely. They would have to choose a place, send a settlement team, purchase a location, build accommodations, gain local support, and finally relocate the Ark, the holy scrolls, the artifacts, the treasures, and various secret items. But he knew he wouldn't be around for the move. He had to convince Benjamin, Ghib-bore's leader, and Rabbi Menasseh ben Israel to resettle where the Lord was leading them.

"Benjamin, you've been like a son to me. It breaks my heart to try to convince you to leave this place," Francis said.

"Are you certain this is the only way? How could we possibly make such an extreme move safely?" Benjamin was confused, emotional, and unwilling.

"I am certain. The message I received in this dream was unmistakably from the Most High." Francis turned to Rabbi Israel.

"Rabbi, there must be a reason that after all these years, you have finally been united with our treasures." Francis waited for a response.

"So you believe that reason is to take the treasure elsewhere?" Rabbi tested.

"The angel said, 'Follow the sun,'" Francis repeated.

*****

Harold was overjoyed when Annie's pregnancy was confirmed by her doctor. This miracle baby reinforced his priories: God first, Annie and the baby second, and serving others third. He also felt that serving the Lord included serving his country. He was elected to do a job not only by the people of South Carolina but also by God. He was still contemplating the offer to be Joe Kennedy's running mate. He had a little more than a year to decide. What sort of challenges would that bring? Where would that fit into God's plan for his life? God directs branches to hold on to the vine, not to produce fruit. Trust the vine and the fruit will come.

He was the world's most unwilling celebrity. The news media pursued him, the paparazzi pestered him, government agencies distrusted him, and Christians swarmed him. Everyone wanted a piece of him. Some for good reasons, others for not so good reasons.

Harold understood where his popularity came from. He, too, was stunned by the outpouring of the Holy Spirit on those three occasions. But he knew the outpouring of the Holy Spirit was not meant for his own glory but to glorify the Father and the Son. It also validated the gospel message he shared with the world. Now, more than ever, he had to be careful what message he sent out. It had to be good seed. His every word would be publicized, scrutinized, analyzed, and criticized. He prayed he wouldn't be paralyzed. He prayed that God would superintend his every word and guide his every choice.

Harold was having trouble deciding what he would say as the keynote speaker at the annual meeting for the Coalition of African American Pastors (CAAP). The meeting was in Memphis, Tennessee, in two days. Harold had written three speeches and tossed all three. He knew this was a time to speak from heart, not from the head.

He knew this engagement would bring to focus his southern roots. His ancestry was deeply entrenched in the south. Some facts about his ancestry were clear, some more cloudy. His people were taken to the West Indies by Spanish slave traders to harvest sugarcane. They were later transferred to the colonies to build a new city in Carolina. Later, they became rice farmers and eventually, somehow gained their freedom. It was unclear to him how that feat was accomplished, but they later moved to Alabama. He figured they became sharecroppers and eventually owners of their own humble plantation.

God had placed him in the "here and now" for a purpose. He knew God loved him and had a plan to prosper him and not to harm him. He also believed God knows the end from beginning. How was he going to convey this knowledge and this hope to the confused and hopeless world? How could he let them know God was listening?

*****

Harold was the center of attention in another realm. Mammon was not wasting any time. His agents were on the move. An occult group of followers under the influence of demonic power were planning Harold Washington's assassination in the next few days. It would appear racially motivated. It would be publicly viewed, and it would be earth shaking.

Mammon didn't know how far this attack would be allowed to go. But Mammon was given his position of power to get results. Some previous schemes had failed, but as a whole, the Rebellion was gaining ground. Marriages failing, families disintegrating, education devolving, governments crumbling, the Bible losing credibility, and Christian believers losing hope around the world to mention a few areas of progress. The only question was whether he would be allowed to squeeze the life from Pastor Washington personally.

Mammon was a giant. He was fed by greed. And there was plenty of greed in America. Greed chocked out truth. Greed redirected the desire for life's good and honorable things to obsessions for possessions. Greed carried with it the hollow hope of happiness even though it never delivered. Mammon used greed like a maestro uses his musical instrument. It was the driving force behind many glorious disasters.

His own personal greed was only matched by his pride. He decided he would take care of the "Pastor Harold" problem personally. By personally, he meant alone. He would demonstrate to the entire demon world that he could accomplish alone what all the demon armies couldn't accomplish together.

The bomb was already in positioned. The triggering device already in place. Since human agents prepared the assassination, demon involvement was minimal. He was sure to maintain a very low profile. Therefore, guarding angels weren't alerted.

Congressman Pastor Harold T. Washington, DDiv., was the keynote speaker. His wife, Annie, accompanied him to the stage. Lights, cameras, reporters, TV, radio, streaming services all waited to hear what he had to say. There were already rumors about him running for the vice presidency or being appointed the new ambassador to the Mideast. This speech could be a jumping-off point. It was a very big event.

Angel had followed the pastor to Memphis. He placed his guards around the entire area. They scouted the city, looking for unusual demon activity. What they found to be unusual was that there was no demon activity. It was like demons had been ordered to leave the city entirely.

Blue was following up on Dagon's replacement. Mammon was a dangerous demon. He stopped at nothing to get his own way, and nothing got in his way. She thought it was suspicious, however, that when he did leave his cavern, he only roamed through the South. Tonight, he went alone.

"Angel, where is the pastor?" Blue reached out.

"We are in Memphis, at a speaking engagement. Is there a problem?" Angel asked.

"Something is wrong. Mammon is coming your way, alone," Blue warned.

"The pastor is about to speak. We will redouble our protection." Angel ordered another centurion and his troops to join them.

*****

"Remembering our past is important, but planning for the future is vital," Pastor Harold began after greeting and thanking the dais.

"What others did to us is our history, but what we do for ourselves is our destiny. We cannot change the past. In truth, we cannot control the future. We can only resolve to do what is right today. And the Bible tells us what is right.

"The Bible tells us that if we live with clean hands and pure hearts, we will receive a blessed life from God. If we, who call ourselves Christians, will humble ourselves and pray and seek God's face and turn from our wicked ways, then He will hear from heaven. And He will heal our land.

"When we go through the flood, He is our ark. When we cross the sea, He is the wind at our backs. When we are cast into the furnace, he is our asbestos jacket. And when we go through the Valley of the Shadow of Death, our Good Shepherd goes with us.

"Drawing near to God is a heart attitude. Resisting the devil is decision of the will. It is time for us, as preachers and teachers, to lead by example no matter what trials we face. Because the power of God is at our disposal. The gospel is our power." Harold took his signature pause and then continued.

"If God is for us, who can be against us."

At that moment Angel heard "power" and thought "bomb." He immediately visualized the building, the auditorium, the podium, the stage, under the stage.

There it was, a bomb! Angel called out, "Shields!"

Ten of the closest guardians jumped into action. They dove under the stage, jumped on the bomb, and formed a protective encasement around the entire device with their shields. Angel grabbed Pastor Harold and Annie and covered them with his wings. They tumbled off the stage together.

The explosion was deafening. The stage lifted two feet in the air and came crashing back down. People on the stage were tossed out of their seats. People in the auditorium were pushed back by the shock wave. Those standing were flung down by the concussion. And then, silence.

Mammon hovered over the scene, waiting for the opportunity that never came. In a flash, hundreds of angels attacked him. Blue shot frozen arrows into his knees. Lightning swords sliced through his body. Chains wrapped around him. He was captured. There was no escape, and no one was there to come to his aid.

Pride goeth before a fall, Blue thought.

*****

The bomb specialist and the crime scene investigators had no explanation for what had happened. The power of the detonation was strong enough to demolish the entire building. The explosion jettisoned shrapnel outward at the speed of sound. It should have destroyed, maimed, crippled, or murdered everyone in the building. Inexplicably, there was no damage. Projectiles from the explosion traveled a few inches and stopped in their tracks. Injuries amounted to a handful of bumps and bruises. It was as if the hand of God shielded the entire congregation and its keynote speaker. The word "miracle" was being used by the media and the people there. Fingerprints on what was left of the device were still traceable. Within days, the entire terrorist group was apprehended.

Harold and Annie knew it was God's direct intervention. Just a fraction of a second before the explosion, they both felt a warm embrace. They were lifted into the air and gently brought down to safety. Playback from the multiple cameras present actually showed them being thrown by the explosion and landing thirty feet from the stage. It was a miracle they weren't injured.

The blogs and newspaper headlines read "A Miracle! If God Is for Us, Who Can Be Against Us." TV news coverage hesitated to use the "M" or "G" words but did call the incident unexplainable and amazing.

After personally checking on everyone's well-being, Harold and Annie headed home.

After driving for an hour, Harold decompressed and asked Annie, "How are you, really?"

"I'm confused by what happened. I really believed God, the Holy Spirit, or a ministering angel lifted us out of harm's way. He was literally, 'our strength and our shield,'" Annie said.

"Yes, He did. And yes, He protected us. And the baby?" Harold was driving but turned to watch Annie's expression.

Annie said, "Harold, can you pull the car over for a second?"

Harold heart dropped. Did they lose the baby? He pulled over to a safe place on the road. He turned off the car and turned toward his lovely wife and asked again, "And the baby?"

Annie put her hand on Harold's knee and said, "We're fine."

Visibly relieved, Harold said, "Thank God." Harold had to affirm one more time, "You and the baby are fine."

Annie smiled. "Love, I'm fine and so are the babies."

*****

Angel and Blue stood before the Council once again.

"Gog, Beelzebub, Jinn Sing, the Kraken, Satin, Diablo, and Morto are presently the highest-ranking demons on earth," Eli said to Angel and Blue. "And they are all after you two."

"Sir, may I respectfully remind you that their charge, Pastor Washington, seems to be a lightning rod for these evil's attack. And we don't know why," Joel, the Watcher General, said.

"Yes, indeed. We don't have the entire story yet. I intend to meet with Gabriel and find out what he knows about this escalation of evil." Eli studied his new Colonel of Warriors and Commander of Guardians. "Do either of you have any insight you could share with us?"

"General, I am certain it has something to do with the preparation of the third temple in Jerusalem. I've made some headway, but whenever I get close to an answer, I hit a brick wall," Blue said.

"Angel, do you have anything?" Eli asked.

"General, as you know, I've been guarding the church and its people for over 350 years without a single demon appearance. As soon as Pastor Washington showed up, it's been one battle after another. I believe he has a bigger part in all of this than any of us originally suspected," Angel stated.

"Well, Commander, do you need more warriors or guardians?" General Debra asked.

"Madam General, I wouldn't know what to do with more troops. We really need more information." Angel hadn't vocalized his thoughts until now. "Pastor Washington is being led by the Holy Spirit. He is on a mission. I don't believe he even knows what his mission is. This is all a mystery. But the best we could do is continue to continue. Be vigilant, and the truth will eventually be revealed."

"In the meantime?" General Samson asked.

Blue answered, "Be proactive, and take it to the enemy. Do whatever it takes to squeeze information from their slimy little brains."

"Colonel Blue, any activity must be within the guidelines set by the Almighty," General Seraphima reminded Blue and the Council.

"Of course, Madam General." Blue stiffened a little. She hoped she hadn't overreached. "They still haven't realized I've been redeemed. I believe I have access to their world. Demons talk. I'm certain I could find out what their plan is and why they are focusing on the pastor."

"Blue, you must be careful. If anything happens to you in the underworld, I'm not sure we could come to your aid," Chairman Eli warned.

"I'll be as careful as possible, Chairman. Besides, Angel will be with me," Blue assured the Council.

Angel peeked at Blue out of the corner of his eye. He thought, *What has she gotten us into now?*

*****

Even though Francis expected the move to take three years, it took five to leave Warwick safely. Three families from the Ghib-bore along with Tobias Menasseh Israel, the eldest son of the current high priest, all relocated to the colonies with their precious cargo. These four families financed the eight men sent by Charles II. Known as the Lord Proprietors, they were commissioned to build a new city, strategically placed to protect the southern exposer of the colonies. The land was rich and fertile and would soon become the center of commerce for the South. Charles Towne in the Carolina territory became the Ghib-bore's new home.

For the next ten years, they defended the city from assaults by the French, the Spanish, the American Indians, and pirates. They built fortified walls around the city, military fortresses, various community buildings, residential buildings, and churches.

The three Ghib-bore families and Rabbi Israel were able to keep their true identities and their families' origin and purpose secret. They changed their surnames. They became landowners, bankers, attorneys, politicians, and persons of influence. For all practical purposes, they owned and ran the city of Charles Towne.

Like everyone in the Carolina Territory, the families utilized slaves brought to the city by the British from the West Indies to help build the territory and raise tobacco, cotton, and rice. While Europe was struggling through their "Enlightenment Period," the "Reformation," religious turmoil and political hostilities, fortunes were made on top of fortunes in Carolina.

In spite of all of this, the Ghib-bore family leaders never lost sight of their purpose. They were entrusted to protect what God had given them and to be prepared to return to Jerusalem when called. Emissaries and dedicated followers in Jerusalem watched and prayed for the day all Jews would return to their city and the temple would be built again. Angels stood at the ready, watching.

*****

"Mammon failed." Apollyon grew larger as he shifted his attention to Gog. "And where were you through all this?"

"Ambassador, I was following your orders. I was in my own district in the North searching for the enemy's agents and connection to whoever has been protecting the pastor," Gog answered.

"And what have you found?" Apollyon asked. It was clear that tensions were building in the room.

"We have isolated it to a guardian. He has received greater power and weapons than we normally encounter and at least a thousand warriors. I still don't believe he is accomplishing this on his own. We have hundreds of demons stronger than him and a million demons to match his troops. We will match him and then some. The next time we meet, he will be destroyed. As soon as we are ready, we will attack him and his pastor." Gog was growing more confident as he spoke. This somewhat satiated Apollyon's anger.

"Good, we must work together on this." Apollyon banged a fist on the table. "Satin has been assigned to North America. I want you to work with her. She will take the lead in this effort. This is your last chance. If I don't have results by the next Blood Moon, you will both be replaced. Before the pastor is destroyed, I want to know who he really is and why he is so important to the enemy."

"Next, Beelzebub, have you found the Ark?" Apollyon shifted into his dragon beast form and turned toward the King of the South.

"We have not. In fact, almost certainly, it has been destroyed," Beelzebub answered.

"Almost certainly? Did you say almost certainly?" A menacing green vapor spewed from Apollyon's nostrils.

"Ambassador, there hasn't been a sighting of the Ark since AD 70. Titus Caesar Vespasianus most probably destroyed the Ark along with the temple at that time." Beelzebub began to stammer.

"I want proof!" Apollyon demanded.

"How can I prove something doesn't exist? If it's not there, it's just not there." Beelzebub thought he was right. It turned out he was dead right.

In a streak of green lightning, Beelzebub was decapitated. His body never hit the ground. He was consumed on the spot.

It took a few silent minutes for Apollyon to recover from his fit of rage. No one in the room moved a claw, wing, muscle, or eyelash. Finally, he addressed the remaining six demon leaders.

"I believe I just demonstrated how to prove something doesn't exist. 'Almost certainly' and 'most probably' the same will happen to you if I don't get results."

*****

"Pastor, what can we do to help you decide what to do?" Jim asked.

Jim, Sam, and Richard sat in Pastor Harold's office drinking iced tea. They had just spent an hour recapping Pastor's last three months and the White House's offer to run for vice president.

"Pray for wisdom," Harold said. "If I run for vice president, my duties here at church will be greatly affected."

"Together, we can handle it. This is a once in a lifetime opportunity. We've had Christians at the helm of this country many times in our history, but there has never been a time like this. America has never had an active pastor help run our country. This is a 'God thing.' You are clearly blessed by God. You are His man. You've been affirmed by the Holy Spirit more than once. The world, Christian and non-Christian alike, recognizes you as a genuine man of God and not just another politician out for personal gain. I believe people want someone they can trust for a change. I believe God has a special purpose for you even beyond DC." Jim was leading the charge.

"Jim, what is our membership as it stands today?" Pastor Harold asked.

Jim turned to Sam and waited for an answer. "Actual members, we've got 2,469 and an additional 245 in membership class who plan to become members," Sam said.

"Then this is what I'd like to do," Harold said. "Let's bring this to the members and ask them what we should do. A simple 'run or not run' vote."

Jim knew there was more to Pastor's plan than a vote, "Fair enough?"

"And if we get 2,469 votes to run, I'll do it. Why should we be the only ones God directs?" Harold smiled.

"A unanimous vote? We never agree 100 percent on anything," Richard Bridgewater said.

"That will make it all the more special," Pastor Harold said. "If one member is uncomfortable with the idea of their pastor as vice president or if God doesn't want this to happen only one, 'not run' vote will let us know." Harold felt like he was on the right track. He was immediately at ease for the first time in weeks. He looked at his three closest friends and said, "You know, a fleece."

"We got it, Pastor. A fleece," Jim said.

*****

Satin was one of the most beautiful angels I had ever known. In fact, she became my muse. She was an awesome worship leader. She wrote songs that magnified the glory of the Almighty. We spent many hours together discussing them. She would sing them for me and asked my opinion. We began to write and then rewrite verses and choruses. She could play every instrument imaginable. I couldn't play one. However, her beauty, her voice, her talent, her total persona brought out the poet in me. I discovered that I had a creative side.

I was most saddened when the Rebellion swept her away. Apart from Blue, whom I thought was my life partner, I missed Satin the most. When I heard Satin was now the new demon commander of North America, I was shocked but at the same time not shocked. She was never the most skilled fighter, nor the most talented strategist, but she was the most determined leader I had ever known. She accomplished whatever she set out to do. She would find a way to get others to follow and support her. So even though fighting wasn't her thing, I knew she could lead fighters to do whatever she decided needed to be done.

One thing was for certain, she would recognize me if we ever met again. That's why I couldn't believe my ears when Blue said, "We need to infiltrate the North American demon headquarters and find out what Satin is up to."

"That's not possible," I said. "Satin would recognize me in a second. We were close. In our past life, I mean."

Blue looked at me, smiled, and said, "I'm counting on it."

Blue was smart, cunning, even crafty. Where Satin would get others to do what she desired, Blue would do it herself. "Never ask anyone to do what you can do yourself," Blue always said. And Blue could do anything.

"I think I'm missing something here," I said.

"Do you trust me?" Blue asked.

"Yes, of course I do," I said.

"Then give me your shackles and put your hands behind your back."

*****

Tobias Menasseh Israel was nothing like his father. Physically, he was tall, slender, and somewhat sinewy. His father was short, stout, and a formidable power of nature. Unlike his charismatic father, Tobias was timid, reserved, and unassuming. However, he did inherit his father's genius. It would take Tobias twice as long to make a decision, but he never made the wrong one.

His father wanted a large family. To that end, Tobias was the eldest of four brothers and three sisters. Tobias, who celebrated his thirtieth birthday on his overseas journey to America, was not yet married. Any one of a dozen available young ladies, who traveled to the colonies with Tobias and Ghib-bore family members, would have gladly been courted by Tobias. But Tobias was dedicated to his studies and realized that being the eldest son of the legitimate high priest of Israel carried serious duties and heavy responsibilities. Additionally, there was the cargo that accompanied them. He was intrinsically bound to its safety and its future. Romance was the furthest thing from his mind.

In Charles Towne, Tobias found that the woodworking skills he developed in Amsterdam became very practical in the New World. His natural talents as an engineer and architect became invaluable. He helped design and build multiple buildings. He soon earned a reputation as the most capable builder in the region.

Tobias never pursued wealth, but that didn't stop wealth from pursuing him. He left his finances in the hands of his dear friend, Benjamin Schumacher. Benjamin convinced Tobias to build a home for himself and gently suggested he consider finding a life partner. Benjamin reminded Tobias that as the heir to the high priest, he had a duty to have an heir himself. For a thirty-year-old, Tobias knew that eventuality lay in his future, but for the present time, he had his studies and responsibilities and work to occupy him full time.

*****

Claire was the daughter of African slaves in the West Indies. Her family worked the sugarcane fields, but because of her natural beauty, she was always favored by her owners. She was moved into the house. There she learned to cook, clean, read, write, and play the piano. She helped raise the children of the house and, after a time, became the children's nanny. She was watched closely by the mistress of the house and was never inappropriately treated. She was regarded as a gem.

When her owners were asked by King Charles II to relocate their import/export business to a southern town in Carolina, they viewed it as an opportunity to improve their status and join the British elite. Claire had no other family but the Moores. She was delighted and excited to change her world once again.

After five difficult years in Charles Towne, sickness took Mrs. Moore. Mr. Moore was devastated. He decided to take his grown children back to England, enroll them in the finest college. There he planned to recreate himself in London. Sadly, he decided to leave his slaves in Charles Towne but sought to place them in secure, respectable homes before he left. His own architect and builder Tobias Menasseh was in need of a house manager. Mr. Moore suggested Claire.

"She was loved by my dear wife, taught my children, managed our home. She is proficient in all areas of domestic support, bookkeeping, language arts, music, politics, and is a student of the Good Book. I pay her for her work and give her room and board. She knew our intent was to let her buy her own freedom when she turned twenty-one. We hoped she would choose to stay with us." Edward Moore began to tear up just speaking of his wife and the plans they had for the future.

"But now I must ask you to follow through with the promise I made to my Mary. Claire must be provided for. I don't know what would happen to her without a sponsor once we leave. She is a strong girl but not invincible. She will need protection. If you catch my drift." Edward took a sip of brandy and stared at the fire in the sitting room hearth. "Of course, I will pay for any added expense you may incur."

"This is a little sudden. I do need help running this place. I'm rarely home. And when I am, I dedicate myself to my studies." Tobias ran through a number of scenarios in his head that could possibly work. "I don't know how I feel about owning a slave," Tobias said.

"Tobias, you misunderstand me. She won't be your slave. I have already bought her freedom, legally. I've already spoken to her about this proposal. She amenable to this opportunity. Of course, she wants to come with us to England, but she realizes that there will be no us once the kids move away. It will just be her and a doddering old fool." Edward lost himself again in the fireplace flame.

"Nonsense, 'Weeping may last through the night, but joy cometh with the morning.' You're headed to a new life with your children and many future grandchildren. Many men would gladly exchange lives with you. I would love to have a family like yours someday." Tobias tried to cheer Edward on, but now he seemed to feel a little melancholic himself.

After a few more minutes and a few more sips of brandy, Edward asked, "Tobias, you're a good man. Maybe the kindest man I know. This is the right thing to do, for all of us. Will you take her on?"

Something, almost unearthly, moved in Tobias's heart. Whether it was the sadness for his friend's loss, the fact that Edward was moving to England, or the possibility of having someone else living under his roof, he couldn't place it. But at that moment, he knew he would accept his friend's offer.

*****

"A million sets of ears listening to a billion conversations for two thousand years and not one word about who or where he is? The silence tells us all we need to know. He's being hidden from us!" the Kraken searched the eyes of his board members for a response. The King of the West was a patient beast. Destroying everyone on his board would gain him nothing but temporary relief from his frustration and leave him with the momentous task of replacing each of them with similar incompetents. He tried it before.

"Either he doesn't exist or the Jews have out maneuvered us. I don't believe that the Jews would allow the 3,500-year-old office of high priest to simply vanish."

The Kraken's twelve arms roamed through the room, sensing every emotion being experienced. Fear, anxiety, anger, and hate were normal reactions to his presence. But wait. Was that guilt?

"Or," he paused, trying to find where that last emotion was coming from, "am I being betrayed? Is someone holding out on me?"

One could gage the danger of the moment by watching the color of the Kraken. Black was the safest, red the most dangerous. The change was normally gradual, but it could be sudden. It was deemed best to keep quiet, keep your head down, and keep living. He had just turned green. This meeting wasn't going well. Someone had to say something, or this meeting would end very messy.

"Sire, may I speak?" Vapus asked. The Kraken nodded.

"I also believe he exists. There are 15 million Jews alive today. Out of which about 1,000,000 are actual Levites. Only a portion of those come from the line of Aaron. I estimate there are 100,000 true Kohens. Only a fifth of these are firstborn males. Only a portion of those are living a kosher life. Meaning, alive today, there are approximately 20,000 qualified individuals who can become the high priest. I've been developing a list of who and where those individuals are." Vapus waited for an indication from the Kraken.

"Go on," he said, gesturing with one of his twelve tentacles.

"Only 5,000 live in your kingdom. I suggest we focus on them, their immediate families, their friends, their synagogues and see where that leads." Vapus looked up and noticed the Kraken was black again.

"Why not kill them all?" Luminous asked. The possibility had entered almost everyone's mind in the room.

The Kraken interrupted the conversation. "We tried that. What winds up happening is that we lose important information. The death of a few Jews only launches a population increase of Jews elsewhere. We need to find this coward priest and follow his activity. If he is who we think he is, he will eventually lead us to the Ark, the plans for the building of the temple and the way to destroy it all. This must happen to avoid the Enemy sending His Son, again."

Vapus thought, *He's on board. This is good. As long as he's talking, he's not killing.*

"Prepare a similar list for each kingdom. I want to hand it to the Ambassador, personally. You and Luminous organize our demons to find and follow the 5,000 in our kingdom and report back to me before the next Blood Moon."

*****

Satin had just dismissed her monthly executive board meeting. This month, it was hosted by Slate in Utah. Satin was reviewing her notes and wondering just how aggressive her search could get without attracting the enemy's attention.

"The answer is out there," she said to herself.

"I believe I've got it right here," Blue said.

Satin was startled but didn't show it. She said, "Blue, how nice of you to drop by." But thought, *Slate's security must be amped up.*

"Is this a scheduled meeting or just a friendly visit?" Satin asked.

"It's a follow-up meeting I was scheduled to have with Dagon. Since Dagon is no longer with us, I thought I'd follow up with you. I've brought you a present." Blue removed the hood off Angel's head and pushed him forward.

Satin was visibly moved when she saw Angel. And then she drew her sword.

"Well, I haven't seen you in centuries. How have you been, old friend?" Satin composed herself when she noticed the shackles and Angel's lack of weaponry.

"Busy," Angel said.

"Blue, did you want to explain?" Satin asked.

"Lover boy here is the pastor's guardian. He's got a ton of help. I haven't found out what the ultimate plan is yet, but I will," Blue said.

"What about his back-up?" Satin asked.

"What you see is what you get," Blue said.

"Leave him with me," Satin said.

"Sorry, he is my prisoner. I will complete what I've started. And I work better alone." Blue stiffened.

Satin raised an eyebrow. "I see," she said as she stared at Angel. Memories of a previous life came flooding back. "Pity. Look, I don't know what Dagon told you, but we need to know who's backing the pastor. He's causing quite a stir. Tongues, divine appearances, miracles, something big is going on. We need to know what it is. But our main objective is to find and destroy the Ark. We know it isn't here in North America, but maybe we can discover where it is."

Blue knew Satin's guard was down and that Satin always loved playing the big sister. "Why do you want to destroy the Ark? People would idolize it. It could be a modern-day Golden Calf," Blue asked.

"Obviously it must be destroyed. No Ark, no temple. No temple, no return of the Enemy's son." Satin was now gloating.

"What makes you think the pastor and the Ark are connected?" Blue just wanted Satin to keep talking.

"The pastor was in Jerusalem. He was poking around the temple site, asking questions," Satin said.

"And?" Blue did the rolling movement with her free hand.

"And?" Satin continued, "There is no 'and.' We must find out who's protecting the pastor, obviously Angel isn't doing this himself." Satin looked at Angel and said, "No offense."

Angel responded with a smile, "None taken."

Satin's gaze dwelled on Angel a second longer and continued, "Hmm, well, if we don't find out who else is involved, what his mission is, and if the Ark exists or not, Apollyon assures us heads are going to roll."

"By when?" Blue asked.

"The next Blood Moon," Satin answered.

"That's in November, right?" Blue said.

"October 31," Satin confirmed.

"I'll find out everything you need to know by then." Blue gave Angel's chain a tug.

"Good," Satin said. "Keep this between us. And when you've completed your inquiries, I need you to report directly to me. And then, Blue, I want you to hand Angel over to me."

Blue looked at Satin and nodded. "Oh, I will."

*****

Tobias was impressed by Claire. She was not only intelligent, talented, and well-read, as Edward described her, but she was also very beautiful. In a place like Carolina, there was an amazing mix of people. People from England, France, Spain, Africa, and the natives themselves. Each with their own cultural influences, cuisines, and aesthetic.

As an architect, Tobias appreciated their differing artistic approaches; as a woodworker and builder, he was enlightened by their varying skills and talents; as a Jewish believer, he recognized the beauty and diversity in the Almighty's creation.

After a few months, Tobias asked Claire to sup with him. She did. Dinner together became a regular occurrence. After dinner, they often sat by the fireplace and talked. Tobias felt at ease with Claire. She didn't judge him. She didn't require any extras from him. She just seemed to enjoy his company as much he did hers.

"Mr. Tobias, may I ask you a personal question?" Claire asked.

"Now, Claire, that depends on the question." Tobias took a sip of brandy. He always enjoyed their banter.

"Do your scriptures condone slavery?" Claire asked.

"Well, that's a question. As you undoubtedly know my people were slaves for four hundred years. It took ten awesome plagues from God Almighty to convince their masters to free them. The masters immediately changed their minds and set out to recapture them. That didn't end well for the masters.

"I'd say God allowed slavery to teach His people to be dependent only on Him." Tobias continued, "I am drawn to the comment Joseph made to his brothers. Do you remember, Joseph's ten brothers sold him into slavery?"

"I do, but please, go on. What did he say?" Claire asked.

"Well, twenty-two years after they beat him, threw him into a pit to die, changed their minds, took him out of the pit, and sold him into slavery, God's providence brought them together again. This time, he was not a seventeen-year-old kid but a thirty-nine-year-old governor of Egypt. Second in power only to pharaoh himself. When Joseph's brothers realized who he was they became fearful. But Joseph said to them, 'Do not fear for I am in the place of God. As for you, you meant it for evil against me, but God meant it for good.'" Tobias could see Claire was thinking about it.

She then said, "So God has a purpose in our lives, and He uses the circumstance of our lives to achieve that purpose, no matter how difficult?"

"Yes. I believe that is absolutely true," Tobias said as he studied her closely. She had lovely brown eyes, high cheekbones, and a slim body but definitely female. Curly ringlets outlined her lovely face. Her skin was cocoa in color and always seemed to be shining. She smelled like a field of wildflowers. Her voice was honey sweet. Tobias was attracted to women but always put his duties as the next high priest, ahead of personal needs. But Tobias had never been attracted to anyone like he was attracted to Claire.

"Then can I assume God has a purpose for our being here tonight? Can I also assume that the obvious attraction I have for you, and may I say, that we have for each other is in His plan?" She was now staring at him with intent.

Tobias took a gulp of his brandy rather than a sip. "Claire, I am bound to the Almighty in a special way. I must maintain 'clean hands and a pure heart.' My life must be beyond reproach."

"So you can never marry?" Claire asked innocently.

"I can," he stammered. "The woman I marry must love God wholeheartedly, be pure, and a believer, willing to follow God's law, and of course, she must love me."

"Can she be an African?" her intent had grown words.

"If she can fulfill all the requirements I mentioned and convert to Judaism, then, yes." Tobias could hardly find his voice.

"She can," she whispered. "When Adam and Eve were in the garden, they pledged themselves to their creator and to each other. Can a couple be married if they do the same before the Almighty wherever and whoever they are?" She stood up and moved toward him. She reached her hand out to Tobias. She waited for him to respond.

He did.

*****

"If you're sick, you're a sinner. If you're poor, you don't have enough faith. If you're being persecuted, God is punishing you. And if you're dying, God abandoned you."

On this Sunday morning, Pastor Harold was testing his people.

"No," a few brave parishioners spoke out.

"You disagree? Let's ask a few people to be sure."

"Bartimaeus, what was it? Was it your sin or your parents' sin that caused your blindness? You don't know? It was probably both of you all.

"Mary, you're a teenager, you've got no husband, no money, no home of your own, and you're pregnant. Where is your faith? Your quoting Bible verses now, but it's too late and the baby is coming.

"Stephen, you're going down. The stones are flying. Why is God punishing you? You don't know. Think again.

"Lazarus, you've been laying in a tomb for four days. Why has God abandoned you? You can't figure out why you were left to rot?

"Paul, why do you still have a thorn in your flesh? You asked three times to be healed and you still need someone to dictate your letters to."

Pastor Harold turned around and pointed to the verse hanging below the cross on the church's front wall. "Jesus has the answer. He said, 'My grace is sufficient for you, for my power is made perfect in your weakness.'

"But, Jesus, I thought you were the Prince of Peace. Where is my peace? Jesus said, 'In this world you will have trouble. But take heart! I have overcome the world.'

"But, Jesus, why have you deserted us? Jesus said, 'I will never leave you and I will never abandon you.'

"And yet they hung you on a cross." Pastor Harold pointed to the cross behind him.

"But, Jesus, where did you go? Jesus said, 'I go and prepare a place for you, I will come again and will take you to myself, that where I am you may be also.'"

Pastor Harold scanned the auditorium and asked, "Who do you believe in? What do you put your trust in? Where will you turn to?

"Bartimaeus was blind so that God could be glorified in his healing. Mary was chosen to demonstrate the presence and power of the Holy Spirit. Stephen was martyred to fan the flames of Christendom. Paul was debilitated to demonstrate our dependence should be on Jesus alone.

"If you don't know Jesus, come down the aisle and meet Him. If you need prayer, come down the aisle and we will pray for you. If your marriage is failing, come down the aisle and be reconciled. If you've lost your job, come down the aisle and be blessed by God's love for you. If your body is breaking, come down the aisle and find comfort. If your heart is aching, come down the aisle and find real peace that surpasses all understanding. I will meet you there. The elders will meet you there. Jesus will meet you there."

Pastor Harold unhooked his mic and came down the pulpit stairs. There he met Richard, Jim, and Sam. The four of them began praying with aisles full of people. More of the elders came to assist. Then Annie and the elder's wives joined the prayer team as hundreds were on their way down the aisle for prayer. A full hour passed, people began to sing and praise God.

This time, the rumble occurred in their hearts. This time, the light shone in their souls. This time, the Spirit of God spoke to people's hearts. People began to repent of their sins and receive Jesus as Savior and Lord. This time, a true revival began.

*****

The list was extremely detailed. Some of the list was written in Kabbalah Qadosh. It could only be open in the holy chamber. It could only be viewed by one person at a time, under specific circumstances. No one could speak a word while studying it. Communication was limited to signing. No notes, photos, or recordings could be taken. Elohim was constantly being praised in song by a cantor, who stood in the center of the chamber, 24/7. Four rabbis were stationed at the four corners of the chamber reading different portion of scriptures aloud. The holy men of the temple knew demonic forces were seeking the information found in the list. While well thought out and well executed, these precautions were unnecessary. The chamber and the work it produced fell under the protection of an extremely powerful archangel, Gabriel.

For centuries, the existence of this extraordinary list remained secret. It tracked the lineage, the periods of service, and the location of every high priest: the tribe of Levi, family of Aaron, eldest sons and duly qualified individuals. Rabbi David's theory was that if he found the current high priest, he would be able to locate the Ark. Once located, they would have the final pieces to the building of the temple.

He was allowed forty minutes to gain all the information possible. He took an oath never to speak of the list's existence or seek to view it again. David decided that the best way to go about this unique opportunity would be to memorize the list's information from present day back to as far as he could retain. He began reciting in his head, "Rabbi David Masinter, the current high priest in Johannesburg, service 1949 to present, Rabbi Benjamin Kohen, service 1899 to 1949, Oslo, Norway..."

After thirty-five minutes, David was pretty comfortable with the information regarding the last ten high priests. He had five minutes left. He decided to revert to locations only, starting from the destruction of the Herod's temple. He only noted changes in countries, and that is when he saw an unusual jump. He traced the high priest locations from the temple's destruction in Jerusalem to Spain to France to the Netherlands to the United Kingdom. But around 1650, there was a fifty-year gap. When the list resumed, it started in the Netherlands, then to Sweden to Norway. The list failed to describe the relocation from the UK to the Netherlands. And it was missing the link between the two high priests, a gap of fifty years. Rabbi David felt a tap on the shoulder. His time was up.

*****

The Council had convened to hear Angel's and Blue's report.

"Well, thanks to your daring exploits, we now know what the Rebellion is looking for and why," Eli said.

Angel confirmed, "They want the Ark if it exists, its treasures if they exist, the identity of the true high priest if he exists. They want to destroy the pastor, his ministry, anyone attached to his ministry including the church and its surrounding property." Angel turned to Blue and asked, "Am I missing anything?"

Blue slowly shook her head in disbelief. "Yes, Angel, they want to destroy you."

"Oh, right." Angel agreed, "They want me."

Eli turned to Debra. "How secure is the information?"

"Chairman Eli, it's so secure that none of the guardians, including their general, know where any of what Angel mentions is or if it even exists," General Debra reported.

"So this a matter for the throne room. But we can still continue to fight for the pastor's safety. We can still protect the church and its property. We can still aide the revival that's begun," Eli said.

"General, may I make a suggestion?" Blue asked as she scanned the members of the board.

"Go ahead, Colonel," Eli nodded.

"I believe we can be a little more proactive. Why don't we pick a convenient place and increase our activity around it? Station warriors, guards, and watchers. Feign to keep the location secret and safe. Draw the enemy's attention. All along preparing for an attack. We can fake them out. When they make their move, we can be ready to break them." Blue pounded one fist into the palm of her other.

"Colonel Blue has a great idea, Chairman Eli. I would personally like to be involved," General Samson interjected.

Blue nodded to General Samson, thanking him for his support.

"Very well, the Council would like to see the complete plan before we give full approval. I would rather have the unanimous agreement of the Council as to location, timing, and resource allocation," Chairman Eli said. "Let's say by next week's meeting?"

Everyone nodded in agreement. "Angel, this is still your responsibility we are depending on your knowledge of the pastor and the church's history."

Angel saluted by placing his right-hand fist across his heart and bowing his head. "Yes, Chairman, to Him be the glory," he said.

"For His glory. Amen," Eli said. "Dismissed."

*****

Tobias and Claire vowed to love and honor each other for the rest of their lives. Their vows were taken privately. When Tobias received word from his father, he called his friends together and announced their union. Tobias's three closest friends, the Ghib-bore, shared in the couple's joy.

Mr. Petersen who became the town's first mayor wondered how their marriage would affect Tobias's duties as heir to the high priesthood. He wondered how this union could affect the security of the Ark. He wondered how the two of them would handle the union of a Christian, which Claire definitely was, and the heir apparent Jew high priest. He could see how much the couple loved each other, but he wondered how his friend would work this all out. In short, Claire and Tobias were from different worlds.

"Our people populated North Africa in 1500 BC. We were 3 million strong. Even though we became slaves to the Pharaohs, we engineered and built the most powerful kingdom of the day. When our people left Egypt, they took the best of the land with them. When Moses met the Almighty face to face on Mount Sinai, he was promised a land flowing with milk and honey. Through the centuries, we gained and lost that land. We look to the day we can return to that land. And when we do, we will rebuild the temple and reestablish the old ways. My heir will carry the hope and the promise of the high priesthood into the future. I pray we will be found worthy by the Almighty," Tobias explained.

"Has your father blessed your marriage?" Mr. Schumacher asked.

"He has. He said that we all came from one father, Adam. We all survived the great flood through one man, Noah. We all share in one promise through one man, Abraham. We were all led to one land by one man, Moses. His people all follow one truth, His holy word. The high priest's direction to us is that Claire become a convert and that we both live kosher. I shall continue in my prayers and studies," Tobias explained.

"And have babies." Mr. Bridgewater raised his glass of brandy in a toast. They all laughed as they moved into the dining room where their families were settling in for a feast.

*****

Angel spotted Blue on her favorite mount top in the Andes. He approached her from behind.

"What have you been doing?" Angel asked.

"Planning," Blue said.

"Anything you'd like to share?" Angel put his arms around her and held her close.

"The 'where' has to be perfect," Blue stated. "The Vatican is too intimidating. A battle there could easily escalate into something much bigger. Egypt and the pyramids are too obvious. Jerusalem has been gone over with a fine-toothed comb. The Rebellion would never be fooled into thinking the Ark is there. The Far East isn't tenable. I'm thinking a museum or secret treasure chamber in France or England," Blue said.

"You want to do battle with the Kraken?" Angel asked.

"He may be powerful, but he's not invincible. In fact, I've been toying with the idea of the Tower of London. There's loads of rooms, chambers, secret passages. It overflows with the history of crusaders returning from the Holy Land. It's a pretty believable choice. Don't you think?" Blue didn't wait for Angel's response. "Neither side dominates there. And I have the perfect plan to lose." Blue looked away as she mentioned "lose."

Angel was momentarily stunned. He couldn't believe his ears. But then he collected himself as he was reminded that Blue was the smartest, strongest, and most cunning angel he ever knew. She would never plan to lose.

"I think you had better fill me in on the details." He suggested. "I'd rather not be filleted alive by the Council," Angel said.

"What is it that we want the most out of this conflict? Victory? In the end, victory is assured. When the Lord returns to earth, the victory will be His." Blue turned to give Angel her full attention. "If not victory, then what?"

She gave Angel time to think.

"To always do the Almighty's will? To serve and protect His chosen?" Angel guessed.

"Right! But if we eliminate the enemy's target, the enemy will have nowhere to go, no one to shoot at. They will lose their purpose and their focus for years." Blue waited for the light to go on in Angel's lovely head.

Angel thought for a minute. He slowly began to realize just how brilliant Blue was, literally and figuratively. "It will take a lot of preparation," Angel said.

"You still have a thousand angels at you command, right?" Blue raised an eyebrow.

"Yes, I do," Angel answered. "It may take more."

*****

"Ratcliff, what do you make of this?" Weezer was reviewing the three hundred daily activity logs taken around London. "The records showed an increase in enemy activity near Buckingham Palace and the Tower of London."

Weezer and Ratcliff were low-level demons given the most tedious task of organizing surveillance reports. Weezer handed the file to Ratcliff. "Looks to me like something of interest is going on in the Tower," Weezer said.

"Maybe there was an arrival of a foreign dignitary. Are any new demons poking around the Palace or the Tower?" Ratcliff looked through the reports and nervously pulled at his whiskers.

"Not that I know of." Weezer took the reports back.

"I'll go and ask around." Ratcliff got up to find Roku or Séance.

"Hold on." Weezer grabbed Ratcliff by his tail. "We don't want to draw any undue attention to ourselves." There was an ominous foreboding in Weezer's voice. "You do remember what the Kraken did to Charlemagne. And that was for merely mentioning the possibility of a raid and Charlemagne was right!"

"Right. So what do you propose we do?" Ratcliff asked.

"That's simple. Let's go over to the Tower and see for ourselves," Weezer suggested.

*****

The chamber in the Tower's dungeon was ready. Angel artisans worked for weeks fashioning artifacts that resembled the temple treasures. They were made of the finest of gold and bronze, ancient-looking curtains hung against the walls. They were made of twisted linen and gold. There was a chest made of gopher wood clad in gold and inlaid with gems. There was a portion of a golden cherubim wing half melted down. The wing was placed next to a petrified wooden staff. There were musical instruments, pitchers, a censer, and a menorah. There was also a jar of granite dust and marble chips. There was no manna, no Ark, no budding rod, no stone carved tablets, no scrolls.

However, there was a feeling of authenticity in the chamber. Purple linen covered any exposed portions of walls. There were paintings on display throughout the chamber. One of Moses holding the two tablets of the Ten Commandments, one of a high priest offering sacrifice at the Ark of the Covenant in the Holy of Holies, and a final painting that depicted the architectural layout for Solomon's temple.

A small gap, barely perceptible, was left open in the dungeon floor. It led to the open tunnels below.

It didn't take long for Weezer and Ratcliff to find that gap and weasel their way past the guards and into the chamber.

Weezer couldn't believe his eyes. He was awestruck. "We've finally found proof."

"Of?" Ratcliff was studying pieces of jars and other implements placed around the chamber.

"These pieces of Jewish relics prove that the Ark is gone. Probably destroyed by our Roman friends centuries ago. The enemy is trying to hide the fact that they are without their temple treasures. Which means they can't legitimately build a temple." Weezer was living up to his name. He was so excited, he began to choke on his own saliva.

"Quiet, man! You'll get us killed!" Ratcliff whispered.

A moment later, Weezer calmed down. Two moments later, guards came bursting into the chamber. All bedlam broke loose.

Ratcliff sprayed the guards with poisonous fumes. The guards dropped in their tracks. More came crashing in. Weezer grabbed the half-melted wing and dashed for the gap in the floor. He came face to face with Angel.

"Going somewhere?" Angel asked.

The golden angel standing before Weezer was one of the most powerful-looking beings Weezer had ever seen. The Kraken was a huge giant, intimidating beyond belief. But this angel had an inherent power that was not to be challenged.

"I can't let you leave with that." Angel lifted his chin toward the cherubim wing. Angel was holding a sword in each hand, in ready position at his sides.

"Great, I didn't know it belonged to you. Take it."

In a flash, Weezer threw the wing at Angel and dashed through the gap in the floor. Ratcliff wasn't as lucky. A half a dozen arrows penetrated his body in a nano second. He went down in flames.

Angel looked at the other guardians and then at the gap in the floor Weezer just dove through. Angel smiled and said, "Follow him. I want to know where his boss is. Report back to me as soon as you find out."

*****

"Harold, it's David." Rabbi David couldn't contain his excitement.

"David, how good to hear from you. How's the family?" Harold asked.

"Great, everyone's great. Harold, forgive me, but I must make this quick. I need to speak to you about the thing I was looking for." David hoped Harold would catch his meaning without much difficulty.

"Oh, the 'thing.' Can I assume you've made headway?" Harold quickly realized David was worried that their conversation was being listened in on.

"Yes, but I've got a problem. Are you planning a trip over the pond soon?" David hoped.

"Why yes, I am. I'm speaking at the Summit of World Religious Leaders next week in London. Did you want me to pop over to see you?" Harold sensed the urgency in David's voice.

"No, it's not safe here in Jerusalem. I'll come to you. Where are you staying?" David asked.

"We'll be staying at the Winfield House in Regent's Park. I could meet you…"

Harold was cut short by David. "Don't say it out loud," David said. "Send the time and location to me by registered mail. I have a special place to open it. We must be cautious about this."

"Okay? Cautious how?" Harold's concern was mounting for his friend.

"Let's just say, we need 'prayer cover.' Do you have any close friends that could pray for your safety and the secrecy of our meeting? They must be strong believers. This may put them in some danger." David's tone had turned more serious.

"I do, they're the best," Harold answered.

"Good, see you then," David said. "And, Harold, be careful."

Harold did two things in the next few minutes. First, he wrote a cryptic note, "St. Dunstan in the East Garden Church, June 16, 10 p.m." and planned to send it via currier to David's home immediately. Second, he called Jim, Richard, and Sam to come to his home that evening for prayer.

Angel wonder what Rabbi David had discovered. He was clearly spooked by something or someone. Was he being oppressed by a demon? After Blue's little charade, was the Kaken convinced there could no longer be a third temple? Was the Kraken planning to destroy the dig site or ransack the hidden chamber in London? Was Gog going to raid the Temple Mount? Or had Rabbi David found the qualified heir to the high priesthood? Was Rabbi David at risk? Angel would have to send guards to Rabbi David's home immediately.

Two other things Angel knew for certain: he would have to be at St. Dunstan in the East Church Garden on June 16, 10 p.m. And invited or not, Blue would be there too.

*****

Weezer was relieved to escape with his life, but he was angry at himself for not keeping the golden angel wing. He was certain the Ark was destroyed. That angel wing was most likely part of the "Mercy Seat" that sat on top of the Ark. That and the other broken and scattered artifacts all but proved that the enemy had failed to protect their most valued pieces of Jewish treasures. And that they had lost the single most important item needed to complete the third temple.

The question now was how could he inform the Kraken without losing his head. If he merely sat on the information the Kraken would eventually find out he withheld information. The Kraken would have him for lunch for not reporting to him immediately. If he told the Kraken what really happened and the fact that they were found out and had to run off, the Kraken would still have him for lunch.

He decided the best thing for him to do was to lie. If he was good at one thing, it was lying. And the perfect fall guy would be his former partner, Ratcliff.

The Kraken's Headquarters in London was one hundred feet below the Thames at the Traitors' Gate. Weezer prepared himself for the performance of his life; it had better be.

"State your business." The gate guard stopped Weezer in his tracks. Weezer had cut himself on the arms and across his face. He allowed the blood to dry on his cloak and tore a hole in it for good measure.

"Tell his eminence I have come with critical news regarding his search." Weezer feigned weary exhaustion.

"What search is that?" the guard demanded.

"'Need to know' and you don't want to know," Weezer chanced.

"Very well, it's your head." The guard turned to his partner and said, "Watch this guy. Don't let him leave. I'm going to see what the boss wants to do with him."

Weezer sat on the floor and rehearsed in his mind what he would say. If done right, he would get all of the credit and none of the blame.

The original guard returned after twenty minutes and said, "His eminence is on his way. He should be here in a few minutes. This better be good or you're toast."

About an hour later, Weezer was placed in a bubble chamber and ushered into the Kraken's office. It was underwater. The Kraken preferred water to land and was more comfortable breathing water than air. He was a duodecumus, a twelve-armed demon. His arms could sense emotions and thoughts. They could also crush rock. His beakish mouth could puncture steel. He lived comfortably underwater, but like most demons, he could soar to the heavens or dwell in a desert. He became the King of the West because he eliminated all rivals. He aspired to become the Demon Lord's ambassador.

"If I'm not convinced your interruption is worth it, you will die. You've got sixty seconds," the Kraken said. He began looking through a report on his desk.

"Your eminence, I'm sorry to disturb you but I have nowhere else to turn. My partner found out about a chamber filled with enemy treasure. He wanted to run off and keep it for himself. He was planning to leverage it into great favor with the Ambassador himself. I tried to stop him, but he attacked me and left me for dead.

"I followed him through the tunnels under the Tower and to a secret passageway. The chamber was full of treasure. It was amazing. There were golden candle holders, pokers, pitchers, and chests. There were paintings of Jewish heroes and priests offering sacrifice. Ratcliff picked up a partially melted figure of a golden angel's wing. Before I could intervene, guards appeared and killed him. They noticed me and began to shoot their arrows at me. I grabbed a piece of chest armor and used it as a shield. I escaped and flew away for my life. I could only assume the guards couldn't leave their posts to follow me, so I was saved."

Weezer thought his performance was fair and decided to stop before his minute was up.

The Kraken reached out into the air bubble and grabbed Weezer by the throat. The Kraken felt the demon's fear, worry, and regret. If this demon was lying, the Kraken wasn't sensing it.

"What kind of a wing?" the Kraken asked.

"A stretched-out angel's wing. Like it was forming a covering over something. It all happened so quickly, I really couldn't tell much else," Weezer squeak out.

"Could you find this chamber again?" the Kraken let go of Weezer's throat.

"I'm sure I can," Weezer confirmed.

"Let's hope so," the Kraken said.

*****

"If it is possible, as far as it depends on you, live at peace with everyone."

Congressman Pastor Harold T. Washington was addressing a stoic group of religious leaders at their annual summit. He knew they were not all his friends. There were accusations in periodicals and daily newspapers that he was a charlatan. Suspicions were voiced that he was seeking personal and political gain. He was being called an anti-Semite, a homophobe, a xenophobe, a spy. But his Master never promised smooth sailing on his journey. He did know his mission was to speak the truth with love.

"If it is possible," he repeated. "What is possible? We are to speak the truth, that's possible. We are to speak with love, that's possible. We are to avoid vain conceit, that's possible. So if I speak at all, I must not speak to you about my life, my plans, my desires. I must speak to you about the only one that can give us what we need the most, peace. I must speak to you about the Prince of Peace.

"The Prince who left His throne in heaven to live a peasant's life on earth. The Prince who left His palace to not even having a place to lay His head. The Prince who left the presence of adoring angels to be subjected to hateful, jeering crowds. The prince who exchanged a crown of glory for a crown of thorns.

"His Father asked Him to humble Himself. He became a man. His Father asked Him to deny Himself. He became a penniless itinerant preacher. His Father asked Him to lay down His life for a world filled with death and decay. He went to His death as silent as a lamb to slaughter.

"He didn't come to show us the way. He is the way. He didn't come to speak the truth. He is the truth. He didn't come to improve our lives. He is life. He who is perfect took our imperfection upon Himself and was nailed to a tree. He who was sinless bore the penalty of our sin, and not our sin only, but the sin of the whole world, and hung on a cross. He never spent a second away from His heavenly Father, but on that day, His Father turned away from Him. He spent three days and nights in hell and the grave. For us."

Pastor Harold had a very unusual gift. He was able to speak from his mind and heart and soul and still be in constant communication with the Spirit. He asked the Spirit to continue to guide him as he spoke. And that's when he heard the Holy Spirit say, "Tell them to stand." It was as if someone had come up behind him and spoke directly in his ear. His voice was kind, concerned, involved. He should have been spooked by the sudden command, but it was like a parent telling his child, "Take my hand."

Pastor Harold paused, looked out among the thousand or so religious leaders in the auditorium, and said, "Please stand."

The leaders looked around to see what the others were doing. Most hesitated, a few stood. Slowly, everyone in the auditorium stood.

"I would like you to be honest. People are looking, cameras are recording, your friends are curious, your enemies are already accusing you. But God is watching."

Harold spoke silently to the Holy Spirit, "I really hope this is your idea and not mine."

"If you've ever stolen anything, please sit down."

Some people chuckled; others became sober, hundreds sat down.

"If you've ever lied, please sit down."

Priest, rabbis, imams, monks and reverends sat down. Harold looked out among the leaders. Half were still standing.

"So you're going to make this hard on me. All right then, if you've ever had sex with a woman, other than your wife or a man other than your husband, please sit down."

No one moved.

"Or if you ever lusted after a woman or a man that wasn't your wife or husband, please sit down."

There was some movement.

"If you ever killed anyone," Pastor Harold paused, "or hated your neighbor, or became angry with your brother or sister, please sit down."

Half of those still standing sat down.

"If you've ever coveted your neighbor's possessions, wife, husband, success, please sit down."

By this time, only a few older gentlemen were still standing.

"Finally, if you haven't always loved God with your whole heart, mind, soul, and strength, and your neighbor as yourself, please sit down."

Harold looked up. No one was standing. He turned away from the lectern, took a chair from the dais, and sat down in front of the stage where everyone could see him. With his head in his hands, he prayed.

"Father, we are all as an unclean thing. All our righteousness area as filthy rags. None of us can stand before you and your perfect law. No one can measure up to you and your perfect holiness. There is none righteous, no, not one. Father, we acknowledge that our sin has separated us from you, the giver of life, the source of life. We are dead in our trespasses and sins.

"But you loved us so much that you gave your only Son, that whoever believes in Him will not perish but have everlasting life. Father, although we are divided by our doctrine and our understanding of you, this one thing we can agree on. We need you. We need your love. We need your mercy. We need your forgiveness. Holy

Spirit, illuminate our minds, open our hearts, tear down the barriers that are blocking you out and let your Son shine in. Amen."

At first, people just sat. Some began to weep. Some got up to hug another. Some openly asked for forgiveness. Even cameramen and reporters and technical staff person laid aside their immediate duties to participate and pray.

Not wanting to quench the Spirit, Harold got up and quietly walked out of the auditorium. No one noticed him leave, no one but God.

*****

At 10 p.m., four persons walked into the ruins of St. Dunstan in the East Garden Church. Two were human, two were not. Angel and Blue made certain the area was clear of any eavesdroppers. Harold and David sat on a bench near a stream.

"Harold, thanks for coming. I didn't know who else I could turn to," Rabbi David said.

"David, it's fine. I just hope I can help you, whatever the issue," Harold said.

David went on to show Harold the scroll he constructed from memory of names tracking the high priest from Caiaphas to the present.

"This is remarkable. It reminds me of the genealogies of Jesus found in the gospels. How did you come by this?" Harold asked.

"I am bound not to say. But look at 1670. The line goes from Amsterdam to London to the colonies. Then there is a break. The succession of high priests picks up thirty years later. But the location is back in Amsterdam without a definite predecessor or any idea why the shift in location. This could be very important. If the line is broken, we could have lost the identification of today's true high priest," David explained.

"I could see after all this record keeping, that would be a tragedy. I just don't know what I can do about it," Harold said.

"Harold, I know you're well connected to President Kennedy. He has access to resources that I can't even hope to have. The Library of Congress, the Smithsonian, the National Historic Society could have records and writings that go back to the colonial days. In 1670, England was in a big push to colonizing the US. I'm certain England has records of barons, nobles, men of influence dating back that far. Maybe, the president could get you access to those records. I need to track the last known high priest in this chain before the break. Rabbi Menasseh ben Israel went from Amsterdam to London. I need to discover what happened to his heir. If my suspicions are correct, his eldest son broke the chain either in London or the colonies." David continued, "Harold, we must be discreet. If the wrong people get a hold of this list, they may try to discredit our efforts or even eliminate the current heir."

Harold ran his finger down the scroll. He pointed to the final name on the list: Rabbi David Masinter, Johannesburg.

"Him?" Harold asked.

"Yes. A real live person. Now you could see why the secrecy," David said.

"But you also believe there are spiritual forces at play here. Don't you? That's quite a turn for you. Right? What caused such a change of heart?" Harold probed.

"You. I have come to believe that there is a greater spiritual side to everything I've been doing. The Temple, the Ark, the priesthood, the history of my people. It's not all just archeology and science. It's God."

David lowered his head. He slowly shook it back and forth. It was a troubling thought. It had lingered in his heart for weeks now. Barely audible, David said something he had finally realized. "Maybe you're right. Maybe when Mashiach comes, he will have pierced hands. I just don't know. If we've got this lineage wrong," David pointed to the scroll in Harold's hand. "If the chain has been broken, maybe Mashiach is the only true high priest."

"I believe He is coming back. I believe Jesus is the Anointed One. And I believe he is the true and final high priest," Harold said.

David said, "Do you think you can help us figure this out?"

"I don't know. But I can try." Harold assured David.

"Thanks, Harold." David paused. "Now what about this 'stand-up thing' you did tonight?"

"Blue, do you remember Chairman Eli said he was going to speak to Gabriel and find out why Pastor Harold was being targeted?" Angel asked.

"Yes," Blue answered.

"Well, Pastor Harold keeps getting deeper and deeper in this thing. I'm not sure where it's going to lead us, but I have a feeling we're going with him," Angel concluded.

*****

The Kraken needed to recover the treasure Ratcliff had uncovered. The next Blood Moon was fast approaching. The Kraken knew this was his last chance to discredit the other leaders and gain the Demon Lord's attention. He could, once and for all, prove the Ark no longer existed and the construction of third temple was an impossibility. He would spare no cost to accomplish his goal.

Angel was preparing for an all-out attack. This would be very difficult. He didn't want to lose any warriors or guardians, but he wanted to present a strong opposition to Kraken's strike. He knew if his defense wasn't strong enough, it would cause suspicions. Possession of the fake treasure would put an end to the Rebel's search for the Ark and the high priest. It would put an end to the continued disruption at the Temple Mount. And it would put an end to the attacks on his pastor and his church.

"But how?" Angel said aloud.

Blue heard Angel and immediately knew what Angel was thinking. She was in a quandary herself until she wasn't.

"What if we don't defend the treasure at all?" Blue purposed.

"Don't you think that would look a little suspicious?" Angel said.

"Not if we make it appear as if we miscalculated the enemy's move. What if we were so confident that the existence of the treasure was a secure secret that we only maintained a skeletal guard?"

"And do nothing when attacked?" Angel questioned.

"I didn't say 'do nothing.' What if we attack the Kraken's lair as he is attacking the treasure chamber?" Blue explained.

"It would appear as if we had been outsmarted, allowing the Kraken's forces to plunder the treasure chamber with as little or no loss of his troops or ours." Angel completed Blue's thought.

"And we would get to destroy the Kraken's lair in the process. What fun!" Blue said.

*****

Even though it was late, Pastor Harold couldn't sleep. He lingered in the Church Garden. He was compelled to pray for David's salvation, the safety of David's family and those affiliated with his dig. He felt evil powers were at work in high places. He felt like things were coming to a head. He wished he could call upon his friends back at home to pray with him. Unknown to him, he was only a few meters from the Tower of London and Traitors' Gate. There was a battle about to ensue in both locations.

Harold then realized it was 8:30 p.m. back home. He made a quick call to Annie and asked for prayer. Without hesitation, she went to her knees and prayed.

"Father, please be with Harold and David right now in a special way. Give them courage and strength. Build a hedge of protection around them. Send your angels to defend them against the evil one. Father, give Harold the wisdom and the words to bring David to a saving knowledge of our precious Lord and Savior. Remove the scales from David's eyes and help him see Jesus as Messiah. Amen." Annie continued, "Harold, I love you, please be safe."

"I love you too. Do you think I should call the others?" Harold asked.

"Call Jim. He'll reach out to the others," Annie suggested.

"I will, thanks. I love you. Bye." Harold called Jim.

After explaining the situation to Jim, Jim said, "Pastor, we can't ignore the Spirit's prompting. If you can find one open at this hour, get to a church and start praying. You'll know when it's safe to leave.

We'll have you covered in prayer from here. Anything else we should know?" Jim asked.

"Jim, don't repeat this to anyone, but I physically heard the Holy Spirit speak to me tonight. I was in the middle of my speech and He told me what to say. I didn't plan it. But I obeyed," Harold said.

"You did the right thing, Pastor. It seems to me like you should be praying for us." Jim wasn't surprised by what Pastor told him. He knew his pastor was special.

Harold continued to walk and pray. It was past midnight, and he was anxious, mentally exhausted, and physically spent. He thought he heard music and decided to follow it to the source. He was led to a beautiful old stone church. The plaque next to the door read, "All Hallows by the Tower, Since AD 675." Harold tried the main door. He could hardly believe it opened. He slipped in and was instantly taken aback. Candles were lit throughout the church. Beautiful music was coming from the organ loft. But what left him speechless were the worshippers in the pews. The church was full. It was clear that they were signing praises to the Almighty. They all wore similar dark gray cloaks with hoods over their heads. The music itself was heavenly. The voices were harmonizing as if they had been signing together since the beginning of time. Their focus was so intent on worship that no one noticed his presence.

He sat in the last pew and listened. He thought he recognized the melody, but the words weren't English. The words were closer to Greek or even Hebrew than anything else, a heavenly language. The overall effect was pure beauty. He closed his eyes and let the music soak into his soul. He began to weep. Not tears of sadness but of joy in the presence of the Lord.

Harold's mind drifted toward heavenly thoughts. His head slumped forward, his body began to lean to the side. Seraphima gently lowered his body to the pew, and he fell asleep.

*****

If the guardians weren't pre-warned and prepared, the explosion would have been disastrous. Hundreds of demon warriors rampaged through the chamber. In minutes, they emptied out the contents of the entire chamber. As instructed, the raiders took the treasure to a cavern three hundred feet below Stonehenge. The site was well protected and free from the enemy's presence. Of course, there was no physical damage to the Tower of London. No human noticed a thing. The battle took place in a different dimension.

The only problem with the Kraken's plan was that the Kraken himself was left without a guard in his own lair. He was confident enough in his own power that no enemy could be a threat to him.

"Bad decision," Angel said, as he entered the Traitors' Gate lair.

"Who are you?" the Kraken asked with a smile on his face. "A golden angel? A guardian at that? I'll give you ten seconds to get out or you will die."

"My name is Angel. And it's you who's going to die." Angel drew both swords from behind his back.

"Oh my," the Kraken said standing to his full height, "you're going to need help."

"How about me?" Blue appeared opposite Angel across the lair. She unhooked a bluish silver whip from her belt with one hand as a lance materialized in the other.

"You're Blue, aren't you? I heard you were a decent fighter, but I thought you worked for Dagon. Does Satin know you're here?" The Kraken unsheathed twelve black swords, one for each tentacle. Blue had no doubt the blades were poisonous. "I'm going to teach you some manners. You will bow to your king before you die."

"We only bow to the King of kings, you wretched creature." Samson materialized in front of the Kraken in an instant.

Samson's lightning sword struck out and removed three of the Kraken arms.

Seemingly unaffected, the Kraken struck Blue across the face with one sword and thrust another sword toward her body. Angel blocked the thrust aimed for Blue's heart with a golden sword of his own. With his other sword, Angel struck down aiming at Kraken's head. Angel's strike was blocked. Blue was losing consciousness but managed to sink her lance into the Kraken's body. Samson blocked three more poisonous swords swinging in his direction. He blasted the Kraken with blinding pure light. The Kraken fell back, and Samson sliced off another three of the Kraken's arms.

Samson shouted out to Angel, "His heart is in his skull!"

Angel dove in front of Blue, shielding another blow aimed at her. Angel swung his sword wildly and managed to remove another one of the Kraken's arms. "Why didn't you say so earlier?" Angel yelled back at Samson.

Samson didn't respond. He was hit. Angel had one more chance to finish the Kraken. There were seven missing appendages. The loss alone didn't seem to slow the Kraken down in the slightest. But it did leave his right side vulnerable to an attack.

Angel sought to take immediate advantage, and in a split second, Angel launched himself toward the Kraken with both of his swords aimed into the Kraken's head. The Kraken did the only thing he could. He drove his remaining swords into Angel's body.

*****

"Man proposes, but God disposes." Tobias was very familiar with this scripture, and it haunted him. He planned to proselytize Claire so that they could be married in the Jewish tradition and according to Jewish law. He proceeded to teach her the Torah, the Law and the Prophets, the Books of Wisdom, and the traditions and teachings of his predecessors.

As far as their racial difference, he had his father's blessing. Racially mix marriages were not common, but they were also not unheard of in England. Many of the Jews had Egyptian, Moroccan, and Arabian ancestry. England was rife with examples of mix couples in society. English poetry and literature dramatized it, such as *Othello* and *The Merchant of Venice*. The Bard himself, William Shakespeare was in love with the "Dark Lady," as he referred to her in his most intimate writings. Not to mention King Solomon's love who said, "Look not upon me because I am black."

The most troubling issue Tobias faced concerning Claire wasn't her position in life or her race but her intelligence. She not only absorbed the material he taught, but she understood it, seemingly better than he did. Her questions were gentle and non-confrontational but nonetheless, challenging.

"Who does God refer to when he told Eve that 'her seed' would crush the head of the Serpent?"

"Isn't the seed from a man?"

"Wouldn't the Serpent's crushed head be lethal?"

"How could God be so inconsistent, being merciful to Noah while still visiting judgment on the rest of the world?"

"Why were the sins of the people placed on the scapegoat who was saved from dying and the spotless goat sacrificed for the sins of the people?"

"Who is scripture referring to in Isaiah 53, or Psalm 22, or Micah 5:2?"

Tobias had studied and memorized the scriptures but never looked to the scriptures for the deeper meaning of life. He never searched the scriptures to find the Almighty. Life was getting very complicated. But Tobias was nobody's fool. The English Bible translations, the Geneva Bible and the Authorized Version, had been available for a hundred and fifty years respectively. Tobias also had a scholar's understanding of ancient Hebrew, Latin, and Greek Aramaic. There were few people as prepared as Tobias to research the meanings of these troubling passages in Holy Scripture.

He spent the better part of a year researching every reference to the coming King in scriptures. And then categorized every reference made in the New Testament to the Old Testament. One night, he came to a decision.

"Claire, I can no longer deny that Jesus Christ is truly the Mashiach and is coming again," he said.

Tobias was seated at the hearth. Claire put down her knitting and walked over to him. She put her arms around him and quietly said, "I know."

"But where does that leave me? You know I that am to be the next high priest of Israel," he asked, feeling a little traitorous.

"It leaves you right where God wants you. You must decide what you're going to do with this knowledge," she answered gently.

"I think I must go speak to my father," he concluded.

"That's a good idea," Claire said. "How long would you be gone?"

"Four months at the longest," he answered. "Is that acceptable to you?"

"Yes, dear, it's acceptable." She smiled. "I just wouldn't want you to miss your baby's birth."

Tobias dropped his glasses and his brandy.

*****

It was October 31. In a few hours, the Blood Moon would haunt the nighttime sky. The earth's shadow would completely cover the full moon. Demons on the earth and their followers would celebrate their dominance over the earth. It was also the night the Ambassador, Apollyon, was expecting answers: Did the Ark of the Covenant still exist? Was there still a high priest on earth? And who was protecting the pastor and why?

It was a few hours before the celebration when mayhem would begin. But now, the seven principals were convening for their meeting with the Ambassador.

The meeting was at Stonehenge. The King of the West had been sent to the pit in a brutal battle with the enemy. His second in command convinced the Ambassador that after all was said and done, having their meeting at Stonehenge would not be a disappointment. Apollyon agreed to the meeting place. Besides, Stonehenge was a great place to celebrate. It had been consecrated in human blood and orgies many times over, down through the centuries.

Amon, King of the South, leaned over to Vapus and said, "I hope you know what you're doing."

"When this evening's meeting is over, I will be the next King of the West," Vapus said.

Amon thought Vapus seemed overly confident. Amon knew that caution rather than confidence would win the day and assure a tomorrow. Their conversation was cut short by the entrance of twenty elite guards. They were the Special Forces of Demon's Teeth, assigned to protect the Ambassador. The guards scanned the room. They allowed the seven principals to stay seated but confiscated their personal weapons. All others guards and assistants were escorted out of the room.

Moments later, a green hue overshadowed them. Oxygen seemed to be sucked out of the room and replaced with sulfuric gas. The vapor swirled through the room and began to organize itself in the chair at the head of the conference room table. And there he was, Apollyon.

"Let get this started," Apollyon said. "Vapus, make your presentation."

"Yes, Ambassador, may I bring in the exhibits I prepared?" Vapus asked. Apollyon nodded.

Vapus got up and went to the door. He signaled his assistants to bring in the exhibits. In minutes, treasures were arranged on the table. Vapus placed the half-melted angel wing in front of the Ambassador and said, "This is what remains of the temple treasure. As you can see it isn't much, but it is impressive. What you have in front of you, Ambassador, is part of the Mercy Seat which covered the Ark of the Covenant. Proof that the Ark is no more."

For a moment Apollyon was nonplussed. He slowly reached out and touched the golden wing. He immediately pulled his hand back. It pulsed with "angel." When he finally spoke, he said. "Where did you find all of this?"

"The Tower of London," Vapus said.

"So the rumors were true," Apollyon said aloud, to himself.

"Yes, Ambassador. We believe the crusaders brought the temple treasure to London for safe keeping. As you can see, it just wasn't safe enough." Vapus smiled.

"And the Kraken?" the Ambassador asked.

"A hero. He led the charge to recover all of this. With his last dying words, he commanded me to secure what he so valiantly fought for," Vapus dramatically waved his arms over the treasure, "and bring it to you."

Well done, Amon thought, *this demon could be dangerous.*

After Apollyon composed himself, he asked, "And what of the high priest?"

"We found carvings in foundation stones documenting the suicide of the last high priest and his heir at Masada. There has been no evidence of any further movement on that front. The Romans did our work for us." Vapus was gaining more confidence by the moment.

"And the pastor?" Apollyon leaned forward in his chair. Vapus knew this meeting would either end in his promotion or his death. It all depended on his final answer.

"I believe the Restrainer may have some interest in the pastor and his so-called revival. But since the Kraken killed the pastor's guardian, a low-level guardian angel, and Warrior General Samson who tried to come to the angel's aid, I doubt we will have any more trouble on that front." Vapus waited for a response.

"Any other enemy casualties?" Apollyon followed.

"There may have been a few others we haven't been able to identify. We have our spies looking into it." Vapus was hoping he could hide the fact that none of this could be confirmed.

"Very well. Let's keep eyes on the pastor. The Kraken had accomplished much, he will be missed. Vapus, I am placing you in charge of the West. We will see if you can handle the district as well as your master did." Apollyon continued. "Satin, the pastor is your responsibility. I expect you to come up with a plan to either kill him or, at the very least, make certain the revival is quenched."

Apollyon looked over the chamber. He was satisfied with the progress they had made. He would have good news to report to the Demon Lord and some real treasure to offer him.

"I will report our progress to the Demon Lord. But right now, I am hungry for souls. Tonight will be a night of celebration. You are dismissed."

Apollyon and his guard took the treasures and vanished.

"So that's it," Vapus said to the principals in the room. "The search is over. We can get back to business as usual. You're all welcome to stay and celebrate with us this evening."

The principals were already planning how to destroy Vapus before he could be permanently installed as King of the West. The last thing any of them wanted was another powerful rival who threatened the status quo.

*****

Congressman Washington with a nod from President Kennedy was given access to all the historical records from the Smithsonian Museum in DC and the British Museum in Bloomsbury, London. His search focused in on the time period between 1600 and 1700. With Annie's help, they found the information that David was looking for.

Rabbi Menasseh ben Israel was born in Portugal in 1590. His family moved to the Netherland in 1610 under pressure from the Spanish Inquisition. There he became a printer and a successful businessman. With the support of Oliver Cromwell, Rabbi Israel opened access to England, not only for himself, but for an entire community of Jews.

Around 1650, Rabbi Israel sent his eldest son, Tobias Menasseh ben Israel, to establish a community in the colonies. Sometime around 1670, Tobias vanished from the official historical record. Rabbi Israel's younger son, Joseph, appeared in Amsterdam in 1680 as a rabbi and as the next in line to become the high priest. He became an extremely successful printer, publisher, and landowner.

Searching for more information on Tobias, Harold found that he had designed and built many private and public buildings in the then Charles Towne. He also became a landowner and, in his lifetime, established many plantations throughout the southern colonies.

When Harold privately tried to reconcile this information with the list given to him by David on that night in London, he was able to focus in on the time of the gap. The office of the high priest lineage transferred from Rabbi Israel to Tobias in 1650, but then in 1670, this transfer was expunged. In 1680, Rabbi Joseph ben Israel appeared as the qualified high priest in the Netherlands. But the odd thing was Tobias hadn't died. If he would have died without an heir or a wife, one could explain the transfer of office from one brother to the other. But that wasn't the case. Tobias had lived well into his eighties with his wife and family. But no further mention was found of him as a rabbi or even as a Jew. There was no information about what happened or why.

"I'm sorry, but that's all there is, David," Harold explained over the phone. Harold had sent a full report to Rabbi David via secured courier.

"I seriously appreciate what you did. But I really don't know what to do with the information you found. It's not ideal. If we are one day called upon to reveal the qualified 'you know what' and I don't have the right 'you know who,' it won't matter what we build 'you know where.'"

"What if the 'you know who' has already been determined? The Psalmist tells us the 'forever priest' will be 'in the order of Melchizedek,' with 'no beginning and with no end.' The writer of Hebrews tells us that this means our Great High Priest is already before the throne of glory, a throne not built with human hands and that He is ever interceding for us, even now. How will that affect your plan?" Harold asked.

"I don't know, I guess I will continue to continue and I will pray. Like Nehemiah, I will have one hand on the trowel and one hand on the sword," David said.

"Well, good luck, my friend. I will also pray for you and that your efforts won't be in vain," Harold said.

"Let's keep in touch," Harold said.

"We most definitely will. God be with you." David disconnected their call.

Harold prayed to the true High Priest, right then. "Lord, be with David. Shine your light on him. Make his path straight and show him your way."

*****

Angels don't dream because angels don't sleep. Angels don't dance on the heads of pins. When we do dance, it's typically before the throne. Angels don't sit on clouds playing harps. The ones that do play harps lead thousands of worshippers to the Almighty's praise and glory. And angels don't think about how many wings they have. Not unlike humans who don't think about how many arms they have. But angels do heal, when possible.

Blue was struck and poisoned in her fight with the Kraken. But when Samson blinded the Kraken with pure light, it also neutralized the poison on the Kraken's swords. Even though some of the poison was already in Blue's system, the cut was shallow enough that the pure light dissolved most of the effects of the poison.

Samson's wound wasn't fatal, thank the Almighty. And my armor limited the penetrations of the Kraken's final blows. I was stabbed in five places. If his swords would have still been poisonous, I would have been permanently retired. But I am still on the job. I was knocked out of commission for a time, but I return today.

Our ruse had worked. The demonic search for the Ark and the current high priest had been terminated. But the enemy's desire to destroy Pastor Washington and my church had redoubled.

My mission hadn't changed. I needed to guard the church, the church property, and the pastor, his family, and the parishioners. But Blue and I were being summoned to meet with the Generals' Council again. I was getting used to this. I was actually looking forward to seeing General Samson and thanking him. But things didn't quit work out the way I expected.

"Angel, it is good to see you out and about. How are you feeling?" Chairman Eli asked.

"Thank you. I'm doing well. And I wanted to thank General Samson. He literally saved our lives."

I turned to the General and motioned to Blue.

General Samson smiled and gave Blue and I a nod of recognition.

"Angel, I'll cut to the chase. We are promoting you to colonel and increasing your responsibilities," Eli continued. "The Council has decided that it's time to take the fight to the enemy. We need you and Colonel Blue to drive the Rebels from North America. This current revival has increased our prayer cover. The Holy Spirit has been blessing your pastor's ministry, and demon leadership is in disarray.

It's time to strike with impunity. We don't believe the enemy is ready to escalate this into a worldwide battle. It's time to take back North America."

"General, thank you, but I've done very little to warrant such a promotion. And as General Debra will attest, I am a guardian at heart, not a warrior. I'm sure someone else would be more qualified for such an endeavor." I knew I was stammering, but I couldn't help it.

"Your 'very little' has accomplished 'very much.' And we have paired you with Colonel Blue for tactical and moral support. You will have the full support of this Council. We have much to do that you are not aware of. But we need you to complete your piece of this puzzle. Do we have your cooperation?" Eli wasn't taking no for an answer.

"Yes, Chairman General, as you command," I answered.

The Chairman turned to Blue and said, "Colonel Blue?"

"Delighted, General." Blue snapped to attention.

"Indeed," General Eli responded. "Let us know what your plans are. Dismissed."

PART 6

Angel and the Candidate

The five of them met in Pastor Harold's living room. Jim, Richard, Sam, Harold, and Annie. Not counting Angel and Blue. Jim brought in five ballot boxes full of marbles. Each box weighed about twenty pounds.

"This should go pretty quickly. There are about five hundred marbles in each box. The marbles are either green or red. Green means that Pastor Harold should run for the vice presidency with President Kennedy. Red means he shouldn't run. Pastor Harold has insisted on a unanimous vote for 'should run' by our church members in order for him to agree to run. I think we'd all agree the chances that there will be all green marbles and not one red marble in any one of these five boxes would be astronomical," Jim said.

"Or a sign from God," Pastor Harold said.

"Or a sign from God," Jim repeated. "Each member knew what was at stake and given the opportunity to privately vote by placing a red or green marble in the box."

"We didn't tell the membership that Pastor would require a unanimous vote to run," Sam said. "We thought that it would put too much pressure on any one person."

"And it could have affected the outcome," Jim added.

"So how do we do this?" Annie asked.

"Oh, right," Sam said, knocking his forehead with the palm of his hand. "I'll be right back."

Sam ran to his car and returned with an old-fashioned galvanized washtub.

"No counting necessary. We just need to pour out the marbles one box at a time. And look for a red one," Sam explained.

"Wow, that's smart," Annie said.

"They didn't make me a CPA for nothing," Sam said.

"Are you sure you haven't lost any of your marbles?" Richard quipped.

"Ha," Sam responded. "There all there, all 2,714. I guarantee it. I bought them myself and the boxes are locked. I'm the only person who has a key to all five boxes. The boxes have never left my possession. I didn't want any suspicions of impropriety when all was said and done."

"Should we pray first? Annie asked.

"Yes, Pastor Harold, would you pray for us?" Jim asked.

"It would be my pleasure."

They took each other hands. All seven of them bowed their heads as Pastor Harold began.

"Father, we are not putting you to the test here. We are seeking your perfect will. We want what you want. We want you to cast your vote before we decide on our own what to do. Please give us peace in whatever the result is. In Jesus's name, we pray."

And they all said, "Amen."

Jim turned to Sam and said, "Well, Sam, since they're your marbles and you have the key, can you pour out the first box?"

"Sure thing," Sam said.

Angel and Blue were just as anxious as the rest of those in the room. They were hoping to get some direction themselves as to what to do. The result here would be a big step in that direction.

As the marbles hit the washtub, they made a loud pinging sound and then a softer sound as glass marble began to hit glass marble. But the overwhelming sound in the room wasn't made by the marbles but by the occupants. There was an astonished silence at first, then gasps. Tears began to form in Annie's eyes.

Jim said, "Unbelievable."

Sam looked at the others and said, "I don't know how this happened."

Harold said, "Pour the next box."

And so it went, until all five boxes were emptied into the washtub.

"No one would ever believe this," Richard said.

"I don't know if I believe this," Sam mumbled.

Annie looked at Harold. "What does this mean?"

Harold looked into the wash tub again. There were no red marbles. But then again, there were no green marbles either. All the marbles were white.

"Sam?" Harold looked at Sam.

"Pastor, I promise you, there were only red and green marbles. I bought one hundred pounds of red marbles and one hundred pounds of green marbles. The boxes never left my sight. I moved them from the church to my study last night and from my study to here tonight. That's it." Sam looked at everyone in the room.

"Sam, I believe you. We believe you." Harold looked around the room. Everyone nodded their head. "This is a sign from the Lord beyond what I could have asked for. He has placed His blessing on our effort, and He has cast His vote. I think you'd all agree, His vote is truly the only one that counts."

"Honey, what does this mean?" Annie asked again.

"I take it to mean the Lord wants me to run but run His way. Sam, how many votes did you say there were?" Harold seemed to be thinking about something important.

"Well, with the new members, we have 2,714 votes from our people," Sam said.

Harold got up and grabbed his well-worn Bible off the shelf.

"Not 'our people,' Sam, 'God's people.' Second Chronicles, chapter 7, verse 14 that is 2, 7, 1, 4 says, 'If my people, who are called by my name, will humble themselves and pray and seek my face and turn from their wicked ways, then I will hear from heaven, and I will forgive their sin and will heal their land.'"

"Friends, Annie," Harold said, "I think I not only received God's direction to run for office, but I also received my campaign platform. Let's keep the white marble thing to ourselves. I think it was only meant for us."

*****

"Father, I've come back to Amsterdam to let you know I must disqualify myself as the next high priest." Tobias decided to just tell his father the truth as clearly and as quickly as possible.

"Have you lost your faith, my son?" Rabbi Israel looked up from his work, took off his glasses, and laid both of his hands on his desk.

"In truth?" Tobias asked.

"Please, Tobias, the truth." Rabbi Israel motioned Tobias to sit down and continue. "You are safe here. I love you."

"Very well, Father. I have found that the Holy Scriptures reveal the plan Elohim has for the world. A plan of redemption, a plan of salvation, a plan of love." Tobias felt he wasn't saying this right.

"So how has this perspective disqualified you from your life's path?" Rabbi Israel struggled to open his mind to understand what his eldest son was telling him. Tobias had always been the smartest student he had ever taught, a serious thinker. He never just accepted what others told him without considering all the other options. But as long as that process took, once he made up his mind, he became firm in that belief.

"It's led me to Jesus. He is the true Mashiach." Tobias unconsciously firmed his jaw and clenched his fists. This was the moment he was dreading for the last three months. The student in him wanted to run out of the room, the son in him brought tears to his eyes for hurting his father.

"Tobias, I love you. As much as I love you, I know you better. A decision like this and turning your whole life upside down could not have been chosen lightly. You know the official consequences of this decision. What you don't know is that I have spent years evaluating the possibility that Jesus is the Messiah as He claimed. I have my doubts concerning both positions. But for me, duty outweighs doubt. I must choose to carry the mantle of high priest. I want you to have peace in your life, the peace that could only come from Elohim

161

and a clear conscience. Whatever the official ramification of your new belief, I want you to know you are still my beloved son. We shall wait to see together what the Lord has in mind and where this journey will take you." Rabbi Israel got up. Tobias froze where he stood as his father moved toward him. Rabbi Israel threw his arms around Tobias and kissed him on both wet cheeks. After a moment, he asked, "Tell me, are you doing this for Claire?"

"No, Father, I'm not doing this for Claire, rather I am doing this because of Claire. Her faith has given birth to my faith. She is loving to all people. She is kind and gentlehearted regardless of how people treat her. She has a powerful prayer life. She knows our scriptures and the New Testament backward and forward. And she lives it out." Tobias was missing Claire tremendously.

"So have you thought about how this will affect your assignment?" Rabbi Israel asked.

"Yes, I don't see how this should change anything. The three Ghib-bore families you sent with me are all Christian. They are dedicated to doing their duty as they committed themselves before the Almighty, and so am I. We will be ready to answer the call, when needed." Tobias assured his father.

"Good. This is a little fast for us, but I think we must speak to your brother, Joseph."

*****

"Will things ever go back to the way they were?" Angle mused as he held Blue. They were at the top of a mountain in the Andes, Mt. Aconcaqua. It had always been Blue's favorite spot on earth. It was now Angel's. It was peaceful, secluded, and the blue of the sky matched her eyes.

"Goodness, I hope not," Blue said.

"I don't mean back to then. I mean back to before then. No war, no discontent, just peace," Angel explained.

"I knew that's what you meant." Blue squeezed Angel's strong arms that were wrapped tightly around her. "We need the King of kings to take his throne. Then we will have peace. Until then, we must prove ourselves worthy. Little else matters."

"You matter," Angel corrected.

"You matter." Blue leaned her head back and allowed Angel to gently kiss her lips.

After a short time, Angel asked Blue, "So what are we going to do?"

"We're going to take out Satin and then rout her army," Blue said.

"But how? Do we have a plan?" Angel was becoming a little anxious.

"We are going to her headquarters, take her prisoner, or worse. And then your troops will do the rest," Blue said.

"That place is a fortress. Twice as many warriors as I have wouldn't be able to breach its defenses," Angel tried to explain. "Trust me, I know defense."

"Angel, fortresses are built to keep invaders out. They're not designed to keep invaders in." Blue smiled to herself and relaxed back into Angel's arms.

Angel tried to imagine how that fact explained anything.

*****

"Harold, that is great news. This is a marriage made in heaven. Wow. Did you tell Joe?" Chip asked.

"Not yet. I thought I'd call you first and find out how to handle this whole deal." Harold was home and preparing to get back to DC in a few days for the scheduled Congressional meeting, the first Monday in December.

"This is great. We're in Utah today, California tomorrow, and back in DC Wednesday. Let's meet up with Joe, say, Wednesday night, at his place. We can work out the details then." Chip was ecstatic.

"Okay. I'll bump my flight up a few days and see you Wednesday at 7, Okay?" Harold asked.

"Sounds great, Pastor. See you then. Bye." Chip signed off.

Harold felt relieved that Chip was so excited. *This was definitely a God thing,* Harold thought.

*****

Slate's assignment was to track the president's activity. He happened to overhear Chip's phone conversation. He saw it as a huge opportunity. He thought that this could be his last chance to get what he really wanted. If he could eliminate the pastor, he would surely be promoted to General of North America instead of Satin. He could then do as he pleased, and he could finally have Satin for himself.

"With the guardian gone," Slate thought out loud, "and General Samson eliminated, the enemy is at their weakest. Once the pastor took to the air, he would be away from his church and not under guard, at his home in DC."

"But what if the Restrainer is protecting him?" Jabulon asked.

Slate had forgotten where he was for a moment. Jabulon was Slate's superior. But Jabulon had no concerns for earthly or even unearthly politics. Jabulon was the Grand Architect of the kingdom. His work dated back to the days of old and the Tower of Babel. He had designed and was maintaining an organization that had become a quasi-religion. His influence could be felt through the entire world. He was an entity of great power, on the same level as the archangels of the Realm.

"Jabulon, my apologies. I didn't realize you were there. Why would the Restrainer concern himself with a lowly pastor from a rundown city like Charleston? Who cares about what happens in Charleston? He's been lucky, and I have a feeling his luck has just run out," Slate said.

"If I were you, I wouldn't rely on a feeling. This is clearly an all or nothing proposition. Rasputin was destroyed taking on the pastor in the air," Jabulon advised.

"That was the pastor's guardian, not the Restrainer. His guardian is gone. Besides, Rasputin was a fool. He let anger get in the way of good judgment," Slate reasoned.

"And what about greed and lust? They can also get in the way of good judgment," Jabulon warned.

"My personal desires sharpen my judgment. They don't cloud it. You'll see," Slate responded.

"A word to the wise is sufficient." Jabulon tired of this conversation and dissolved.

Slate called his lieutenants and began to plan his next move.

*****

It was midnight. The daytime demon activity was winding down. The evening shift was gearing up. Satin was alone at her New York office. She was in the lower chamber below the historic New York Stock Exchange Building. She was sitting at her desk listing the demons she considered to be a threat to her permanent installation as queen over North America. Slate was at the top of her list. She knew he was attracted to her and she was trying to work out how she could use that fact to her advantage without killing him. Her thoughts were interrupted by a guard knocking at the door.

"Enter," she said in an annoyed tone.

"Ma'am, sorry to disturb you. There is a visitor at the gate with an angel in bonds. She said you would want to see them." He felt like he was on borrowed time but concluded quickly, "She wouldn't give us their names."

"Bring them here," she said. Satin assumed it was Blue. Blue had probably come to turn Angel over. Satin was already contemplating weaving Angel into her silkened cocoon and having her way with him. He would talk. When she was through with him, he would be her slave.

Moments later, a pair of guards brought Blue and Angel to her office.

"Leave us," Satin ordered her guards. With a wave of her hand, she sealed and soundproofed the room.

Blue was standing in front of her with Angel shackled to a heavy iron ball. "He doesn't know a thing," Blue said. "He claims his assignment was to guard the church and its people. He says the pastor has been relying on him for protection. They've had a real run of good luck."

"And you believe him?" Satin asked.

"Look, I told you I'd bring him back to you after I interrogated him. Here he is. You deal with him." Blue unlocked Angel's shackles and released him from the iron ball.

Satin was shocked by the suddenness of Angel's release. He produced two golden swords and a smile.

"Did you want to ask me something?" Angel asked Satin.

Satin shot two twisted ropes of silk at Angel. Like pythons, they wrapped themselves around Angel's legs and quickly wove their way up his body. Angel cut the ropes leading back to Satin and twisted his way up and out of the silk enclosure. Satin wasn't ready for the golden chains Angel threw at her. The chains locked themselves around her. She immediately slipped out of her satin gown and flew up and away from the cage of golden chain. She was now positioned above Angel and Blue. She threw a silk web at Angel. The instant the web touched Angel's body, it burst into golden flames.

Satin turned to Blue and yelled, "Are going to help?"

Blue shrugged and said, "No, I think Angel's doing fine."

"Traitor!" Satin yelled.

"I was, but I've been redeemed," Blue said as she swept her arm around and froze Satin in a block of ice. Satin struggled to release herself with darts of silk jetting into the ice, but they couldn't penetrate it.

"Now this is what you need to do," Angel said. "Unlock the room and wait here for your escort to take you away."

"Release my hands, and I'll let you leave," Satin said calmly, looking totally defeated.

"Done." Blue partially melted the cube, imprisoning Satin's upper torso.

Satin immediately threw out dozens of webs. Some grabbed Blue and some tangled Angel. Satin then pulled as hard as she could on a web that sealed itself to the front wall and smashed herself and her ice tomb against the wall. The ice exploded, destroying half of the office and knocking Blue to the floor. Dazed but freed from her prison of ice, Satin grabbed Blue from behind and wrapped her arms around Blue's throat.

"Drop your swords or I'll choke her out," Satin threatened.

"Okay, don't hurt her." Angel was definitely concerned. He dropped his swords and held up his hands.

Satin smiled to herself and thought, *That was easier than I expected.*

Blue thought, *This is going to hurt.* She crisscrossed both arms in front of her body so she could grab both knives strapped to her biceps. She then reached behind and backhand both daggers into Satin's upper torso. The daggers turned to ice crystal as they entered into Satin's naked body.

Satin gasped and went down hard. "Help me." She looked at Angel.

"Unseal the room and we'll get you help." Angel hardened his stance and his resolve.

Satin knew that this was her last chance to live. She could open the room and hope that her guards would neutralize the invaders, or in a worst-case scenario, Angel would keep his word and get her help. Satin dropped to the floor, unsealed the room, and passed out.

*****

Just as Blue had predicted, Angel and Blue easily cut their way through Satin's unsuspecting guards. They opened the gateway out of Satin's headquarters. Half of the demons were on break and the other half were unaware of what was happening. In the end, it was a total rout. The entire North American demon command center fell to Angel's army. Satin's demons were either destroyed or taken prisoner. As for Satin, her wounds were tended to and she was sent to the Council for further questioning.

From that point, the demon hierarchy in North America was in disarray. Demons resorted to aimless raiding parties and ineffective counter attacks. Some continued to tempt and discourage Christians. Some fought to maintain an influence over their followers. But for the most part, evil was being driven out of North America.

"It will take years to restore North America to its original glory," Angel said to Blue.

"That depends on the strength of this revival," Blue responded. "There hasn't been one like this since the Great Awakening."

"All the more reason to protect the pastor." Angel was eager to return to Charleston to reconnect with Pastor Washington as soon as he and Blue were debriefed by the Council.

"He's in good hands. Eli, Debra, and Samson said they would personally protect him until we returned," Blue assured Angel.

"I know, but I'll feel a lot more comfortable once I get back," Angel explained.

*****

Slate couldn't believe his good fortune. Satin was captured. Her army destroyed. The void in leadership ready to be filled. Once he killed the pastor, he would most certainly be given the reigns over North America, but first things first.

"Where is the pastor now?" he asked Henchman.

"He's heading for DC any minute. He is about to leave for the airport now," Henchman reported.

"And his guardian?" Slate asked.

"Nowhere to be seen. Probably still in Council," Henchman said.

"Is the limo on the way?" Slate asked.

"It is. We've disabled the driver and have replaced him with our own man." Henchman beamed with his accomplishment.

"This is too important for a human to handle. I'll take over myself," Slate decided.

"As you wish, sir," and Slate was gone.

*****

Harold was packed. He had minutes before the limo arrived. He ran up the stairs to check one last time on Annie.

"How are you doing, honey?" Harold asked.

Annie was in their bedroom reading a book in her rocker. "Fine. Are you ready to go?" Annie asked.

"Yes," Harold said. He walked over to her, offered his hand, and lifted her up into his arms. "I'll miss you, but I'll be back in three days."

Annie didn't say a word.

"Annie, what's wrong?" Harold pulled away from their embrace and looked into her eyes.

"I don't think there's anything wrong," Annie took a long pause, "but I think it's time."

"Yeah, the limo will be here any moment." Harold checked the time on the nightstand clock.

"No, dear, I think it's time." She stared at him intently.

Harold was thunderstruck. "Time? You mean time, time? It's two weeks early! Oh no. Can you walk? Can you get to the car? Where are your bags? I'll call the doctor. We've got to go!"

"Calm down, the contractions are about twenty minutes apart. They're not real intense yet. My water hasn't broken. I think we have time, but we should go." Annie took control of the situation. "I'm pretty sure this isn't a false alarm. I'm sorry."

"Sorry? I'm just glad I'm not on the plane to DC." Harold was excited, worried, and relieved at the same time. "We've got to go. I'll call the limo company and explain from the car."

And off they went.

*****

Slate pulled up to the parsonage in a black limo and beeped the horn. He was tickled. *This is too easy*, he thought. He checked the Ruger 9 mm, screwed in the silencer, and laid it on the console. This had to look like a political assassination. "When would humans learn?" He did this before in '68. It almost destroyed the country. He hoped this time it would. "They can run but they can't hide." He thought, *One in the heart, two in the head and done.* He laid out some anti-Israeli/American propaganda on the passenger seat next to him. He beeped his horn again. It began to rain. He saw the outline of two

169

angels on the steeple, one at the church entrance and two walking the perimeter. "Invisible in plain view. Act natural and they won't even notice you," he said to himself.

Before long, he saw the pastor come out of the doorway with a bag in one hand and an umbrella in the other. Slate popped the truck, got out of the limo, grabbed the pastor's bag, and stowed it away.

"To Charleston International, Reverend," Slate said as he shut the back passenger door and got back into the driver seat and drove off.

Slate drove north on Church Street for a mile and turned right on North Market. He slowed down and pulled over into an empty parking lot. He put the limo in park, slowly turned around, pointing the Luger at the pastor, he asked, "Pastor, just a quick question before you die, who's been protecting you?"

"I don't really need protecting, Slate," a voice came from the back seat.

"We'll see about that." Slate shot three times: one in the chest, two in the head. Then it dawned on him. He panicked as he said, "Wait, you know my name."

The interior in the limo filled with light, a white hot, burning light. Slate's last memory was of a gleaming white archangel.

In seconds, the limo was completely empty. There was nothing on the seats, in the truck, on the console. There was no evidence that anyone had been in the limo or even driven the limo to where it now rested.

Above the limo, in the church parking lot, where the limo sat was a neon light that glowed through the night rain, declaring, "Jesus Saves."

*****

Annie was right. They made it to the hospital in plenty of time. Harold was a little more shaken that expected, but he survived. Compared to how most first births normally went, the delivery was quick. Compared to how most first births of twins normally went, it was miraculously quick.

The babies were healthy and sleeping, Mom was resting, Dad was trying to recover. Pastor Harold roamed the family waiting room wondering what he should do next: call Chip, call the elders, call the grandparents, buy flowers, buy candy, pray.

"Right, pray," he decided.

The Medical University of South Carolina (MUSC) Hospital had a nice chapel. He had been there many times consoling, counseling, comforting families and friends of patients. This time, he was going to go there for himself. The way things all worked out, Harold felt as if he were being held in the loving embrace of the Father.

Before he even got to the chapel, he prayed. "Father, I am so grateful. Help me be a good parent to these precious boys you have given us. At an early age, let them come to know you and receive your Son as their Savior and Lord. And lead them to grow strong in You and serve You. Let them become Your mighty men of valor. Amen."

He could hardly believe he had two sons. Annie and he hadn't really decided on names. They knew they were having boys. Harold wanted to wait until they could see them before naming them.

As he walked into the chapel, he saw an older gentleman seated by himself in the front pew.

"Don't be shy, Pastor. Come sit with me." Without turning around, the gentleman motioned to the seat next to him.

Harold was used to people recognizing him. He was certain he had never met this man before. Yet somehow, the man's voice sounded familiar. "I'm sorry, I don't remember your name." Harold walked over and sat beside the man.

"Names are important. Mine is Melchizedek," he said.

"Pleased to meet you. That's quite a name to live up to," Harold said.

"Yes, the great-grandfather of Abram, no beginning, no end." There was a smile in his voice. "So, Pastor, have you decided on names for your boys?"

Melchizedek was looking straight ahead. Harold noticed, for the first time, that he wore dark round sunglasses and was holding a white cane. *Blind,* he thought. *Wait, he recognized me but didn't see me. He knows I just had twin boys, but I haven't told anyone. And his name is very telling. I had better tread softly. This is beyond strange.*

"No, not yet. Sort of waiting for an inspiration. Annie and I haven't decided. I'm going back in a few minutes," Harold said.

"I'm pretty sure God will let you know what's best," Melchizedek said.

Melchizedek held out his hand and said, "Well, Pastor, may the Almighty bless you and Annie and your two beautiful boys."

Harold shook his hand. "Thank you, Mr. Melchizedek, may our Lord bless you and keep you also."

Harold got up to leave. When he got to the exit, Melchizedek said, "And, Pastor." Harold turned to face the old man. "God has already answered your prayer."

Harold didn't know what to say. So he nodded his head and left the chapel.

That was surreal, Harold thought. *I'm not entirely sure if I just experienced it or dreamt it.*

As Harold got into the elevator and headed up to the Maternity Floor, he felt a warmth in the palm of his right hand. He held out his palm and saw etched in glowing letters, "Mat. 17:3." And then they faded away.

*****

"Why would I want to spend my last years of freedom fighting a losing battle?" Jabulon asked.

"We're not losing! We've got a real chance to rewrite prophecy," Apollyon argued.

"We lost this fight Easter morning. It just hasn't gone the full twelve rounds yet. Besides, I've got my followers, I've got my own religion. I've got all I need. I couldn't care less how many humans you take to the pit with you or how many angels you destroy. They can't defeat me. You can't defeat me. The Demon Lord doesn't interfere with my comings and goings. I want you to leave me alone," Jabulon insisted.

"What if the Demon Lord tells you to take command of North America?" Apollyon jabbed.

"Has he?" Jabulon challenged.

"Not yet," Apollyon countered.

"We've got a deal, he and I. I took care of something big for him. He agreed that he would leave me be." It was as if Jabulon hit Apollyon with a roundhouse.

"Okay, just think about it. No one has been able to penetrate this pastor's defenses. We've lost some of our best leaders. And now we're losing control of North America." Apollyon had one more shot at trying to convince Jabulon to take the North American post.

"Fine, final offer. You've got big interest here and Europe. What if I could increase your territory?"

Jabulon showed some interest; he was bored with the status quo and wondered what the "final offer" could be. "Increase how?" he asked.

"What if I got you access to the Vatican?" Apollyon waited, holding his breath.

Jabulon froze in place. "You can do that? That's over a billion humans."

"Vapus is under my control. He'll do anything I tell him. You'll get North America, you can continue your influence in Europe through your organization and be given access to the Vatican." Apollyon knew the Vatican had many layers of protection. Efforts to take control had been stymied for centuries. If Jabulon thought he could do better than the thousands before him, let him try. It would be a win-win.

"And I can do anything I want? My way? Without interference?" Jabulon was already developing a plan.

"Get North America under control and you've got it." Apollyon was counting out Jabulon in his head, *Seven, eight, nine…*

"All right, I'll do it." Jabulon said.

Ten, and you're out! Apollyon thought. He smiled.

"Great," Apollyon said, "I'll make the announcement tonight."

*****

Chip met Pastor Harold at Ronald Reagan National Airport and warmly welcomed him. "Pastor, how are you? How are Annie and the boys?"

"I'm feeling blessed. Annie and the boys are doing great. Annie's parents came in to help her this week. Everyone is so excited," Harold said.

"Great, so are we. I mean, so am I." Chip grabbed Pastor Harold's bag and threw it into the truck. As he settled into the back seat with the pastor, he asked, "Have you named the boys yet?"

"We sure have, Moses and Elijah." Harold was beaming.

"Wow, big names for small boys. Family tradition?" Chip asked.

"Well, let's just say, a new tradition." Harold thought back to his meeting with Melchizedek.

"And let's hope new traditions don't stop there. We can't wait to discuss our campaign strategy. Joe will be free for dinner tonight. We can kick off then. I'll take you to your place. You can relax a few hours and I'll send a limo at 7. Okay with you?" Chip was already on his phone requesting a pick-up.

"Sure, I'd like that," Harold said.

*****

A private dinner was set up for Harold and Chip at Joe's private sun deck at the White House. The conversation was casual and amiable. As the diner dishes were being cleared Joe asked Harold, "Pastor, I'd be interested to hear if you have any ideas about our campaign?"

"I'm glad you asked, I would like to put politics aside and focus on people," Harold answered.

"Ah yes, 'People are more important than politics,' to steal a page from your book," Joe said.

"Exactly. I'd like to encourage the people of this nation to lean on God rather than the government. 'In God We Trust' should not only be our national motto, but also our national goal," Harold stated.

"That would be chancy, Pastor," Chip injected. "'Church and State.'"

"Chip, the separation of church and state was meant to keep the 'State' out of the 'Church' and the 'Church' out of the 'State,' not God out of our country. I believe the majority of Americans are discouraged by the way we've handed our country over to godlessness. I believe that the people of America have a strong spiritual desire to bring God back into their lives and their government, not to exclude God altogether."

A large piece of key lime pie was placed in front of Harold. "Are you trying to tell me shut up and eat?" Harold joked.

"No, please, Pastor, go on. How do you propose we get God back into government?" Joe asked.

"By example," Harold said. "As public figures, we must be transparent, honest, clearly stating our purpose, seek what's good for our country, not merely what's expedient. As leaders, we can demonstrate how we believe in God's goodness and grace and His blessings on America."

"Won't we lose vote by making such a firm position of faith?" Joe asked.

"Joe, I don't have to tell you, but 65 percent of this country identifies as Christian, 2 percent Jews, 1 percent Muslims, the rest are pretty much undeclared or outright nonbelievers. I don't believe we are doing the wrong thing by demonstrating we are the Party of Faith. Those that are opposed to religious beliefs will not be convinced to believe, even if Jesus himself came down on a cloud. But those on the fence need to see our faith in action. Sincere seekers will follow sincere believers."

"What issues, specifically, would you like to champion?" Joe asked.

"The same issues I've been championing most of my life. Eliminate government funded abortions, restructure welfare policies that have decimated the family nucleus, end human trafficking, revisit drug laws and penalties, address big pharma and the real crisis of drug use and abuse. Just tell me when to stop." Harold paused.

"I would just a soon step in front of a freight train." Joe laughed. "You're in a unique position. People listen to you and hear a man of God speaking the truth in love. How are you planning to separate your ministry from your political life?"

"That's simple, I'm not," Harold said.

Chip raised his cup of coffee in a toast. "Well, gentlemen, to a successful campaign. May we make more friends than enemies. And may the enemies we have forget where we live. God bless America."

*****

Tobias returned to a very pregnant Claire. He felt truly blessed. He finally had peace of mind. His father had lovingly respected and accepted his decision to follow Jesus as Mashiach. He would continue his duty as overseer of the Ark and its treasures while his brother Joseph had gladly taken on the mantle of future high priest. Tobias was with the woman he loved. They were expecting their first-born. The Ark and its treasures were secure. And an exciting future lie ahead.

His professional life was also being blessed. His reputation, as a good architect and builder, kept his services in high demand. He expanded his business into more towns. He also purchased another plantation. He bought as many slaves as he could and gave them their freedom. Most of them, in turn, stayed with him as hired work-ers and sharecroppers. It was an ideal model as to how to eliminate slavery, one person at a time.

After Wycliffe Tobias Israel was born, Claire took on greater interest in Tobias's business. She became an astute manager who was loved by friends, clients, employees, and neighbors. She was also accepted by the Ghib-bore and became a trusted ally.

Her acceptance into the Ghib-bore made eight total members in the colony. The three original Ghib-bore and their wives, Tobias, and now, her.

One evening, the Ghib-bore got together for dinner. Claire quipped to the group, "I just realized, Noah's Ark protected the eight on board with its treasure through the storm of a lifetime, we eight are protecting God's Ark and its treasure through our storm of life."

Tobias added, "And let's not forget, Gabriel is protecting us and ultimately the Lord is with us."

They all nodded in agreement. Tobias raised his glass in a toast and said, "Unto Him who is able to keep us from falling."

Lester Petersen, the eldest Ghib-bore, added, "To the only wise God our Savior, be glory and majesty, dominion and power, both now and ever."

And everyone said, "Amen."

*****

Apollyon called the meeting to order.

"You all know by now Satin has been captured. We can assume she isn't coming back. It's a sad loss for us all. That being said, we are increasing the strength of our North American army by reorganizing under new leadership. Jabulon will take over the North American District." Apollyon gestured outward for Jabulon to speak.

Jabulon was a high-ranking demon at a level equal to an archangel. He never adopted a permanent form but rather chose to take on various creature shapes and sizes at will. His preference, however, was to possess humans. Use them as he saw fit and then dispose of them. Nimrod was his first. He directed the building of the Tower of Babel. He was also responsible for guiding Judas Iscariot to betray Jesus of Nazareth, which gained him favor in the Demon Lord's eyes.

Jabulon materialized in front of the board as a specter. Black as night with glowing red eyes. His most troubling characteristic as a specter was that he didn't have physical boundaries. He could be wherever he decided at any given time. His voice had no directional element to it.

"I have one request of you. If the pastor winds up in your district for any reason, any reason at all, do not engage him. I need to be notified. I have reliable information that he has high level protection." Jabulon thought it was possible that the Restrainer had a personal interest in the pastor, but he didn't express it.

"I intend to squash this revival and destroy the pastor. There isn't anyone in the Realm that can defeat me. So I can't have anyone blundering into a losing battle over this adversary. Any questions?"

The group of six nodded in the affirmative, but they all wanted the pastor's scalp for themselves. If he ventured into any of their territory, it would be "game on." Then they could discredit Jabulon's claim to be the only worthy match for the pastor.

"Vapus," Apollyon said, Vapus almost jumped out of his skin, "I am assigning you the full-time position as King of the West."

"Yes, Ambassador. Thank you, Ambassador." Vapus recomposed himself.

"Don't make me regret it. Dismissed."

Vapus was beside himself. He started off as a mid-level demon. The only skill he really had he kept to himself. He could become invisible and undetectable to most demons and angels. He worked his way up through the ranks by spying, gaining information, using that information to his advantage. He had no other special power or ability to speak of. But with what he could do combined with his political acumen, he knew he could go a long way, maybe all the way. He did favors for others that also benefited himself. This promotion to King of the West was the product of years of hard work. But it wasn't his final goal. He aspired to be ambassador.

"Patience, Vapus," he said to himself, "tout vient a qui sait attendre" (all good things come to them that wait).

*****

Harold did not go on the campaign trial. True to his word, he let the president take care of the politics. He made it clear to Joe and Chip what he believed and how he would approach the election. He would continue his ministry as senior pastor of First Congressional Church of Charleston and perform his duties as Congressman of the State of South Carolina. He would preach the word and minister to the people as the Lord led him.

On the Sunday after the president introduced him as his running mate, Harold climbed the steps to his pulpit to bring the sermon. His heart was bursting with compassion for God's church and the all those that needed to hear the Good News. As he climbed the curved steps up to his pulpit, he counted out loud, "One, two, three, four, five, six, seven, eight, nine, ten, eleven, twelve.

"I just climbed twelve stairs to get up to this pulpit. Those twelve stairs are significant to me. I could spend a lifetime searching scriptures for the spiritual significance of the number twelve in the Bible, but that would be a waste of my life. Yes, there were twelve tribes of Israel, twelve apostles, twelve thrones in heaven, twelve stars in the crown of the mysterious woman in Revelation 12, twelve gates in Jerusalem and twelve pearl gates in heaven, twelve months of the year, twelve constellations, twelve eggs in a carton of eggs." Pastor Harold paused as the congregation chuckled. "But those aren't the reasons the number twelve is significant to me.

"These twelve steps are significant because when I climb them, I get to talk to the people God loves. When I climb those twelve steps, I get to talk to you. I get to talk about how much God loves you. God loves you so much. In the past, He gave us His Son. In the present, He gives us fullness of joy. In the future, He will give us pleasures forevermore."

Pastor Harold was feeling the presence of the Holy Spirit. He continued to explain the path to eternal life through repentance, believing, receiving Jesus as personal Savior and Lord.

"If I ask you, 'Who are you?' what's the first thing that comes into your mind? American? Mother? Anesthesiologist? Or is the first thing that come to your mind is, 'I am a child of the living God.' 'I am a Christian'?

"Who would people say you are? 'He's my neighbor.' 'He's my mechanic.' 'She's my wife.' Or would they say, 'He or she is a Christian.'

"What's the name you are called by? God says, 'My people are called by My name.' He says, 'If My people, who are called by My name, will humble themselves.' He says, 'If My people, who are called by My name, will humble themselves and pray and seek My face and turn from their wicked ways.' There are great promises to be had.

"This is the creator's promise to His creation. This is the Almighty's promise to His subjects. This is the Father's promise to His children. This is your Savior's promise to you.

"He promises to hear you from heaven, forgive your sins, and heal your land. Yahweh promised this to the Jews 2,400 years ago, but God is the same yesterday, today, and forever. His promises are relevant today."

At this point in the sermon, Harold intended to invite people to pray, seek God's presence in their lives, and turn from their wicked ways. But he heard a voice call to him from behind, "And be baptized." He quickly spun his head around. He wondered if a choir member shouted out something. There was no one behind him and no choir member seemed to be addressing him. Then he heard it again, "And be baptized." Harold was convinced that the Holy Spirit was speaking to him again.

And so he continued, "God says to repent and be baptized. By being baptized, you are declaring to the world that you have received Jesus as your Lord and Savior. You are driving your flag into His holy ground. You are declaring yourself to be His child, called by His name. You are wanting others to know you are a 'Christian,' the best way to tell the world 'I am a believer who is called by my Savior's name is to be publicly baptized.'

"There is a beach not ten minutes away from here. Go home, get on your swimsuits or whatever you chose to wear and come and get baptized. The elders and I will be there to do the baptizing. Those of you who are in places other than Charleston, find some water and ask your pastor or someone you know is a believer to baptize you 'in the name of the Father and the Son and the Holy Spirit.' All over America, declare yourself a child of God. Identify yourself as one who is 'called by His name.' Then humble yourself, pray, seek His presence, turn from your sin and watch what the Lord will do in your life.

"He is watching. He is listening."

That day and during the weeks to follow, hundreds of thousands of people in the country did just that. A revival had taken hold. The papers and the internet were filled with reports and recordings of people getting baptized and praying to God. The report was "not a body of water in America could be found without people being baptized." It was truly a phenomenon.

*****

Jabulon was a fallen angel. He was a leader in the Rebellion. He was one of the Demon Lord's elites. He didn't normally take a form but chose to drift in and out of people, places, and things. He possessed people who were not wholeheartedly committed to the Almighty. He oppressed weak believers. He entered people's homes though items he attached himself to. He had human followers who freely gave him control of their will. He had demonic followers who served him without question. He controlled entire cities, buildings, homes, temples, and even churches. He controlled historic places, new places, governments, wherever there was a place that he could master and that would serve his purpose. So when he decided to attack the pastor, he planned to do so alone and approach as an invisible cloud of evil.

One night, not long after the revival started, he was notified by his spies that the pastor was in his study, trying to decide on his next series of sermons. He was also told that the pastor seemed physically run down, worried, anxious, and was beginning to doubt the effectiveness of his ministry. Jabulon knew he could get through the enemy's defenses and do some real damage, maybe even kill the pastor before anyone could come to his aid. Suicide wasn't out of the question. If worse came to worse, he would kill the pastor's wife and children, leaving the pastor a sorry excuse for a human.

He drifted onto the church property just before midnight. He kept low, following the natural movement of the trees, leaves, flowers, and grasses caused by the wind. He followed the shadows of the clouds as they traveled past the moon. It took him over an hour, but his stealthy tactics paid off. It was unexpectedly easy. *The fools,* he thought. At midnight, he slipped under the door of the pastor's study. The pastor was sitting at his desk with his Bible in his hand and staring at the empty screen of his laptop. Jabulon then sensed another spiritual presence in the room.

"So you decided to come by yourself," a voice spoke out to Jabulon.

"I can take care of this without any help. You will find that out, shortly. Identify yourself before I teach you a final lesson," Jabulon said.

"My name is Angel." Angel slowly drew both swords.

"Angel, as in you are an angel? I figured that part out myself." Jabulon began to grow inpatient with this interruption.

"No, as in 'My name is Angel.' As in the last person you'll see before you're sent to the pit," Angel said.

"Ah, Angel, you must not know who you're dealing with. I am Jabulon. I am the Demon Lord's top commander. I took possession of Nimrod, Jezebel, Nebuchadnezzar, Judas, Hitler, and many more. I control whatever I decide to control. I do whatever I want. There is no one that can stop me, much less defeat me." Jabulon formed himself into a massive warrior. He looked like a combination of Genghis Kahn and a Jinn. "And I will kill you."

"I'm not planning to fight you," Angel said.

Angel struck the floor and then the ceiling with his two swords. They turned to solid gold. He then spun around and slashed at the four walls. They, too, turned to solid gold. Before Jabulon could react to this strange behavior, they were both encased in a cube of gold. This pure "angel gold" cube transported them to a spiritual dimension that acted as a seamless prison.

Jabulon screamed and attacked the walls with a scimitar. The walls held. He then turned toward Angel and charged him. To Jabulon's surprise, Angel slid through the nearest wall before Jabulon could reach him. The ensuing collision was horrifying. Jabulon lost his form. As he recuperated from this self-inflicted blow, he realized he was trapped. He tried screaming out for help, but to no avail. The walls were soundproof in all dimensions.

Angel stepped aside and wrapped the cube in his golden lasso and slowly pulled. The cube began to shrink. Not a sound could be heard from inside the cube as it eventually shrunk and disappeared. Jabulon was sent to the pit.

Oblivious to the battle that had just transpired around him, Pastor Harold looked down to his Bible and read a familiar verse he had previously highlighted, "The angel of the LORD encamps around those who fear him, and he delivers them" (Ps 34:7). He knew he had his next sermon and was comforted.

*****

The Lord said, "I know the plans I have for you, plans to prosper you and not to harm you, plans to give you hope and a future."

Tobias Menasseh Israel was very familiar with this verse and claimed it as his own. And the Lord was very familiar with Tobias and kept His promise.

Tobias and Claire had a wonderful life together. They had six children, three boys and three girls. The eldest, Wycliffe Tobias Israel, grew to manage the family business. Like his father, he also became a scholar, an architect, a builder, and a plantation owner. He freed twice as many slaves as his father had and continued to expand the family's empire. Wycliffe never forgot his family's humble beginnings and gave God all the glory.

When he had a family of his own, he began the tradition of naming his firstborn son after his own father, Tobias. From that point on, Wycliffe's heirs either named their firstborn sons "Tobias" or included "Tobias" as a middle name.

The years passed, through the American Revolution, the Confederation Period, the Civil War, and the Reconstruction Period. During the American Revolution, Tobias's great-grandson was named Tobias Washington Israel in honor of America's first commander in chief. Before the Civil War, the family moved a great deal of their wealth North while most of the family held interest in the South. After two centuries of family growth, knowledge of Tobias Menasseh Israel and his story faded. The relationship between the Ghib-bore and Tobias's family also faded. One thing, however, remained the same and even strengthened: the family's commitment to the Lord and the Lord's commitment to the family.

*****

When Pastor Harold returned to DC on Monday morning, he was greeted by his fellow congressmen. Bill Cartwright was the Representative from Massachusetts and a good friend of the Kennedy family. He and Harold had also become friends. After a few pleasantries were exchanged, Congressman Cartwright asked Harold, "Pastor Harold, would it be possible for you to baptize me here at the Capitol?"

"Bill, if you've received Jesus as your Savior and Lord and if you want to obey the Lord in baptism, it would be my honor. Just let me know where and when," Harold said.

"Well, Pastor, Sandy Point State Park in Annapolis has the closest beach to DC. The water has warmed. If you're good with it, I can make a few calls," Cartwright said.

"Wow, that would be a first. A congressman baptized in a state park. Is it allowed?" Harold asked.

"To my knowledge, it would be a first. But we are citizens taking a dip in the Chesapeake Bay. But under these special circumstances, I believe we could get permission first," Cartwright answered.

"What 'special circumstances'?" Pastor Harold asked.

"Well, I'm not the only one who wants to be baptized. There are others from the House and Senate," Bill said.

"Oh? How many of you want to get baptized?" Harold asked.

"Including both the House and the Senate? Fifty-seven," Cartwright answered.

Harold was almost knocked off his feet. "This is special, a specially good thing. The leaders of our nation proclaiming themselves to be Christians in such a public and bold way. Has anyone run this by the president?" Harold asked, more to himself than to Bill.

"Pastor, I think you missed the memo. It was President Kennedy's idea. He didn't want to pressure you into saying yes. So he asked me to breach the subject," Bill said. "The president wanted me to ask you to baptize him first."

*****

That evening, Joe, Chip, and Harold met for dinner at the White House. Over dessert, Joe brought the subject up. "Can I ask you a few questions regarding baptism?"

"If they're not too hard," Harold said.

"I was baptized as an infant. Is it permitted to be baptized again as an adult?" Joe asked as he glanced over at Chip and shrugged.

Harold swallowed his bite of cheesecake and took a sip of black coffee. In previous conversations with Joe, he knew his friend was sincerely seeking the Lord. He had spent time laying out the "Roman's Road" with Joe and offered to pray with him to receive Jesus as his Savior and Lord. But Joe hesitated because of the possible ramifications with his family and with public opinion.

"Look, Joe, I know you were raised Catholic. And I know that the sacrament of baptism is important to you and your family. Infant baptism carries a lot of significance for some. But when you were baptized some fifty years ago, it was hardly your choice. If I were in your place, I'd want to make my own decision to follow Christ and be baptized in accordance with Jesus's instructions. I'd also want that decision to be made public in the same way Jesus made His public.

"So if you've received Jesus as your Savior and Lord and if you want to obey the Lord in baptism, it would be my honor to baptize you. Have you asked Jesus into your heart to be your Savior and Lord, as we spoke of before?"

"I did." Joe looked at his friends and smiled.

"Wonderful, praise the Lord. Then there is nothing prohibiting us," Harold said.

"Nothing but the scrutiny of 350,000,000 Americans," Joe said softly.

"Joe, the only eyes and ears that matter are your Father's in heaven," Harold responded. He placed his hand on Joe's shoulder and said, "He's always watching, and He's always listening."

Harold then turned to Chip and asked, "How about you?"

Chip answered, "Pastor, you had me the day I sent in my dollar."

The three of them laughed together. Pastor Harold said, "Let's pray."

*****

"This is preposterous! I can't believe it! Who knows what happened?" the Ambassador yelled at the top of his voice. The meeting room shook along with everyone in the room.

Jinn Sing, always the calmest in any situation, answered, "We simply don't know. One day Jabulon was here, the next day he was gone. We all knew he was planning to eliminate the pastor and anyone else who stood in his way. We asked his advisors. But they only said he had been asking questions about the pastor's whereabouts. That's all we could ascertain."

"Are you telling me that the enemy was able to eliminate one of our greatest warriors in history without so much as a peep? This is absurd. This is beyond absurd." The Ambassador paused and took a moment to look around the room at his six remaining Commanders. It crossed his mind that one or more of them had conspired to destroy Jabulon for their own purposes.

"How long has he been missing?" the Ambassador asked. He wanted to keep them talking. He wanted to see if he could entrap a possible trader or traders.

Jinn Sing looked around the room for an assist. Vapus stepped up, "I'd say a week. You know he wasn't really a team player. He never shared his intentions with any of us. Quite frankly, we all gave him a wide berth."

"A wide berth," the Ambassador mused. "Let's table this discussion for now. I'm going to have to consult with the Demon Lord. I believe it's time to rethink this whole situation. Where is the pastor now?"

After a beat, Gog entered the conversation, "We believe he is in DC. There's a rumor afoot that he will be baptizing many American politicians there, soon."

"The fools, as if any of that matters. Dry sheep, wet sheep, they're still all sheep." The Ambassador tried to get a reading from the room. He could only get fear. "I don't want anyone to approach the pastor or his church or his family until I figure this out. Is that clear?" the Ambassador ordered.

"Yes, Ambassador," the room responded in unison.

"But I still want you all to try and find out what happened to Jabulon. Dismissed."

*****

"When is someone going to tell us what's really going on?" Blue asked.

Blue and Angel were on their mountaintop. It was where they finally expressed their love for each other. It was where they reunited as a couple. Angel was holding Blue in his arms. His wings were gently wrapped around her. They looked out across the ice-blue mountain range, waiting for the sun to rise. He wished he could stay here with her forever. But for the moment, they could cherish this time together.

"Don't ask me. You're the smart one," Angel said.

"Okay, then let's figure this out. You were assigned to guard the church 350 years ago. Right?"

"That's right, the property, the people, the pastor." Angel had been through this thought process a thousand times.

"And up until Pastor Harold arrived, the assignment had been uneventful," Blue continued.

"Well, except for rebellions and wars and storms and fires and hurricanes." Angel clarified the "uneventful" comment.

"But no assassination attempts, no demon attacks, no meetings with the ruling body, no promotions, no warriors, no armies, and no me." Blue smiled at the thought of them together.

"Yes, no you." Angel smiled at her implication. "It was all worth it."

"Now your pastor has become a world-renowned figure. He is a famous preacher, a congressman, a vice presidential candidate, a true statesman. He led the leader of the free world to our Lord. He unashamedly preaches the gospel to the whole world. He's initiated a worldwide food and shelter program for the poor. He ignited a real revival across America, and he is going to be baptizing Washington politicians. He has assisted in the search for the Ark and the high priest. He negotiated a peace in Korea and the Mideast. He is a trusted person in Jerusalem. Melchizedek appeared to him, gave him his children's names, gave him his blessing. What's next, president?" Blue paused.

"Maybe?" Angel answered.

"That was a rhetorical question. Anyway, we can't deny this is all about the church and the pastor. But it's not only the church and the pastor. There is a bigger picture here. Someone knows what it is. And it isn't us. I've never not been able to discover what's going on. Or find what I've been looking for. Or hit such a dead end. There is a powerful force behind all of this. A force for good, but a force, nevertheless. We need to go to the top and ask what is truly going on, whoever it is, whatever it is." Blue finished her thought.

Angel sighed and said, "Can't we just stay here?"

"We'd die of boredom," Blue said.

"Oh, now you're bored?"

He tightened his hug on Blue and propelled them into the sky. Above the sky and into the stratosphere. There they floated and viewed the wonders of the Almighty's creation.

Angel marveled at the panorama before them. The brilliant points of light on an onyx canvas above, gossamer wisps of clouds floating below, around a deep blue spinning orb. And then there was Blue, the most beautiful creature in all of creation.

"Hello," Blue whispered. "Earth to Angel. Are you still with me?"

"Yes, dear, I'm always with you." Angel slowly brought them back down to their mountaintop. There they continued to watch for the coming of the rising sun and a new day.

*****

The sky above the beach was clear. Not only clear of clouds but also news helicopters, planes, drones, and demons. The Chesapeake Bay was being patrolled by the Midshipmen of Annapolis from the Sanctuary to the Academy. The beach area was secured by the not-so-secret Secret Service. And Angel and his warrior watched for any sign of trouble.

Over one hundred people, politicians, and their families gathered on the beach. Among them were Joe and Chip. The believers to be baptized were barefoot and wore either white slacks and shirts or white gowns. They gathered in four groups and waited on the shore. The four ministers stood in the water: Pastor Washington, Jim Petersen, Richard Bridgewater, and Sam Schumacher. They wore black hip waders, white shirts, and black ties.

Pastor Washington signaled the first four to come into the water to be baptized. The participants and their families spontaneously broke into song.

"Amazing grace, how sweet the sound that saved a wretch like me. I once was lost, but now I'm found, was blind but now I see."

"What do you think you're doing here?" Angel appeared in front of an average-looking demon, who was not an average demon at all. Angel drew his swords.

"Now hold on, you know this is a diplomatic zone. Anyone can be here." Smyth was the head of the DC demon district. Smyth and Angel had run into each other once before at a diplomatic soiree. Angel recognized him as the high-ranking official who told his demons to "stand down" that evening.

Angel did not sheath his swords. "I repeat, what are you doing here?"

"A mild curiosity. We are always interested in those who declare their party of choice. Besides, I enjoy a good baptismal service," Smyth said innocently.

"I've got over a thousand warriors standing by. One wrong move, diplomatic zone or not, and I will give you something you won't enjoy." Angel's intense stare showed he was an eyelash blink away from striking this demon down.

"I don't believe we've been properly introduced. My name is Ambassador Smyth. I am the kingdom's liaison to Washington, DC." Smyth didn't dare extend his hand, but he did politely bow his head.

"My name is Angel. If you know what's good for you, you'll leave, now." Angel's tone was that of a determined guardian warrior.

Smyth noticed a twitch in Angel's right arm. He tried to look around for the other warriors Angel mentioned without turning his head. Smyth doubted this warning was a bluff. He decided that now was not the time to "call."

"Well, Mr. Angel, is it? I do have other matters to tend to. Another time perhaps. Until we meet again, I bid you adieu." And Smyth vanished.

"Adieu to you too, Smyth," Angel said under his breath.

*****

It was August. It was hot. It was Atlanta. The Mercedes-Benz Stadium hosted fifty thousand enthusiastic attendees. Captain Frank Silvestor was a true American hero. From a fighter pilot in the Vietnam War to deputy director of the CIA to vice president, Frank Silvestor served his country like few rarely do. When he got up to the podium, his presence alone commanded everyone's attention. Regardless of political affiliation, Americans respected and admired this man. Everyone at the RNC knew what he was about to say. Frank was retiring from public service.

He thanked a long list of influential people in his political career. He thanked the American people for allowing him the opportunity to serve as vice president. He thanked President Joseph Kennedy for his leadership and friendship. And finally, he thanked his dear departed wife for a lifetime of love and devotion. He turned to Joe and smiled. Joe nodded in a gesture of recognition and encouragement.

Wiping tears from his eyes, he continued, "Moving on to the business at hand." He paused, folded the notes he had in his hands, and placed them into his jacket pocket. He removed his reading glass and continued.

"I've never been so humbled by one person in my entire life. He is a genuine individual. His yea is yea, and his nay is nay. He places the needs of others before his own. I know he will put the good of the American people before any other interest. He is honest and open. He is trustworthy. He is a man of character and worth. And he is a man of God.

"None of us know what the future will bring. What challenges are to come. What friendships are to be made. What enemies will rise up against us. Today, more than ever before, we need people like him to join us in the battle for American ideals: equality, freedom, and right standing before our God. In short, he is a man for our time, and I pray, the next vice president of the United States of America. Pastor Harold T. Washington."

Frank rotated his body to face the pastor seated to his left and extended his hand toward the pastor. Frank motioned for Harold to come and join him at the podium amidst the resounding applause of thousands.

*****

Miles below, in a subterranean castle, another was being beckoned forth. Ambassador Apollyon knelt before the Demon Throne in silence. He waited there in subjugation until the Demon Lord appeared. He heard creatures enter the throne room. They were the Demon Lord's personal guard. They were Anubis, large onyx-like creatures in human form with jackal heads, Urim and Thummim. They were powerful creatures who had been with the Demon Lord since the Rebellion. They were invincible. They spoke for the Demon Lord who was unapproachable.

"You may rise," Urim, the Anubis standing to the right of the throne, said.

Apollyon slowly stood and faced the throne. There was a shadow of darkness seated on the throne. It was the shape of man with a goat's head. He couldn't discern any facial features but could clearly see glowing red eyes. The irises were like burning flames. He couldn't look at them for more than a second before his own eyes began to burn. He had to look away.

"You may speak." Thummim, the Anubis standing to the left of the throne, said.

"Your Majesty, Jabulon has failed to kill the pastor. Jabulon is missing and we assume gone. I am presently leading Northern America. We believe the pastor is under the highest level of protection. We believe we must attack with all of our force."

"It is not time," Urim said.

Apollyon carefully phrased his request, "What is your will?"

"Do it yourself," Thummim ordered.

"Do or die," Urim warned.

"Yes, Your Majesty." Apollyon realized this was his cue to leave. He also realized this could be his last mission. Kill the pastor himself or die trying.

*****

It was a busy week in Atlanta. It was now official. Harold was running for vice president of the United States. The vote to accept him as candidate was unanimous. There was not one "no" vote. For the last two years, Harold tried to drive with his foot on the brakes. But he could no longer doubt which road to take. Keep the senior pastor position at FCCC and become the vice presidential candidate with President Joseph Kennedy. If they won in November, he'd have to reevaluate.

After Annie and he settled their bags, they caught up with the boys and Annie's parents. Things had gone remarkably well while they were gone. Annie decided to make a dash back home midweek and then rejoined her husband for the closing ceremonies. He could not have done it without her.

As everyone turned in for the evening, Harold walked over to church to sit and ruminate. He was dead tired. He sat in the first pew on the aisle and gazed at the cross hanging in front of the church. At this time of the evening, moonlight shone through the stained-glass windows and gently illuminating the cross. Most of the verse below the cross was hidden by the dark but two words. They read, "For Thee." He began to pray and fell asleep.

*****

"Father, before I leave, I had to express my deepest regret, again. I have disappointed you. But my conscience will not allow me to fulfill my duties as the next 'kohen gadol.'"

The young man, Tobias Menasseh Israel, was dressed in black trousers, a white shirt, a silver vest, with a black waist coat and a cravat. He stood in front of his beloved father with tears forming in his eyes. He didn't know if this would be the last time he would see his father, on earth.

The senior was seated behind an enormous mahogany desk. He was dressed similar to his son. In addition, he wore a blue and white patterned prayer shawl around his shoulders. He was a stately man with a long gray beard and a velvet blue yarmulke with long curls on either side of his weathered face. Even though his eyes were steel gray, there was a warmth behind them that offset his face.

"Tobias, your place as the next high priest is a birthright given to you as my firstborn. I love you and trust you. If Elohim has called you onto a different path, I will not stand in the way," the aging rabbi said.

"Even if I follow Yeshua as Melekh Mashiach?" Tobias asked.

"Just so. I need you to be certain that you are not doing this for Claire or being blinded by others in that faraway land." Rabbi Menasseh ben Israel got up and came around his desk, grabbed his son, and hugged him as hard as his aging arms would allow.

"Father, I am certain," Tobias said.

The rabbi paused, gathered himself, and then decided what to do. "Then come with me. We must speak to your brother, Joseph."

Harold stirred but didn't awake. He settled back in the pew again.

"I love you, both." Tobias was kneeling at the side of a bed. A beautiful black woman laid asleep with a newborn babe.

The woman slowly opened her eyes and said, "We love you too." She looked down at their firstborn baby boy. "Shall we name him Tobias after his father?" she asked.

"I've been thinking. I'd like the Tobias name to be carried on for the firstborn males in our family, but not necessarily as a first name. We should allow the parents the joy of choosing their own child's Christian name themselves. I was thinking Wycliffe Tobias Israel, after John Wycliffe, whose writings helped me so much, my father who is the most loving man I know and myself. Is that all right with you?" He caressed Claire's hand and kissed it.

"I love the name and the sentiment behind it, and I love you," Claire said. "Now Wycliffe and I would like to rest."

*****

When Harold awoke, it was morning. He was leaning against the arm of the front row pew. The church was awash in rainbow-colored sunlight. He looked up and tried to recall every detail of his dream. He read the verse below the old rugged cross hanging in front of the church, "My Grace is Sufficient for Thee." Then he remembered the last thing he saw before he fell asleep. The only words illuminated by the moon light coming through the stained glass windows, "For Thee."

Had last night's dream been more than the product of his subconscious imaginings. Could it have been a vision from the Lord, for him? He hurried back to his study and rifled through the notes he had taken while searching for the current high priest with Rabbi David. And there it was, the 1670 gap. Tobias Menasseh ben Israel had been expunged from the records. In 1680, Joseph ben Israel was installed. Joseph's lineage continued to today in the person of Rabbi David Masinter of Johannesburg. End of search, or was it?

What of the second part of his dream? What of the beautiful black woman, apparently Tobias's wife? What of their firstborn child, Wycliffe Tobias Israel? Tobias was the firstborn son of the high priest. Wycliffe Tobias was the next in line to be Israel's high priest. Except for the fact that his father, Tobias became a Christian, the priestly line should have truly gone through Wycliffe. Should accepting Jesus as Messiah disqualify a Jew from his birthright?

Harold hadn't bothered tracking Tobias's linage for Rabbi David since Tobias seemed to be a dead end and therefore a non-factor. But since last night's dream, Harold was determined to track this mystery down to the end.

There were a few other issues rattling around in his head. First, Rabbi Menasseh referred to his son being in a "faraway land." Second, other than Tobias's wife, who were the "others" Rabbi Menasseh mentioned as possible influences? Third, Tobias had a desire to continue the "Tobias" name for all future firstborn sons. Fourth, Rabbi Menasseh's steel-gray eyes were similar to his own. Fifth, Harold knew he was a firstborn son of the firstborn son of a firstborn son. Finally, and strangest of all, although Harold never used his full middle name, his birth certificate read "Harold Tobias Washington."

*****

The next Monday morning, Harold decided to place a call to his friend at the University of Alabama. Chase Watson was an associate professor of American History and American Studies. Harold and Chase spent many evenings together, studying, writing, shooting pool, eating pizza. They were both working toward their doctorates in different majors. They would often bounce ideas off each other, adding perspective to their work.

The University of Alabama was established in the early 1800s and had accumulated records and artifacts dating back to before the Civil War. Harold knew Chase was the man to go to for the sort of help he needed.

"Harold, how are you doing? Congratulations on your nomination." Chase was truly happy for his old pizza buddy.

"Thanks, it's been too long. Last Christmas I think," Harold said.

"Well, you've been busy: TV celebrity, internet sensation, worldwide statesman, vice presidential candidate, and father, twice over. How are Annie and the boys doing?"

Chase was Harold's best man at Annie's and his wedding. He was also the first person Harold told about Annie and how he thought she might be the one. Since Harold and Chase were both from mixed-racial backgrounds, they could honestly discuss the implications of pursuing a romantic relationship with a white Jewish girl from New York.

"Annie and the boys are great. Her parents have been a real blessing. The twins aren't easy, and my work and ministry take me away from home, a lot," Harold admitted.

"Why do I always have to work twice as hard as you to only get half as far?" Chase half kidded. "And I don't even have a girlfriend yet."

"Hold on there. Don't sell yourself short. You do work twice as hard as me, but you get at least three quarters as far." Harold jabbed back. "But that's why I called you. I want to put you to work. I'd like you to track down a possible ancestor of mine."

"That sounds like fun, not work," Chase said. "Who is it?"

Harold explained that he could verify his lineage back to his great-grandfather, but things get a little blurring before World War I.

"But the real challenge is from before the Civil War forward. I believe my first American ancestors might have been Claire, a former slave, and Tobias Menasseh Israel, a Jew from Amsterdam. Somewhere down the line, the last name may have changed, but Tobias was always a marker as a first or middle name," Harold explained.

"Tobias, that's your middle name, right?" Chase asked.

"And my father's and my grandfather's, but that's all I know," Harold said.

"Land ownership?" Chase asked.

"Plenty in the past," Harold admitted. He always felt a little uncomfortable about the inheritance he got from his family's fortune. He never flaunted what he had been given, but compared to how some of his friends struggled financially, he felt guilty.

"Then there should be records. Don't worry, Harold. I got this." Chase was like a bloodhound that just caught the scent.

"I never asked, did you give your boys the middle name?" Chase had picked up a pen and paper and began to take notes.

"Moses Tobias, my firstborn, and Elijah Samuel," Harold said.

"Cool. Weren't Moses and Elijah the two who were on the mount with the Lord?" Chase asked.

"And I believe the two witnesses in Revelation 11," Harold added.

"Scary cool, I'll call you when I get something concrete. And say hi to Annie for me." Chase's mind was already on the job.

"I will. And thanks." Harold disconnected. He thought, *The game is afoot, Watson.*

*****

Gabriel in Hebrew means "God is my strength." While Michael was assigned to protect the nation of Israel until the Lord's return and reign on earth. Gabriel was assigned to protect Israel's important people, places, and things. Some people he contacted directly, like Jacob, Joseph, Daniel, Zachariah, Mary, and Joseph, was to guide them through life when necessary. He protected places like Mt. Sinai, Moses's tomb, the city of Jerusalem, the Temple Mount, Golgotha, the Lord's tomb. He protected things like the temple treasures, the Ark of the Covenant and its contents, Moses's original scrolls, and other important artifacts.

Gabriel didn't accomplish this monumental task on his own but enlisted the help of others. Normally, he asked the Council to assign personnel as they saw fit, with the caveat that he would be notified if any trouble arose or help was needed. In the same way, he knew Michael would aid him if and when he needed help, as he did with the prince of Persia.

At the present time, the First Community Church of Charleston, Pastor Harold T. Washington, Annie, their twins Moses Tobias and Elijah Samuel, Rabbi David Levin, and the Ghib-bore topped Gabriel's list. He knew a storm was coming. He already notified the Council to be on the alert. Time was running out.

More than likely, he thought, *this generation would see it all come to a head and the Lord's return.*

"How have we been guiding the pastor?" Gabriel asked the Council.

Gabriel outshined the entire council. Yes, Eli was an archangel. But Eli wasn't consistently in the presence of the Almighty. Gabriel's beauty came from the glow he reflected toward others and the world around him. His main color was violet with radiant shades that varied from wine to a blinding white. He tried not to display his glory in front of others. But at times, he had no choice.

"Well, beside the Holy Spirit's leading, the Lord's answers to prayer, His holy word, we've used dreams, visions, signs, and of course, Melchizedek," Eli answered.

"And is Pastor Washington receptive to the truth he's been given?" Gabriel followed up.

"Quite, he perceives it to be the Lord's will, and more importantly, he obeys it," Eli said.

"Colonels Angel and Blue, how's my favorite couple?" Gabriel asked.

"Stellar!" Samson chimed in.

"Good. Let's keep alert. I expect a major attack, soon," Gabriel warned.

"We noticed the enemy's involvement is moving up their chain of command," Samson said.

"I'm certain you can handle it. We're not sure this will all lead to a full out war yet, but the enemy is getting very uncomfortable with our progress," Gabriel said. "Let me know if anything else changes. Thanks to you all for your excellent service. To Him be the Glory."

"Amen," the Council responded.

And the mighty archangel was gone.

*****

Demon's Teeth was one million strong. There were ten companies of one hundred thousand demons each. Apollyon met with his company commanders weekly. Unlike the Demon Lord, Apollyon organized Demon Teeth along influential boundaries or disciplines.

The disciplines were Sex, Family, Education, Culture, Media, Government, Commerce, Science, Religion, and Terrorism.

As Apollyon entered his weekly meeting, he thought, *Wise as serpents, harmless as doves. I need to make this as simple as possible. If the enemy is going to match their force to our force, we may fail. They've got numbers. They've got strength. But the earth is still our kingdom. We have control, and we've proven anyone can be killed.*

"Where is the pastor now?" Apollyon's opening demand took the room by surprise.

"DC," Sistern answered. "But he is scheduled for Jerusalem to meet with Rabbi David."

Sistern was commander of the Government discipline. She kept up with all governmental movements and decisions. She was always looking for opportunity to steer any government to her advantage and gain greater and greater influence. The pastor's nomination and his impact on everything he touched was a deep concern for her.

"What does he want with that fox?" Apollyon knew the importance of the temple dig to the Demon Lord.

"We don't know. The pastor is very cautious about broadcasting information," Sistern answered.

"We are monitoring him through his phones, smart speakers, emails, texts, anything we can access. But he seems to know we are listening. And he is strongly shielded," Scammer, the Media commander, added.

"He can run, but he can't hide. I need an available individual in Jerusalem. Who have we got?" Apollyon looked around the room.

"I can offer about a thousand, you choose," Slaughter said. Slaughter was commander of the Terrorism discipline.

Apollyon showed a hint of a smile. "Some other day perhaps. I need someone a little more subtle than a wild-eyed terrorist."

"I've got a cameraman ripe for the picking. He works for i24 News in Jerusalem," Scammer said. "He just found out his wife is cheating on him. And is contemplating murder, suicide."

"You're welcome." Shameless injected herself into the conversation. No one needed to be reminded she was the commander of the Sex division.

"I can work with that. Guns?" Apollyon asked.

"Yes, sir, Jericho 941. He was a rifleman and platoon leader in the Israeli army. He can shoot." Slaughter was still hoping to be selected to assist Apollyon.

"All right, I'll take the cameraman. Scammer and Scythe, you two get me close to the pastor. I'll do the rest."

"Yes, Ambassador Apollyon," they said in unison. Scythe, the Religion commander, already knew how to stir up public interest in the pastor. News broadcasters would be drawn to him like bees to honey.

After the meeting, Shameless approached Scammer and said, "Did I mention that the cameraman's wife, Sarah Kauffman, was the traveling TV reporter for i24 News?"

"No. Why are you mentioning it now?" Scammer asked.

"I can get them both together with the pastor, the moment his plane lands," Shameless said as she sidled up to Scammer.

"What's in it for you?" Scammer asked.

"Credit where credit is due," she said.

"If you get the three of them together in one place, I'll give you more than credit." Scammer looked Shameless up and down.

"Done," she said.

*****

Nathan Kauffman was a proud man. He excelled in everything he did. In school, he got excellent grades. In the army, he was an excellent soldier. He was recruited into sniper training. There he became a platoon leader. After six years of service, he decided to leave the military and pursue a career in media and entertainment. He was presently a cameraman for i24 News Jerusalem and was on track to be promoted to assistant producer. But that's where the successes stopped. He recently discovered, his gorgeous wife of three years and reporter for i24 News was having an affair with the prime-time anchor Bruce Hurwitz.

Nathan was hurt and he was angry. His ego was shattered along with his self-esteem. And tonight, he was drunk. Sarah had gone to a producer's meeting that afternoon and didn't return. Earlier that evening, she texted him to say not to worry. She was going out with the girls.

"She's cheating on you," Apollyon whispered in his head.

"And it's not the first time," Nathan mumbled out loud.

"Even the Torah says a wife caught in adultery should be stoned to death," Apollyon added.

I'm being publicly humiliated. I need to exact judgment publicly, he thought.

"We're filming at the airport tomorrow morning, live. I'll shoot her for real then," Apollyon said.

"And anyone else that gets in my way," Nathan mumbled again.

"And the blasphemous pastor. We'll see if his Jesus will save him from me." Apollyon prompted Nathan to take another drink of arak.

At 10:00 p.m. Sarah texted. "See you tomorrow morning. Sleeping at Salome's tonight. She needs the company since Isaac left her."

Nathan had to read the text three times.

"More like, she'll be sleeping in Hurwitz's bed." Shameless punched through his psyche.

*****

Nathan arrived at the airport a half hour ahead of schedule, hungover. Sarah was already with her makeup artist and Salome, and the producer. Salome was setting up the area for the interview. Influenced by Scythe, Salome had emailed Pastor Washington requesting a quick interview regarding his visit and the growing number of Israeli followers he had gained on Facebook and his streaming website.

Nathan hurried to set up lights and reflectors to frame the shot. He felt for the weapon in his camera equipment bag. Airport security knew Sarah and the entire i24 crew. No one hassled him or checked his equipment bag.

Angel chaperoned Pastor Washington down the jetway through customs. Ben Gurion Airport was one of the most secure airports in the world. Nevertheless, Angel sent Blue ahead to clear the way and check for demon presence. Scammer, Scythe, and Shameless headed back to En Gedi to wait for the report of the assassination to come in.

Apollyon recognized it was now or never. He began to speak to Nathan.

"It is time for justice. Vengeance is mine. This will validate me as a righteous person in everyone's eyes. Sarah will never spurn my love again."

Apollyon slowly took control of Nathan's will. Nathan was now demon possessed. Apollyon was buried deep in Nathan's soul. He was hidden from view. Unless an angel looked directly into Nathan's eyes, he would never sense Apollyon's presence.

"Victory is mine," Apollyon said and Nathan smiled.

As Pastor Washington, the two secret service agents, and Angel entered the airport terminal to find Rabbi David, Salome called out to him.

"Pastor Washington, please, a moment of your time, to speak to the people of Jerusalem."

Pastor Harold looked at the secret service agents shadowing him and gestured for approval. They had been informed that Pastor Washington had agreed to a quick interview at the airport. Their trained eyes checked the three people waiting for their arrival: Sarah Kauffman, Salome, and the cameraman. Sarah was holding a mic and Nathan was holding a camera at the ready, concealing his face.

Peter, secret service officer number one, knew this was only the beginning of a long election season. He saw no threat and nodded. Angel wasn't as sure. He drew his sword.

As Harold moved into the camera lights, Sarah asked into the mic, "Pastor Washington, welcome back to Jerusalem. Your fans would like to know if you'll be speaking during this visit and if you plan to tour our beautiful city?"

With Nathan's right hand, Apollyon slowly reach down into Nathan's bag and pulled out the Jericho 941. He kept filming with the camera on his shoulder being steadied by his left hand. No one noticed. All eyes were on Sarah, as she extended the mic toward Pastor Washington.

Angel reacted first, in a flash; he twisted his shield from his back to in front of the pastor. Shots rang out. Two 9 mm bullets spun through the air into Sarah's back and through her heart. Sarah flew forward, exposing Pastor Washington to Apollyon's line of sight. Two bullets hit Pastor Washington in the chest. Sarah was dead. The pastor was thrown off his feet backward and landed on Jim, secret service agent number two.

At the same moment, Peter yelled, "Gun!" and shot the cameraman twice, center of mass. Apollyon was gone. Nathan was dead. Other cameramen and reporters, who were waiting in the wings in the hope that they could also get an opportunity to interview the pastor, began filming along with dozens of iPhones.

Stunned Harold got to his feet. Jim helped Pastor Washington up, checking for other gunmen and expecting to minister immediate first aid to the pastor. Jim knew the pastor was wearing a Kevlar chest protector which Peter insisted upon. But he was still amazed that Pastor Washington didn't seem to be hurt and that there were no bullet holes in the pastor's clothing or vest.

Harold saw the body of Sarah Kauffman lying face down in front of him in a growing pool of blood. He knelt down beside her. He took off his suit coat and placed it gently over her body and began to pray.

"Father, please spare this young woman's life. Oh, giver of life and protector of Israel, save this child of yours. For your glory. Show the world your love and mercy. Show them your power over life and death. Oh, Jesus, King of kings, Prince of Peace, Healer of Nations, raise this one as you raised Lazarus. Call her back into this world so she could testify to your goodness. Holy Spirit, do not let Satan and his minions be victorious over this day. Raise her up as you raised the Lord from the dead. Please, oh Lord, hear your humble servant's plea." Harold began to cry.

Peter and Jim each took Harold by his arms and gently raised him up to get him to his feet, saying, "Pastor, we've got to get you to safety. There may be other gunmen."

And then Peter noticed the body on the floor, in front of him, move. At first, he thought he was seeing things. Maybe he was in shock. But then she moaned.

"What happened?" she asked.

Jim fell to his knees, soaking in a puddle of blood. He slowly rolled Sarah over, expecting to see a gruesome sight. But other than the blood on her blouse Jim didn't see any evidence of her being shot. Peter helped Sarah sit up; he draped Pastor Washington's jacket over her shoulders as he checked her back. There were no entry wounds in her back nor exit wounds. At that moment, with the sound of the assassin's gun shots still ringing in his ears, Peter knew he had seen a miracle.

"Let's get the pastor to safety," Jim said.

Peter agreed. They were designated to meet Rabbi David Levin at the pick-up area. They hurried out front.

Harold pointed out David's car and they headed for their ride. Jim jumped into the front seat, Peter assisted Pastor Washington into the back.

Peter said, a little louder than intended, "Drive."

Rabbi David quickly pulled away and moved into traffic. He noticed the blood-soaked pants of the agent sitting next to him. Looking into the rearview mirror and saw his friend's face splattered with blood. He quickly turned around to see the other agent's bloody hands still holding a gun.

Rabbi David faced forward, settled himself down, and said, "So how was your flight?"

*****

In the human world, word of the assassination attempt spread rapidly. Ironically, the assassin's own recording taken with his own i24 News camera produced the best view of his attack and subsequent execution. But beyond that amazing footage, for the first time in history, hundreds of recordings showed Pastor Washington praying over a woman who was shot at point-blank range, bringing her back from the dead. It was fully documented. It was a bona fide miracle. Pastor Washington was now being called God's Man for Our Time. People were eager to hear anything he had to say.

*****

In the demon world, most were overjoyed by the Ambassador's failure. The Demon's assembly was beyond excited. They were all waiting for the ambassadorship slot to become available.

Apollyon found himself kneeling before the Demon Throne. This time, the Demon Lord was waiting for him. He dared not look directly at the Demon Lord. He knew he could be destroyed in the blink of an eye. He decided to go down swinging, however. He would be positive, proactive, direct. A demon with a plan, not a loser asking for another chance.

Thummim said, "Explain."

"Lord, I tried the subtle approach, testing the pastor's defenses without any loss of resources. I discovered he is protected by a mighty angel. And that he has direct access to the Throne Room." Apollyon paused to check if his head was still on his shoulders.

Urim said, "Go on."

Apollyon continued his train of thought, "Since the pastor is playing hard to kill, I have a plan to destroy him collaterally. I will chip away at his ministry, destroy his reputation, find the weak link in his chain of command, kill his loved ones, and burn down everything that matters to him. If the head is invincible, I will chop off its arms, legs, and then its torso." Apollyon paused; he didn't want to oversell it.

After a long, uncomfortable pause, Thummim said, "You are living on borrowed time."

Urim said, "Go."

And he was gone. Apollyon would live another day. He would attack the pastor's life with a fury. When he was done executing his plan, the pastor would wish he had been assassinated. And Apollyon would regain face. Time was of the essence. He would have to enlist help from every resource available. The pastor's demise was priority number one.

After all, he had a million demons at his disposal. While he was forbidden to orchestrate an all-out attack, he could initiate any number of sorties. His plan was now to deliver a "Death by a thousand cuts."

*****

In the angelic world, the mood was sober. An assassin, a demon-possessed man, had been able to approach the pastor undetected. Angel had saved the pastor's life by shielding him at the last minute. Even though the Almighty brought her back from the dead, a woman had been killed on his watch. The possessed assassin was executed and sent to Hades awaiting judgment.

"Blue and I were guarding the pastor aboard his flight. I hadn't set up an angelic defense at the airport before our arrival. When we landed, Blue went ahead and did a thorough scan of the airport. She determined that the airport was clear of demons."

"Except it wasn't," Samson injected.

"No, I mean, yes, it wasn't." Angel said. "A demon had possessed the assassin and slipped through human security with a weapon. We had no way of knowing the cameraman was possessed other than staring into his eyes. There were at least fifteen thousand people in the airport at the time."

"Are you making excuses?" Debra asked.

"Yes, I mean no, I'm not making excuses. I just wanted to point out where I failed." Angel paused.

"Please, we are all here to learn where we need to improve. We intend to leave this meeting newly informed and wiser about the enemy's tactics," Eli said.

"Okay, here's what I've learned. First, secure all destination points before any of our guarded persons arrive. Always have a guardian angel no further than a shield's length away from anyone we are guarding. Third, no matter how much angel power is needed, we have to look into the eyes of anyone who is within shooting distance from the persons we are guarding. It's the only way to be certain a human isn't possessed," Angel concluded his presentation with a sigh.

Eli nodded and said, "Blue, do you have anything to add?"

"Well, I deeply regret my failure to identify the shooter. I wasn't looking for a demon-possessed human. That possibility never crossed my mind. Now, it will never leave it. If you need to demote me or remove me from this assignment, I completely understand." Blue lowered her head in shame.

Samson jumped in and said, "We'll have none of that. We are all at fault here. We all share in the victories and we will all share in the defeats. This, by the way, was a victory. The only person lost was the perpetrator. For my part I say, 'Well done. Let's do better.'"

Blue looked up and said, "Thank you, General."

Angel said, "With the pastor's vice presidential nomination secured, Generals, I may need more warriors. I've got one thousand angels now. I believe I'll need twice as many."

That's preposterous," Debra said, "you need a hundred times that." She looked at the other General on the Council. "Would you say one hundred thousand will be enough?"

The Generals looked at each other for a unanimous vote. Each agreed.

Eli concluded, "Colonel Angel, Colonel Blue, execute your improved plan of protection. Angel you will be assigned one hundred thousand warriors. And neither of you ever hesitate to ask for help again."

"Yes, General," Angel and Blue said in harmony.

"And thank you," Angel said.

*****

Chase found the search for the Tobiases wasn't easy, but it wasn't impossible either. After Wycliffe Tobias passed from the scene, his firstborn son, William Tobias Israel, took over the family business. Then there was Tobias William Israel. On and on it went until World War I.

At which time, Tobias Washington Israel was drafted into the army. An army registrar strongly suggested that he change his name. He warned that overseas, his name would be confusing and viewed as almost un-American. Tobias didn't agree but thought the registrar had good intensions and probably knew better than he did. So he changed his name to Tobias Israel Washington. He fully intended to rectify the situation after the war. In a letter to his newly-wed wife which Chase found in the WWI university archives, Tobias explained his decision. He wrote, "There's the right way, and then there's the army way."

Most likely, information about Tobias was preserved because he became the first field commander of color in American history and a decorated war hero. After the war, Tobias became a celebrated war veteran. All his metals and letters from President Woodrow Wilson, American leaders, and foreign dignitary addressed him as "Commander Washington."

"And so, the Israels became the Washingtons." Chase wrote in his report to Harold in an email. "I've got all the documentation to verify this and will give you the full written report when you return from Jerusalem. And congratulations on the 'raising people from the dead thing'. Just kidding, Our God is an Awesome God. Chase."

Harold could hardly believe his eyes when he read the email from Chase. This connected the dots in an unimaginable way. He had more to discuss with Rabbi David than he originally thought.

*****

Rabbi David closed the glass-paned French doors sectioning off his drawing room from the rest of the house. Harold finally sat down with David. David poured them both a Copita glass of sherry.

Harold thanked David and took a sip. "David, you're not going to believe this but…"

"No, Harold, after this morning's events, I'd believe anything you said." David took a sip of his sherry and topped both of their glass off.

"Well, I've done some more research on the lineage of high priests. And with the help of a trusted friend at AU, we've made a startling discovery," Harold continued.

"Hold on. If this is about what I think it's about, we need to move this discussion to a more secure location. Do you think Tom and Jerry can drive us to the Temple Institute?" David asked.

Harold chuckled, "You mean Jim and Peter, they're probably in your driveway waiting to take us to dinner and then you, back home, and me, to the hotel."

"Good, then we're off, to 40 Misgav Ladach Street. And make it snappy."

Rabbi David downed his sherry and moved to the driveway. Harold shook his head at his incorrigible friend, took a sip of his sherry, and followed David to the driveway.

From the car, David called a Rabbi Kohen on his cell. "I've got a need for a secure room." Pause. "Just two people total." Pause. "I can't say." Pause. "Yes, about the information you gave me." Pause.

David turned to Harold and asked, "Can Rabbi Kohen join us?"

Harold thought for a moment and nodded.

"He said he was fine with that." Pause. "Thirty minutes then. Shalom."

"Well, the plot thickens, Eh?" David looked out his window and thought, *This could be the moment of no return.*

*****

The elevator didn't indicate an "LL3" existed, but Rabbi Kohen placed a key in the lock below the elevator control panel and pulled out the red emergency stop button. Instead of stopping, the elevator descended three floors.

The secret chamber hadn't changed since David was there last time. A canter was singing softly, four rabbis were in prayer at each wall. A table with three chairs was set up in the middle of the room. The three of them sat down, and Harold open a family tree type diagram in the center of the table.

"Rabbis, this is a pictorial representation of what we knew, combined with what you gave me, combined with information I got with help from the Smithsonian and the British Museum in Bloomsbury London."

All three of them took a few minutes to trace the lineage as shown.

"Excellent work. It's more complete than anything I've seen thus far," Rabbi Kohen said.

"Rabbi, you ain't seen nothing yet. I had a dream or maybe a vision that caused me to dig further. To what end, I couldn't say. So I wrote down everything I could remember from my dream and asked an American history professor to gather anything that could shine some light on the gap." Harold could hear the deep gasp that came from Rabbi Levin.

"Rest assured that my friend knows nothing about our dealings here or searching for the high priest. I merely asked him to track the 'who abouts' and the 'where abouts' and the 'when abouts' of Tobias Menasseh Israel's progeny up to the present day." Harold drew attention to a branch that stopped midair. Like being trapped in a maze, one was forced back down the tree and up another way.

"Here is where Tobias Menasseh Israel lineage stops, and thirty years later, the lineage jumps the gap and continues with Joseph ben Israel." Harold waited for the two rabbis to track his progress thus far.

"We've always assumed Tobias died in the UK," Rabbi Levin said.

"But wouldn't that mean that the younger brother, Joseph ben Israel, would have to marry his sister-in-law and have a child with her to properly continue Tobias's line of high priests?" Harold asked.

"That's the law," Rabbi David said.

"But the evidence I've uncovered tells us different," Pastor Harold said.

Harold took out a second chart that focused in on the actual lineage of Tobias Menasseh Israel. As they studied this chart, they were astonished by its detailed tracking of who, where, and when. The chart led them to Tobias Washington Israel, 1914, and WWI, they both looked up.

"He changed his name?" David asked.

"From Israel to Washington," Harold said. "He was my great-grandfather. And I am the firstborn, as my father before me and his father before him."

"So if, Tobias would have kept his place in the lineage of high priest, you would be the actual reigning high priest today?" Rabbi Levin asked.

"Rabbi Levin, please understand, I'm not trying to claim the high priesthood for myself. I'm just trying to understand why the Lord has taken me on such a curious journey. I'd like clarity on what my duty is today," Harold said.

"Can a mixed-race Christian pastor be a Jewish high priest?" Harold asked rhetorically.

"What do you think?" Rabbi Levin asked.

"Well, I believe, in my heart, that Christianity is Jewish. The gospel, that is the 'good news' to the world, was meant for the Jew first and then the Gentile. Jesus is not only Jewish, but he is the rightful King of Israel, His disciples were Jewish. The first three thousand believers were Jewish. The first Christian church was in Jerusalem. Jesus's brother, a Jew, was its first pastor. Peter, who opened the door to the Gentiles was Jewish. Paul the missionary to the gentiles and the Jews who wrote more than half of the New Testament was Jewish. All of scripture, Old and New Testament, was written by Jews. The King of Israel will return and reign in the New Jerusalem." Harold let that soak in.

"Do I believe I am the rightful next high priest, destined to offer red heifers in the third temple? Probably not. But I believe I have an important role in representing the true Christ to the Jews. Scripture tells us that in Christ, all believers are 'a holy priesthood, offering spiritual sacrifices acceptable to God through Jesus Christ.' But I still think I'm missing something," Harold said.

"Pastor Harold," Rabbi Levin whispered, "we are missing something too."

Harold leaned forward not to miss a word. Rabbi Levin continued, "We are missing the Ark and the temple treasures."

"I think I knew that," Harold said.

"But the thing is, the legitimate high priest was to always know and be in control of the Ark and its various treasures," Rabbi Levin said.

"And he is not?" Harold asked.

"Pastor Harold, have you ever heard of the Ghib-bore, the Mighty Men of Valor?" Rabbi Kohen asked.

"Do you mean as in Gideon, the mighty man of valor?" Harold asked and answered.

"Do you remember the thirty-two thousand soldiers pared down to three hundred?" Rabbi Kohen challenged the pastor.

"Sure, as a kid down by the local stream, we would be certain to lap water from our cupped hands in order to be chosen by God," Harold reminisced.

"Well, those men's descendants are alive today. And I believe, a select few of those men have always been with and have been protecting the Ark and its treasures. We just don't know who they are or where they are," Rabbi Kohen admitted.

"So the true high priest and this Ghib-bore should be the key to all of this," Harold summarized.

"Should be, that's what I believe in my heart," Rabbi Kohen concluded.

"Rabbis, I need time to think and pray and think some more. My brain is about to explode," Harold said.

"Now that would be quite an explosion," Rabbi David said.

PART 7

Angel and the Vice President

The tidal wave caused by the miracle at Ben Gurion Airport carried President Kennedy and Vice President Pastor Harold T. Washington to victory in the November election. Supporters looked forward to having country leaders who were committed to God. The opposition, on the other hand, was worried that the country would become a theocracy.

Apollyon began to mount an attack on all fronts. In the government, he had his agents push the "Separation of Church and State" issue. In the media, he had his people began to run ads about religious fascism. He even authored articles about "Harold Washington, the American Khomeini." In education, he nurtured accusations that the White House was anti-science, anti-earth, and pushing their own version of "Creationism." Culturally, reports were released citing Harold Washington's family's wealth had come from operating slave-run plantations. In commerce, boycotts were staged against any company that didn't carry the "rainbow flag" on its label.

Apollyon marshalled attacks on the White House concerning their pro-life leanings. He stirred up fear that *Roe vs. Wade* would be overturned. He portrayed both Joe Kennedy and Harold Washington as homophobic, xenophobic, sexist, and were opposed to gender choice. He began rumors that laws were in the making targeting persons in the LGBTT 2/T QQ IAA community.

Even though all this was gaining real friction, Apollyon still looked for an opening to personally attack the pastor and the angels protecting him. He watched the pastor's family. He noted their comings and goings. Demon's Teeth had one million demons under his personal command. Apollyon assigned one hundred thousand demons to each of the seven districts on earth, so that he could monitor and maintain control over his kings and generals. He also placed one hundred thousand demons in the sky and one hundred thousand under the seas. There wasn't a square inch on earth, in the sky, or under the seas that he didn't have covered by his own personal army. In addition, he had the last one hundred thousand demons at his beck and call.

Even so, the Demon Lord had Apollyon's hands tied with the threat of being destroyed for any act of direct disobedience. There was only so much Apollyon could do without breaking the Demon Lord's restriction that an "all-out war" wasn't permitted. But Apollyon was beginning to think, if he didn't succeed in defeating the pastor and his protector, he would be destroyed by the Demon Lord anyway.

If I'm living on borrowed time, why not go down in blaze of glory? he thought.

*****

Angel wasn't created to attack at will. In fact, he was hardly willing to ever attack. He was a guardian not a warrior. But if attacked, he was ready, willing, and able to take control of the situation. Blue, on the other hand, was a warrior. She truly believed the best defense was having the best offence.

"We're going to have to be proactive here. The enemy is gaining ground on public opinion and is clearly planning to attack. If we wait until he is fully loaded, we may not be able to protect everyone and everyplace and everything we need to." Blue was trying to remain calm, even though her anxiety meter was off the charts.

"What do you propose we do, that we aren't already doing?" Angel asked.

"Let's clear out DC. I know it's been a diplomatic zone for years, but that hasn't stopped the enemy from gathering information and planning attacks from there. They are using DC as a home base and a launching-off point for their attacks. Surely, they're breaking some sort of rule by doing that. Besides, Charleston is secure, but the pastor and his family are spending half of their time in DC, which is not secure. The enemy could attack them in DC at any time, and we'd be too late to do anything about it. Who placed DC on the 'no fight zone' list anyway?" Blue finally paused for a much needed breath.

"It hasn't, I know, probably, I agree, they could, we won't, and I never asked." Angel smiled.

"Okay, Colonel, what's your plan?" Blue asked.

"I've also been thinking. Why don't we pick them off one demon at a time? Select the most active and dangerous demons in DC and make them disappear? If they're operating outside the rules of diplomacy in DC, then they've clearly given up their right to be treated diplomatically. If the enemy complains, we can launch an investigation into their activities and put an end to this 'no fight zone' agreement, once and for all." Angel already had his first target picked out.

"Who do you have in mind?" Blue asked.

"Smyth," Angel said.

"Top Demon, Smyth?" Blue repeated.

"Well, if we only get one shot, we should make it count," Angel reasoned.

"Not bad," Blue agreed. "I'll see what can be done."

*****

Sarah Kauffman spent weeks avoiding what she had previously sought, fame. She was racked with guilt, filled with doubt, plagued with questions. She finally decided the only way she could move on with her life was to speak to Pastor Washington. And that the only way to see him was to go to his church in Charleston, South Carolina.

She checked the church's website and pulled up their preaching schedule. The following Sunday, Pastor Washington was preaching on "Obeying the Government or Obeying God." The sermon topic seemed an interesting choice. But Sarah wasn't interested in hearing a sermon. She wanted answers. No, that wasn't right, she needed answers.

So she arrived on Sunday morning at FCCC. She was an hour early and grabbed a front row seat. Her bonnet and sunglasses shielded her identity but combined with her natural beauty she drew quite a bit of attention. People assumed she was a celebrity, but they couldn't place her. After three worship songs, the choir sat and began to discreetly take photos of her with their iPhones and search the internet.

Pastor Harold ascended his staircase and began to address the congregation. He welcomed visitors, recognized dignitaries, addressed those streaming and watching on TV. He nodded to Annie and began to do what he loved best, preach the word of God.

"Let everyone be subject to the governing authorities, for there is no authority except that which God has established. The authorities that exist have been established by God for our good. Romans 13:1. 'But, Pastor, the government doesn't always do what's right,' you say. That's right, but the Bible says, 'Be subject to the governing authorities.' 'But, Pastor, the government takes our money for the kind of spending I don't condone,' you say. That's right, but the Bible says, 'The authorities that exist have been established by God.' 'But, Pastor,' you say, 'I conscientiously object.' That's right, but the Bible says, 'There is no (other) authority except that which God has established.'"

*****

Sarah never heard Pastor Washington deliver a sermon. She was enthralled by Pastor Washington's ability to speak right to her soul. She took in every word. The way he continued to applied passages from the Bible and unpacked the truth in them fascinated her. There were large screens to the pastor's left and right. Verses were being shown and actually highlighted as he explained their meaning.

She remembered the last time she saw him. She was holding out the mic. Right before she was sent into the darkness.

"Pastor Washington, welcome back to Jerusalem. Your fans would like to know if you'll be speaking during this visit and if you plan to tour our beautiful city?"

What is this place? she thought. *What am I doing here?*

Sarah spun around. She was in the middle of a desert. It was night. It was barren. It was very cold and lifeless. Then a voice came out of the darkness, "Sarah, you have been weighed in the balance and found wanting."

"Who are you, Lord?" she asked.

"I am a servant of the Lord, 'God is my strength'. The Lord says to you, 'But for the prayer of the Lord's servant, Pastor Washington, you would now be in this darkness forever. You must turn from your wicked ways. You must find life's true treasure. Tell the one who prays for you, even now, to 'Trust your elders.'"

Sarah was used to drifting off and reliving the time she spent in the dark place. She knew she would have no peace until she finally delivered the servant's message to Pastor Washington.

Pastor Washington was wrapping up his sermon. "You must turn from the rebellion that resides in you. Turn from your lying, your cheating, your adultery and fornications. You must turn from your wicked ways and receive Jesus Christ as your personal Savior. Come out of the darkness and into the light."

Pastor Washington turned to descend the stairs. As he did, he said, "This is the moment you need to listen to the Holy Spirit's prompting. Listen to Him, He is listening to you."

"Meet me down front now. The elders and I will be ready to pray with you and lead you into his presence. Now is the day of salvation. Come."

The choir began to sing softly.

> Just as I am, without one plea
> But that Thy blood was shed for me

And that Thou bid'st me come to Thee
O Lamb of God, I come! I come.

Sarah felt as if two arms lifted her out of her pew. Without any hesitation, she was the first to meet Pastor Washington down front. With tear-filled eyes, she said, "Pastor Washington, would you help me, again?"

Tears flowed from both of them. The sinner and the preacher. Sarah knew enough truth to fully open her heart to the Savior. She knew more than most. They prayed together, and Sarah was born again.

Harold had recognized her the moment he ascended the stairs to his pulpit. He was doing some serious multitask praying as he preached. He hadn't plan to give an altar call but was prompted by the Holy Spirit to change the end of his sermon. He was glad he did.

After the service, Harold and Sarah sat down in the front row pew. Harold called Annie over and introduced her to Sarah. Annie already knew who Sarah was from the hundreds of photos she saw after Jerusalem. Annie was still taken aback by Sarah's beauty. But there was something more than physical beauty in her countenance, there was joy.

"Annie, Sarah has something to tell you," Harold said.

Annie looked at Sarah and waited. Sarah looked into Annie's kind eyes and said, "I have come to the end of my journey. I have found the treasure of a lifetime. I've found Jesus, and I've asked Him into my heart."

Annie and Sarah hugged and wept tears of joy. "Sarah, your search may be over, but your journey has just begun. Please join us for dinner today. I've got loads of reading material I want to share with you. I come from a Jewish background too. I'd like to share some information that would help you see how complete your faith has truly become."

"I'd love to, thank you," Sarah said. "But I must share with Pastor Washington something very important before I do one more thing."

"That's fine, dear. I've got to round up the boys and set the dinner table for our new sister. You two join us when you're done here." Annie squeezed Sarah's hand and said to Harold, "Mom and Dad will be delighted. See you at the house, honey," and she left.

Sarah settled for a moment and said, "Pastor, when I was shot, I was thrown into a dark desert place. A voice came to me and told me I needed to find life's treasure, and I have. Then he told me to give you a message." Sarah's throat tightened a little and her eyes began to tear.

Harold reached for his handkerchief and handed it to her. "Please, go on," Harold said.

Sarah continued her story. "I don't understand it, but the voice said, 'Tell the one who prayed for you, even now. Trust your elders.'"

"My elders? That's it?" Harold was puzzled by the simplicity of the message. "Did the voice identify himself?"

"Yes, I think so. He said he was a servant of the Lord and his name was 'God is my Strength.'"

Harold searched his memories. He knew that verse, 2 Samuel 22:33, but not as a name. Then he thought, *We were in Jerusalem. Sarah is a Jewess. He is a descendant of a high priest of Israel. It's a Hebrew name.*

Harold looked at Sarah and said, "Indulge me for a moment."

Harold pulled out his iPhone and Googled "Hebrew name meaning 'God is my Strength.'"

He got his answer. The screen read, "Origin of the name Gabriel: Derived from the Hebrew *gavrīēl* (God is my strength). The name is borne in the Bible by one of the seven archangels."

"Gabriel," he whispered.

*****

After dinner, Annie gave Sarah some literature from "Jews for Jesus." Annie's parents were more than pleased to explain "Jews for Jesus" to her. Sarah was amazed to find out there were a half of million Jews who were members. And thousands more who believed worldwide. The Cohens explained Jesus is the true Messiah and is due to return to Jerusalem, soon.

After a few stimulating hours of discussion, Sarah said she was going to take some time off and rethink her future. They all exchanged numbers and promised to see each other again as soon as possible. She left for the airport, already flying high.

Annie's parents had put the boys to bed and then excused themselves. They retired to their part of the house together. Harold and Annie sat on the couch together with bowls of ice cream. Annie said, "What a glorious day."

"Indeed," Harold said. After taking a stab at his ice cream, he asked, "Gabriel, imagine. What do you think this all means? What do you think Gabriel's message means? 'Trust my elders'?

"My father and mother are gone. I don't know of very many living elder relatives. Maybe a grand uncle and aunt in Alabama. Maybe there are other relatives somewhere I don't know about."

"Why don't you take a breath and focus on all the things you do know, instead of the things you don't know?" Annie was trying to calm Harold before they went to bed for the evening. She knew they won't be together again for about a week after tonight.

"What time are you going back to DC tomorrow?" Annie asked.

"Peter is going to pick me up for the airport at seven. Why?" Harold asked. It was easy to forget that there were secret service agents outside their door 24/7.

"I thought you could run all this by Jim or Richard before you left, to see what they thought," Annie said.

Harold stopped his ice cream filled spoon in midair. He put it back in the bowl. He looked at Annie.

"What did you just say?" Harold asked.

"What time are you going back to DC?" Annie doubled down on the question.

"No, no, the other thing," Harold said.

"You mean, 'I thought you could run this by Jim or Richard?'" Annie tried to follow Harold's questioning.

"What?" Annie furled her brows. "Is there something I missed?"

"My elders, Jim, Richard, Sam, 'trust my elders'!" Harold felt like a new door had just opened, but he truly had no idea where it would lead.

*****

Smyth was working on a plan to bribe a senator from California. Senator Lester was leading a committee to review funding for the development of a new abortion pill. The pharmaceutical company had already poured a hundred million dollars into its research and development. The company desperately needed approval for government funding. Senator Lester was having serious marital problems and needed to shower his wayward wife with presents and a skiing chalet in the Alps.

The proposed pill would make it possible to abort a pregnancy in the first trimester without any physical harm to the woman or a required trip to the doctor. The million-dollar bribe would allow Senator Lester to buy the chalet in the Alps for his wife.

Smyth sat next to Senator Lester and Abbott Slone from the special interest group. They were in a private room, at an exclusive club, not open to the public. They were about to wrap up the deal. The money was being transferred to a Swiss bank account, and assurances were being given about the upcoming committee vote. All was going well, until it didn't.

Blue stepped around Smyth's two bodyguards with a flirty little smile and ran her sword clear through Smyth's heart. Before the guards could react, Blue cut off both of their heads. In five seconds, all evidence of what transpired was gone including Blue. One of Blue's team members stuck his hand through the laptop on the table in front of them and stopped the money transaction.

The senator waited a few minutes for confirmation that the transfer of money had been completed. The confirmation never came. Everything went up in flames, literally and figuratively. Smyth, his two bodyguards, the laptop, and the deal. Blue vanished without being detected by man, beast, or demon. On her exit, she dropped a business card on the table. The card read, "Charles Gleason,

Operations Officer, International Corruption Unit (ICU), FBI."
Senator Lester shelved the entire bill and funding. The pill itself was
aborted.

*****

"Who's next?" Blue drifted across the room and sat down next
to Angel. Angel had been with the pastor all day. Vice President
Washington was having a busy week. Angel had cleared the pastor's
way of all demon presence. The pastor had just settled down at his
DC residence and began working on his family tree and lineage
charts.

"You are," Angel said, "next to me." He put his arm around Blue
and drew her close.

Angel gestured toward the pastor and said, "I believe he's planning something big when he gets back to Charleston. Look here. If
you take one path, the chart begins with Aaron and goes through
Rabbi Joseph ben Israel, you end with Rabbi David Masinter, who
is alive and resides in Johannesburg. But if you follow the same path
and branch off here," Angel pointed to the branch marked Rabbi
Tobias Menasseh ben Israel, "you end up here." Angel ran his finger
down to the end of the new branch.

Blue leaned over the chart and read, "Harold Tobias
Washington." She looked a little surprised and asked, "Is he the high
priest the enemy's been looking for?"

"Guess so." Angel shrugged. "No wonder my life has become
so exciting."

"And all along, I thought it was me," Blue said.

"And you," Angel responded. "Wait, what did you mean, 'Who's
next?'"

"Smyth and two of his bodyguards have just gone on a one-way
trip," Blue said nonchalantly as she adjusted her wings.

"Blue, did you do what I think you did?" Angel asked warily.

"Well, if you're thinking, I ran my sword through Diplomat
Smyth's heart and cut his bodyguards' heads off, then yes." Blue was
studying her nails intently. "Don't worry, no one saw me."

"Oh my. We need to tighten our defense. Where are the warriors stationed now?" Angel asked.

"We've got twenty-five thousand in Charleston, twenty-five thousand here, patrolling the DC residence, twenty-five thousand at the White House, and twenty-five thousand at the Capitol. We are mobile, agile, and hostile. Now, who's next?" Blue's demeanor went into warrior mode.

"I don't know. You started it. What do you think?" Angel was a little rocked.

"We're doing this to protect the pastor. Let's attack the enemy's strongholds. First, let's free the press." Blue was nodding as she began to devise her strategy.

"Well, as soon as the enemy realizes Smyth is gone, they're going to attack this city full on. We've got twenty-four hours or less to do our best, unimpeded. Take whatever troops you need and get it done. I'll stay with the pastor. Make certain Charleston remains secure. I'll notify the Council and let them know of 'our plan'. And, Blue, be careful."

"Always." Blue was gone in a streak.

*****

Before the sun set, the city was ablaze with slayed demons. Without demonic leadership in the DC area, editors, reporters, columnists, and bloggers were quickly released from demonic influence. In one night, the anti-God influence on the media was eliminated. Within a week, the reporting of the news became just that, reporting what was new. It was truthful, unbiased, and fair.

Blue's attacks didn't end with the media; however, she moved on to the Capitol. Angel had already cleared out the demons residing there. But Blue made certain they wouldn't return. Together, their actions were pushing Apollyon toward a tough decision.

Apollyon had been taken by surprise. His Government and Media divisions were decimated in DC. It seemed like the attack happened overnight. When Smyth disappeared, his organization fell like a house of cards. Apollyon had to decide whether to disobey the "all-out" war mandate issued by the Demon Lord or fall into a totally defensive posture and sustain as few losses as possible. The former meant experiencing the wrath of the Demon Lord. The latter meant losing valuable ground taken during the last decade. He decided to live to fight another day. He called his rulers together.

"It appears we stirred up a hornet's nest," he said. "I'm certain this is only a temporary situation, but I need everyone to be prepared for further attacks by the Realm. We are under orders to avoid an all-out war, but we must not lose the ground we've already gained. If you can't hold on to your own territory, you will be replaced. I have also decided that the North American territory will be taken over by General Rommel. He has proven to be a superior strategist and a relentless war time general."

The Ambassador signaled his guards to usher in General Rommel.

Everyone in the room knew of Rommel's reputation. He never spoke an idle word or had a frivolous thought. He was all business, all the time. And he was totally evil. It was best to avoid contact with him if possible. He never held a grudge or tolerated a competitor. He acted swiftly and destroyed whoever, wherever, whenever. He was called the Fox for a reason.

He walked into the room and bowed first to the Ambassador and then to the other rulers.

"Ambassador, comrades, it is my great honor to serve with you. I am certain we will be victorious. And in the end, we will bring glory to our Demon Lord." Rommel sat in the open chair to the right of the Ambassador.

"Herr General, your first order of business is to strengthen our defenses in North America against these recent attacks and to eventually destroy the pastor," the Ambassador said.

"Ambassador, it will be my pleasure." Rommel bowed his head to the Ambassador.

Apollyon thought, *I really think this will work. Why didn't I make this move earlier?*

To the rest of the rulers, Apollyon said, "If there's nothing else. You are dismissed. Do not let me down."

*****

The first thing Rommel did was to feign an attack on the White House with five thousand demons. In response, twenty-five thousand warrior angels chased the attacking demons out to sea. Which was exactly where General Rommel wanted them. Demon's Teeth did the rest. They dropped onto the pursuing angels from above and slashed up into them from the ocean below. Over three quarters of the warrior angels fell to the demon ambush in brilliant flashes of light. Moments later, the demons were gone without a trace.

To anyone watching, it appeared as if the demons were protecting their territory from an attack of angels, not like the aggressive demon attack it really was.

The second thing Rommel did was to send spies into the ranks of the angel camps. Their objective was to gain information and relay it back to Rommel's headquarters. If the spies were discovered, they had their orders to destroy whatever and whoever they could before being sent to the abyss.

Finally, Rommel wanted to establish an indestructible fortress in the center of North American. Then push outward, taking control of an ever-expanding territory. He would strengthen his position as he expanded boundaries. Eventually, not even the Ambassador would be able to stop him. He planned to take over North and South America. Then move overseas toward the Crown Jewel, Jerusalem.

He started almost unnoticed, by occupying Rugby, North Dakota. Rugby had the dubious honor of being the geographic center of North America. The town was literally out in the middle of nowhere. He sent agents into Rugby to establish a beachhead and begin to take control of the people in the area.

His demons were instructed to kill anyone who resisted them or got in their way. They were happy to oblige. In less than a month, they locked up North Dakota. In two months, South Dakota, Montana, Minnesota, Saskatchewan, and Manitoba were under his control. He moved his entire operation and headquarters to Rugby. The cycle of expanding and then securing small areas at a time was highly success-ful. Rommel estimated that in three years' time, the enemy would no longer have a place to stand in North America. In four years' time Central and South America would be one with North America. In five years, he would overthrow the Ambassador and take Jerusalem. The Fox would finally have his den.

*****

Rommel's presence didn't go unnoticed, however. The Council was already planning a response.

"General Samson, would you please give us an update on your progress?" Chairman Eli requested.

"Yes, of course, Chairman Eli," Samson said. "We've dealt with Rommel before. His weakness is overconfidence. He has clearly over-reached. His borders have become so extensive that it has weakened his core."

"So what's your next move?" Debra asked. "You know it isn't time for the Lord's return. Our response must be measured."

"And it will be," Samson explained. "We will surgically remove the threat at its core. We will hit him with a sudden lightning strike. He is a mastermind, but he is not invincible. This time, he will be destroyed."

"Who will head up the strike?" Debra asked.

"We have one angel in our ranks that can still walk into the enemy's camp unscathed." Samson waited.

"You mean Blue, don't you?" Eli said.

"I've already asked her. She is more than willing." Samson paused again.

"But?" Eli asked.

"She won't do it without Angel," Samson answered.

"But he's not a warrior. He's a guardian," Debra said.

"Yes, true enough. But he'll be guarding Blue," Samson said.

"Don't we have anyone else qualified to take on this task?" Joel, Watcher General, suggested. "They both have their hands full with the pastor."

"I can't think of anyone more uniquely qualified for the job. Blue is still considered a demon in good standing," Samson explained.

"Samson, we can't afford to lose either of them," Eli said.

"We won't. I'm heading the charge. This is not only a fight for North America, it's the beginning of the end for the Ambassador. If we defeat Rommel, the Ambassador will lose face and, most probably, his head," Samson said, hoping to strengthen his case.

"Then I'm going too," Eli said.

"You're an archangel, you can't go into battle unless the Almighty sends you," Joel insisted.

"Let me worry about that. Samson's right, this has become bigger that we all thought. If we could get rid of Rommel and Apollyon and free North America from demonic influence in one fell swoop, we must try," Eli insisted.

"We'll need backup for Angel and Blue," Joel noted.

"I've got that," Debra assured everyone.

"All right, Samson, you've got a green light. Let's do it," Eli decided.

*****

Harold made a call to Jim Petersen just before he boarded his plane home. "Doctor, I need a consult with you, Sam, and Richard this evening at around eight. Can you organize that?"

"Probably, I'll check with the others and text you back. Where?" Jim asked.

"Let's make it in the church basement. It's secluded and I'll need some room to show you what I've got," Harold answered.

"Can we bring anything?" Jim asked.

"An open mind," Harold said.

Harold got to church a little early. He brought coffee cake and made coffee and set them out. Then at two separate tables, he spread out his family tree graphic and lineage chart. He covered them with tablecloths. He set up four chairs around a third table. Physically spent, he sat down and prayed.

"Lord, please help me present this information in a clear and convincing way. If I am mistaken, in any way, give these men wisdom to guide me in the right direction. Cast out any pride or self-interest in me and replace it with humility and obedience. Bless these friends of mine. And let them know that they are appreciated. Lord, we all come here to do your will and good work. Bless our efforts. Above all, Lord, glorify your holy name in all we say and do. Amen."

Harold opened his eyes and saw all three of his elders standing in front of him.

"Amen," they said.

"Men, good to see you." Harold got up and hugged each of them. "Please, help yourself to coffee and cake. The coffee is decaf. Boy, I missed you guys."

"Pastor, it's only been a week," Jim said.

"Yeah, but what a week," Harold said.

After everyone grabbed a slice of coffee cake and a cup of coffee, they sat around the table.

"So, Pastor, what's up?" Jim asked.

"I guess the best way to start is from the beginning. When the president sent me to Jerusalem, the first time, I met a rabbi. His name is David Levin." Pastor Harold went on to bring his elders up to speed to the point of his dreams.

"Whether they were dreams or visions, I couldn't say. But they were as clear to me as if I were standing there. I was in Amsterdam in the 1600s. Rabbi Tobias Israel was explaining to his father and high priest why he couldn't fulfill the duties that would be passed on to him upon his father's retirement."

As Pastor Harold continued explaining his dream to them, Jim shot a look to Richard and then to Sam.

"And so, they went to Joseph, the next eldest son, and explained the situation to him. Apparently, Tobias's father, Rabbi Menasseh ben Israel understood the pressures and requirements of being a high priest without a temple. He decided those duties should be pasted on to Joseph." Harold stopped for a bite of coffee cake and a sip of coffee. "Any questions so far?"

"Pastor," Jim asked. "What does this have to do with us?"

"Patience, Jim, I've got to tell this my way."

The second dream was even more detailed. Harold told them about Wycliffe Tobias being born to Tobias and Claire who was a former slave and the love of Tobias's life. He then explained Tobias's wish to carry on the "Tobias" name.

"So now I'd like to show you what this all looks like put together." Harold moved them over to the family tree graphic. "Here is the 'High Priest Family Tree.' This is extremely sensitive material. I don't have to tell you there are those who would do harm to the present-day high priest should any of this get out."

"Believe me, Pastor, we know," Jim said.

In his mind, Harold thought Jim's comment was a little off. But other than Annie, these were the three people on earth he trusted most. So he continued.

"You see, the tree starts with Aaron and weaves its way to the present-day high priest, here." Harold pointed to Rabbi David Masinter.

"How did you obtain all of this?" Sam asked.

"I had a lot of help," Harold answered. "Look over here, where Tobias Menasseh Israel gives birth to Wycliffe Tobias Israel and the branch stops."

"Was that due to the fact that Wycliffe was part black?" Richard asked.

"I really don't think so. I think it had more to do with Tobias deciding not to follow orthodox Jewish tradition and become a Christ follower," Harold said.

"So the right choice is not always the easy choice," Richard said.

"It is not. And here is where I began to suspect things were getting a little more personal for me."

Harold moved over to the second table and uncovered his own family tree. Starting with himself and moving back in time to WWI. He explained how and why Tobias Washington Israel changed his name to Tobias Israel Washington.

"You may recognize how this chart ties into the family tree on the other table," Harold concluded.

All three of the elders just stood and stared at the exhibits. The elders moved from one table to the other, staring and comparing.

"So," Jim finally said, "you believe you're a descendant of Aaron, the first high priest?"

"Well, yes. I also need to tell you that even though I seldom use it, my middle name is Tobias." Harold pointed to his middle name on the chart and his father's and grandfather's middle names. "But the thing is, if I were the legitimate high priest, I would know where the Ark of the Covenant is, and I would be in contact with a group of Ark Guardians known as Ghib-bore." Harold went on to explain the relationship between the Ark and the Ghib-bore as he understood it.

"Supposedly, wherever the Ark and the temple treasures go, the Ghib-bore follow, and the high priest has knowledge of everything. Don't ask me how I know this, but Rabbi David Masinter, the current high priest in Johannesburg, has no idea of it either." Harold looked over his work and said, "I have one more piece to this puzzle I need to share with you. Sarah Kauffman had an out-of-body experience. When she was shot, she found herself in a desert. Among other things a voice in the wilderness called out to her. I believe it was the angel Gabriel. He told her to give me a message." Harold was holding his coffee cup and noticed it was shaking. He put it down.

"Go on, Pastor, what was the message?" Jim asked.

"Sarah said the message was to tell me to 'Trust your elders.'" Harold took a deep breath and sat down, heavy.

"That's it?" Sam asked.

"That's it," Harold said.

The three elders looked at each other. Jim nodded to Sam, Sam to Richard, Richard back to Jim. Harold looked up at them and asked, "What is it?"

Jim took a moment, looked at Harold, and finally said, "Pastor, we are Ghib-bore."

*****

Blue calmly entered Rommel's camp. The demons who recognized her moved by with not so much as a nod. The ones that didn't know her ignored her. She scouted the camp. She was surprised to see how lax the security was and how easily she moved about the camp unchallenged. She identified Rommel's headquarters. It was a large field tent with his distinctive flag flying at the entrance, a red running fox on a black background. As she approached, she was stopped by two guards.

They were very large. They resembled tigers. Except these tigers were green with black stripes. They were fierce. Standing on all fours, they were a head taller than Blue.

"Identify yourself and state your business," the larger of the two said.

Blue remained calm and poised. *No fear*, she thought.

"I'm Blue. Herr General is expecting me," she said.

The guard looked her up and down and said, "I'm sure he is. I'll let the General know you're here." He told his partner to stay with her and headed for the headquarters' tent. The guard left behind, ogled her for a moment, and glanced back at his partner.

"Bad choice," Blue said and cut off his head.

Immediately, Blue gave signal to attack. The attack descended around Blue like a tornado. A column of warrior angels rained down in a sudden rush of wind. Eli and Samson shot out of the funnel and toward headquarters. Angel landed alongside of Blue. Seemingly out of nowhere, demons rushed them from all sides. Warriors continued to pour down through the column of wind. Angels engaged the rushing demons. They fought hand to hand, one on one. The battle raged on. Within an hour, however, the demons' counterattack waned.

Blue and Angel flew into the headquarters' tent. Samson and Eli were clearly outnumbered but holding their own. Rommel was wounded and being protected by a surround of his personal guard. Angel saw that Rommel's guards had the "running fox" insignia on their chest plate armor.

Not this time, he thought. Angel yelled. "My name is Angel, and no one leaves here alive." He attacked them head on. Blue worked her way behind the melee. She was looking for a direct shot at Rommel.

Rommel yelled at his guards to fall back. He tried to retreat, but Blue would have none of it. Blue threw a series of frozen bolas and ice cuffs at Rommel. He tried to avoid the ice blue barrage. His reaction time was slowed by an accumulation of wounds. He was eventually ensnared and fell to the ground. Angel destroyed the rest of his guard. Blue lashed Rommel with silver cord. Eli and Samson eliminated the rest of the demons in the tent.

Eli and Samson moved to the center of camp and worked their troops out toward the perimeter. After a full day and night of fighting, Rommel's fortress was no more. And Rommel was captured. The brilliant strategist was outwitted and beaten by his own pride and overconfidence.

The victors stood in the center of the camp. Angel turned to Eli and asked, "What do you think will happen to Apollyon?"

"Oh, I don't think, I know," Eli answered.

In the Demon Lord's castle, Apollyon knelt before an empty black throne. He was waiting for the Demon Lord's appearance. He expected to see Thummim and Urim first. They usually preceded the Demon Lord's entrance.

Apollyon had prepared a speech, laying the blame for Rommel's disastrous defeat on the General's overconfidence. But he was never given the chance. First, he heard a swish, and both of his arms fell to the ground. He was shocked. He felt no pain, only disappointment. His legs followed, then his horns. As he looked up, he saw the Demon Lord's burning eyes. His own eyes burst into flames, then came the pain.

PART 8

Angel and the High Priest

"If you're Ghib-bore, then the Ark of the Covenant and its treasures must still exist," Harold said.

"That's correct," Jim said.

"And they must be accessible," Harold continued his train of thought.

"Correct again," Jim said.

"And they must be close by," Harold said.

"Closer than you think," Jim said.

"Where is it?" Harold asked.

"You're standing on it," Jim said.

Harold instinctively looked down. He was puzzled.

"They're in the cellar, Pastor. This place was designed by Tobias Menasseh Israel to house the Ark and its treasures in the cellar," Jim explained.

"Can I see them?" Harold asked.

Jim turned to Richard and Sam and asked, "Did you bring your key pieces?"

They nodded. In the matter of minutes, Sam opened the door to the stairway leading down to the cellar. Richard switched on the lights in the corridor, and the four of them walked up to a hidden door in the stonewall foundation. Jim took the three key pieces and combine them into one.

One of the church guards observing the activity in the cellar flew to Angel's location and said, "Colonel, something's happening at the church. You need to get there right away."

It took less than fifteen seconds. Angel and Blue stood next to the four in the cellar and watched a mystery unfold before their eyes.

Angel dismissed his guard. He noticed the writings carved into the stone above what now appeared to be a door. He asked Blue, "Is this Kabbalah Qadosh?"

Blue answered, "It is. It states that no one can enter, except the archangel Gabriel allows it."

"Gabriel! This must be what the world has been looking for. In my little church? How do we know if this is allowed?" Angel asked.

"I don't see how we could have gotten this far if it wasn't allowed," Blue said.

"What should we do?" Angel asked.

"What you've been doing for the last 350 years, guard," Blue said.

The Ghib-bore and the pastor pushed on one side of the stone door. It pivoted open with surprising ease. Jim grabbed a lighter he took from the kitchen and lit torches along the wall of the room.

"Just as I remembered it," Jim said. "We haven't been down here in at least ten years."

Harold looked around, amazed. He was reminded of passages in scripture instructing Moses to build the tabernacle. The candle stands, tables, tools, knives, tongs, pokers, pots all clad in gold or made of brass or solid gold. And he finally saw the Ark. It seemed to emit its own light. Leaning against the Ark were scrolls and rolls of papyrus. Harold thought it would take a lifetime to document every-thing in this massive cellar chamber.

Harold looked for a place to sit. As he did, his arm brushed a table that seemed ordinary by comparison. A cloth covered what was on it. He looked at Jim and gestured if he could remove the covering. Jim smiled and nodded. Harold's hands began to shake. Removing the cloth, he saw a number of artifacts. A chalice, three heavy spikes, a shroud, a pair of sandals.

"Oh, my sweet Lord." Harold whispered. "Is this…" Harold reverently touched an iron spike. "How?"

Jim explained, "As near as we can tell, High Priest Caiaphas confiscated these items, either to deny their existence or to avoid them becoming sacred items of worship for Christ followers. He had a lot of power before the Romans decided to sack Jerusalem. We don't know what he had planned to do with these Christian artifacts, but we Ghib-bore believe God also has a purpose for them."

"What a tremendous feat, packaging, transporting, preserving all of this. And keeping it secret, safe, and secure. It boggles the mind. Was all of this kept intact, or did it have to be broken down?" Harold was way overstimulated. He couldn't stop his flow of questions.

"It's all been preserved as it was, in its original state. I always wondered how they managed concealing the cross." Jim shook his head in wonderment.

"Did you say cross? As in the 'Old Rugged Cross'?" Harold asked.

"It's more like the old petrified gopher wood cross, but yes," Jim answered.

"Where is it?" Harold almost jumped out of his skin. "Can I see it?"

Sam finally spoke, "Pastor, you've probably seen it every day since you joined us here. It's hanging on the front wall of the church."

Harold was speechless. Angel and Blue moved two floors up and stood before the cross. They were humbled and amazed.

Angel said, "Gopher wood, the cross, and Noah's ark."

Blue added, "Both meant to save God's people from judgment."

Angel said, "Our God is an awesome God."

"So what do we do now?" Harold asked Jim.

"We do what we've always done. We serve the Father, we follow the leading of the Holy Spirit, and we give Jesus lordship of our lives," Jim said.

"And when we are told to return the Ark and its treasures to the temple, we'll do it," Richard said.

"I guess you're right. Nothing changes. I'm still the pastor of this amazing church. I'm still vice president of America. I'm still husband and father to Annie and my boys?" Harold asked.

"And we are still the church elders and Ghib-bore," Sam said.

"Now that you know who the Jewish high priest is and that he is in Johannesburg, are you going to tell him?" Harold asked.

"Knowledge is dangerous. I think we are going to leave that up to the Lord," Jim said. And then he smiled and said, "We're listening."

*****

The six remaining demon leaders of the world sat in the chamber meeting room. They had been notified to assemble and wait for further instructions. They all knew that something terrible had happened. A demonic vacuum was felt around the world. North America was toxic. Word had reached their kingdoms that Rommel had been taken captive and that the Ambassador hadn't been seen after he was called to meet with the Demon Lord.

At this point, no one wanted to draw attention to themselves. It was time to be still and obey. After hours of silence, a low rumble vibrated throughout the chamber. Then the darkness came. Thummim and Urim appeared to the left and right of the Ambassador's chair. They were terrifying creatures. They had gigantic humanoid onyx bodies and jackal heads. They both held scepters in their right hands. Hanging from ribbon belts were flails. The spiked orbs almost touched the ground and were stained with a slimy green ooze.

Jinn Sing wondered to himself if that shade of green matched the Ambassador's coloring.

But even more terrifying than their physical appearance was their stare. It was lifeless yet penetrated through to one's soul. Nothing could be hidden from them. They were the embodiment to evil and death.

When they spoke, whether separately or in unison, they spoke with one voice. This day they spoke in unison.

"The Ambassador is no more. You will receive your orders directly from us. Your orders are as follows: consider North America lost, for now. You must contain its influence by protecting your own territories. Preach worldwide peace and security. Every effort must be made to unite the world against Israel. Jinn Sing, prepare three hundred million soldiers. Amon, build your nuclear arsenal. Gog, prepare your ground forces to attack with tanks and artillery. Vapus, a son will be born in your major city, protect him. Finally, there must not be a temple in Jerusalem. The Dome on the Rock must remain. There will be no questions. Failure is not an option. Now, go."

The Anubis were gone. The leaders were stunned. There were so many questions in everyone's mind.

Jinn Sing said, "It just got really real."

"Clearly, we need to work together," Gog said.

"What do you propose?" Jinn Sing asked.

"First, we need to move the UN out of New York," Gog said.

"We already control the EU. Why not move all activity to Brussels?" Vapus offered.

Gog looked around the room. "Fine, Brussels it is."

"I'm closest to Jerusalem. I'll need help securing the Dome," Amon said.

"Let's build up the guard there." Gog suggested. "Say one hundred thousand from each of us?"

Everyone agreed.

"What about the temple dig?" Amon asked.

"As far as I'm concerned, let the desert dogs play in their holes." Vapus laughed.

Gog said, "Done."

"Does anyone have any idea regarding the 'son' the Anubis spoke of?" Vapus asked.

They all looked at each other. No one knew the answer.

Jinn Sing said, "They said, 'will be born.' It makes no sense worrying about it now. I assume they'll let us know when the time is appropriate."

They all agreed.

Diablo spoke for the first time, "What about the pastor?"

No one had an answer for that question either.

Vapus finally responded, "Well, clearly he's an agent of the Realm. Let's just keep our distance and hope he keeps his."

They all responded, "Agreed."

*****

Chip looked down at his notes. "We've got two hot issues," he said. "The first is new pressure from the Russian-Turkish block to move the UN Headquarters to Brussels."

"Again? We give over fifteen billion dollars to the UN every year. We carry over 25 percent of the overall cost to run the place, and they continue to pressure us to move the headquarters to Europe. Is it urgent?" Joe asked.

"Not sure, but we should at least prepare a response, just in case you get cornered," Chip advised.

"Do we have a report on the political consequence and a cost analysis for such a move?" Joe asked.

"They've got something on it now. The ambassador said she'd look it over and bring it to the next staff meeting," Chip said.

"Good." Joe knew the ambassador was a capable person and that he could rely on a comprehensive report from her. "What's next?"

"In Jerusalem, there are protestors at the Temple Mount, again. They are claiming Israel is planning to destroy the Dome on the Rock. They are demanding international intervention," Chip continued.

"Again? Jerusalem is the capital of Israel. It's on sovereign Israeli soil, it's not international territory. I thought Pastor handled this last time he was there," Joe said. He dropped his pen, got up from his desk, and moved to the window. "Pastor, do you think you can talk sense into these people?"

Harold was sitting quietly in his chair across from Chip. "I'm certainly willing to try. But I don't think sense has much to do with it. There are evil spiritual forces wanting to destroy any possibility of peace in Jerusalem. The Bible tell us to pray for peace in Jerusalem, for a reason."

"Doesn't Jerusalem mean 'city of peace' in Hebrew?" Joe asked.

"Yes, and when the Prince of Peace returns, this name will make complete sense," Harold said.

"Well, until then, we'll do the next best thing. We'll send you," Joe decided. "You'll have the secret service with you, but please be safe."

"Safe and secure. The complete verse is "Pray for the peace of Jerusalem: May those who love you be secure,'" Harold concluded.

"When can you go?" Chip asked.

"Let's see." Harold looked at the calendar on his phone. "I'd like to go after the weekend. How's Monday?" Harold asked.

"Monday's good. It will give us a couple of days to prepare an itinerary," Chip said.

"Before we go, I'd like to remind us of one thing," Harold said. "God promises that if we love Him and live according to His purpose, all things will work together to bring about good."

"How do we know we're doing His purpose?" Chip asked.

"Love God, love your neighbor. Simply walk every day serving God. And maintain clean hands and a pure heart," Harold answered.

"What's simple for some people isn't simple for other people," Chip thought out loud.

"We are not alone. Jesus shows us the right way in every circumstance and gives us the strength to do it," Harold encouraged.

*****

It was a hectic weekend for Harold. Catching up with Annie, the boys, Annie's parents, and the elders was exhausting. The morning's service flew by. Annie's mom prepared a wonderful afternoon meal of brisket, rolls, potatoes, carrots, and onions. Harold loved it. He joked that his mother-in-law was the best Southern cook ever, Southern Bronx.

After the boys went to bed and the in-laws turned in, Harold and Annie retired to their couch. Harold began to feel uneasy. He thought he should check out the church before turning in for the night.

He turned to Annie said, "If it's all right with you, I'd like to check on the church before we go to bed."

"Sure. Is there a problem?" Annie asked.

"No, I just have an inkling. I'll meet you upstairs in a few minutes. Okay?" Harold said.

She rubbed his arm and said, "Don't dawdle."

Harold loved his church. He sat in the front pew, seat one, row one. Knowing what was stored in the cellar below and looking up at what was hanging on the front wall, he thought, *This is the most wonderful place on earth.*

He looked at the cross differently now. A two-thousand-year-old truth had just propelled itself into the present. And he had been placed in the middle of the most unique time in history.

"It is." A voice came from behind him.

He wasn't startled. He almost expected it. He didn't even turn around.

"It's hard to believe that our Lord hung on that cross. I could actually see where the spikes were driven into it. I could see the dark stains in the wood. I've been drawn to this cross from the first moment I saw it. Now I know why," Harold said.

"It was a grievous day in infamy leading to a morning of glory. A tragic moment of defeat assuring eternal victory. The sacrificial lamb crowned with thorns transformed to the King of kings crowned with glory. Sin incarnate hanging on a cursed tree, becoming the Savior seated on His throne of righteousness. All right here in front of me." Harold held out his hands, palms turned up to heaven.

"There are more amazing things ahead," Melchizedek said.

"Good things or bad things?" Harold asked. He still hadn't turned around.

"God things. Wait in Jerusalem." The voice seemed to be fading. Melchizedek was walking out of the church.

"Are we related?" Harold asked. He had no idea why he asked that particular question. It wasn't even on the list of questions he wanted to ask.

"Yes, my son. In more ways than you know." And then, Melchizedek was gone.

*****

Using their own reporters and field agents, Gog and Vapus had successfully stirred up enough false news to make the security of the Dome of the Rock an international issue. Muslims from all over the world started protesting against Israel's totalitarian elitism and international disregard for other nationalities, races, and religions. They were pushing the narrative that the Israelis planned to destroy the Dome in order to build their own temple. The Dome is the oldest Muslim edifice, built in the seventh century. The protestor demanded that it should be declared an international treasure and in so doing be protected by UN forces.

Vapus had hoped that the pastor would stay in America. His presence always spelled trouble. But Vapus's informants reported that the pastor was planning a trip to Jerusalem.

The Anubis did not declare a "hands-off" policy concerning the pastor. Vapus wondered if this would be the perfect opportunity to eliminate the pastor. Air Force Two would fly northeast out of DC over the Atlantic, then over France, Italy, Greece, and into Jerusalem. The flight would be most vulnerable over the Alps.

There were many ways to bring down a plane if one put one's mind to it. In this case, however, Air Force Two was mostly immune. A planted bomb would be easily detected. Ground-to-air missile required knowing the exact time and location of the plane. Storms could be flown over or around. The only way to bring down Air Force Two was to attack the pilot and copilot mid-flight.

The pastor would have a guardian escort, but the pilots wouldn't. Air Force Two was capable of landing itself if need be, but not if the controls were damaged from inside the cockpit. Vapus decided it was worth a try. He would supervise the attack himself. With his special ability, he could get to the pilots before the pastor's guards knew what was happening. If his attack was met with resistance, Vapus could implement brute force. His demons could occupy the pastor's guard until the plane crashed into the Alps.

Harold was on Air Force Two. He was making a list of things he needed to do right away. Contact David and get him caught up. Tell David as much as possible and see if he knew anything about Melchizedek that wasn't found in the Bible. Call Hakim and enlist his help to speak to the head of the Muslims organizing the protesters. Call Sarah at i24 news and find out the best way to speak directly to the people of Jerusalem. Reinforce the idea that there is a world-wide need for peace in Jerusalem.

*****

Angel and a squad of twenty of his finest warriors were escorting Air Force Two to Jerusalem. Angel had a list of his own. A troop of warriors was at Ben Gurion International. They were keeping watch and keeping it secure. Another troop scouted the land along the flight path. They were looking for the possibility of any threat from land. A third troop scanned the atmosphere for any unnatural weather conditions, hostile aircraft, or incoming missiles. Angel had already checked for explosive devices on board the plane. All was secure.

As they approached the Alps, the rear guard spotted a group of demons following them. At the same time, Angel also saw two groups of demons, one starboard and one portside.

Colonel Angel shouted, "Warriors, ready!"

He put out a "Mayday" for reinforcements.

So this is their play? he thought. *Crash the plane? Not on my watch. Lord, help me.*

He ordered his warriors to engage the enemy. Five in each of the three directions. He would stay with the pastor. He sent two of his warriors to guard the pilot and copilot and three to keep watch over the diplomats and aides in the cabin. He drew his swords and prepared for battle.

Vapus had already entered the cockpit. In his stealth mode, he was undetectable. But in this state, he had no ability to affect the material or spiritual world. As soon as he saw the two warriors enter the cockpit, he materialized.

Five of Angel's warrior fought like fifty. The rear guard had detained their attackers. At over 400 mph, the plane shot away from their location. They were removed from the battle as a threat. The troops to both sides of the plane, however, needed assistance. A dozen demons were already terminated but not without taking three warrior angels with them. Angel ordered the guards in the cabin to replace the losses outside. He would protect the cabin alone.

Vapus struck first. He dealt one ending blow into the first angel and slashed at the second. The second angel was clearly outmatched but fought bravely. He got in a damaging thrust. He wounded Vapus's right wing, but in so doing, left his own chest exposed. Vapus ran him through. The second angel burst into a brilliant light and was gone. Vapus turned on the pilot who was oblivious to the battle. Vapus didn't have permission to kill the man directly, so he temporarily stopped his heart. The pilot slumped in his seat. The copilot look up and grabbed for his friend. Vapus dropped a logbook on the copilot's head which was stowed on a shelf above him. The copilot was knocked unconscious. He then pushed the controls forward, initiating descent.

His plan had gone so well that Vapus considered going into the cabin and finishing off the pastor personally. But seeing that the plane was headed for the Alps below. And taking into account his wounded wing, he decided to call an orderly retreat.

Vapus had forgotten he was no longer in stealth mode. As he slowly lifted himself out of the plane with one wing, he was lassoed around his legs and yanked back in.

"What do you think you are doing?" Vapus asked. "I am Vapus, King of the West. Untie me."

Vapus tried to transform himself into stealth mode, but the golden rope wrapped around his legs had a power and mind of its own. It resisted Vapus's effort to change and held him firm.

"My name is Angel. And I've got the other end of this rope." Angel pointed his sword toward Vapus and pulled on the rope with all his strength. Vapus accelerated toward Angel and his sword. Vapus was impaled through the heart and burst into flames.

Angel heard them before he saw them. The reinforcements had arrived. The remaining demons were killed or scattered.

"Get under the plane's wings and lift," Angel shouted.

Ten warriors dashed under each wing and leveled the plane's descent.

"Get us to Ben Gurion," Angel said.

Angel then did some damage control. He set the plane's controls on automatic and revived the pilots. They would have to try and figure out how they both lost consciousness at the same time. Angel left them to their thoughts and went to check on the pastor and the other passengers.

For the next few minutes, he monitored their conversation. They were unsuspecting of any demon attack or angel-demon battle, but they had felt the plane's descent. They had all stopped what they were doing and looked out the windows. The only thing they saw through the clouds were the Alps. The Alps were very jagged and covered with ice and snow. They were beautiful but intimidating. Trusting the flight crew, they settled down and went back to their business.

When Angel returned to the cabin, the pastor was still looking out his window. Angel smiled at him in relief. The pastor slowly turned from the window and looked into the cabin. The pastor spotted a golden figure standing the sunlight coming through the window. The figure was holding a sword in a non-threatening way but was frightfully mighty. The pastor looked Angel right in the eye. Angel froze. In all of his years, he had never been seen by someone he was guarding. The pastor lowered his head and whispered, "Thank you, Lord."

Angel responded to the pastor's prayer in the only way he could, "Amen."

*****

Rabbi David could hardly wait to see his friend. This time they were meeting at the American Colonial Hotel. David wasn't surprised when he saw the guards and security agents, but he was impressed when he was escorted to the executive suite. Harold told David he had a matter of importance to discuss with him. David couldn't imagine what it was.

"Good afternoon, Mr. Vice President." David intentionally emphasized Harold's title.

Harold responded, "And a good afternoon to you, Your Dr. Rabbi-ship."

They both laughed.

"Kidding aside, Pastor, how are you doing?" David asked.

"Dazed and confused, I thought being a congressman was a busy job. But being vice president is just nuts," Harold said.

"Well then, they've got the right guy. Raising people from the dead on national TV. I'm certain that didn't help calm things down."

David couldn't help but bring up Harold's latest controversial incident.

"David, you more than anyone know that wasn't me, but God," Harold corrected.

"Harold, one thing I do know. Sarah was dead and now she's alive. And she has quite a story to tell," David said. "A desert, a voice, a message, what's going on? What was the message?"

"I wish I could tell you, but I can't. I could tell you that your work is important and not to give up. Besides sharing a meal with you, I wanted to pick your brain." Harold waited for permission to proceed.

"Slim pickings, but go ahead," David said.

At that moment, they were interrupted by Harold's PA with a well-planned-out luncheon service. Harold chose the menu. It was hot dogs, hamburger, fries, and cheese pizza with Coke. For dessert, Hostess Cup Cakes, Twinkies, and Starbuck's coffee.

"Wow," David said, "fancy-schmancy."

"Just for you, my friend. Nothing but the best. Let's dig in." Harold gibed.

An hour later, over coffee, Harold asked. "Okay, I was hoping you could you tell me all you know about Melchizedek. I don't mean what we can read about him in scripture, but anything else."

"You don't ask easy questions, do you? We've not found any other information about him in written history. But there have been multiple stories about him appearing to help and guide the faithful. After all is said and done, he is a mystery. What we do know is that his name means 'God is my Righteousness.' He was the King of Salem before there was a Jerusalem. He was the High Priest of God before there was Moses or the Ark or a temple for that matter. Abraham paid him homage and a tithe. We don't know his lineage or if he had progeny. There are three theories bandied about.

"Theory number one, he was a theophany. God appearing as a man, with no father, no mother, no account of his birth, no account of his death. Like the person who wrestled with Jacob. Jacob later says, 'I have seen God.'

"Theory number two, he is an angel. Throughout scriptures, angels are constantly doing God's work and ministering to man, like Gabriel and Michael.

"Theory number three, he is a man who never died. Like Enoch and Elijah who went to heaven without dying, except Melchizedek didn't go to heaven. He is staying on earth to serve God."

"Interesting, which do you think is most likely?" Harold asked.

"I don't believe he is God. Scripture tends to identify those instances. As in the Garden of Eden, as in the visitor to Abraham, as in the wrestler with Jacob, as in the burning bush, or as in a column of smoke and fire. So I eliminate theory one, right off the bat.

"Theory two, angels are cited 108 times in your Old Testament and an additional 177 times in your New Testament. We only know two by name, Michael and Gabriel. I believe, if Melchizedek were an angel, he would have said so. Also, Abraham paid homage to Melchizedek. On earth, it's proper to pay homage to a superior, like a king or ruler or one's parents. But is would never be acceptable to pay homage to an angel. That would be blasphemy. For these reasons, I don't believe theory number two fits.

"The last theory, as unlikely as it seems, is the most logical. He is a man who was born but hasn't died. Quite possibly, he could be traveling earth doing God's bidding now.

"Please, tell me. Why the sudden concern over this ancient character?" David asked.

"I will tell you as much as I could. But you must be sworn to secrecy. Do I have your word?" Harold asked.

"Only if your life or the life of another is not in danger. You have my word," David said.

Harold considered David's exception and nodded in agreement. He looked David in the eye and said, "Melchizedek has appeared to me more than once."

*****

The five remaining rulers were called to the Demon Lord's chamber. The question on everyone's mind was "Would any of them be leaving?" This time, the shadow on the throne appeared to be a vicious dragon. The dragon was constantly shifting shape. Its color was nondescript, like smoke taking on the color of what it enveloped. The dragon had ten horns, a muzzle full of needle-sharp teeth, fire and smoke coming from its nostrils, flaming red eyes, and two large wings. Its two forelegs ended in long black eagle-like talons. In each of its claws was an entrapped demon. The dragon's talons pierced the demons through. The demons were writhing in pain and appeared to be screaming, but no sound could be heard. The entire scene was terrifying. No one spoke. No one moved. Everyone waited.

Thummim spoke first, "Vapus was a fool. His demise was well deserved. He was told to leave the pastor be, but he disobeyed. Does anyone else have a plan we are not aware of?"

After a long pause, Urim spoke, "Then let's move on to the business at hand. Manitou will rule North America. His orders are to retake what was lost in that district."

Thummim then spoke, "Ghidorah will take Vapus's place. She will control the West. She asked to have a word with the rulers at this time."

A hydra entered the chamber. A three-headed serpent resembling a dragon slithered into the empty seat next to the Demon Lord. She was green with iridescent blue scales. She looked like she came right out of a cursed sea. She had intelligent eyes, and she matched everyone's stare. The hydra's tongues continuously jetted out of her mouths, tasting the air and everyone in the room. It was very intimidating and made the rulers uneasy.

Each of her heads spoke, one at a time,

"Come into my district, you will die."

"Challenge my authority, you will die."

"Get in my way, you will die."

Thummim and Urim spoke in unison, "Ghidorah will be a surrogate mother to my son. She will have the solely responsible for his growth and safety. On all matters concerning my son, you will obey her without hesitation or die."

The two Anubis scanned the room. Everyone was nodding in acceptance.

"Gog," they continued, "are you prepared to take the current protest at the Dome to the next level?"

"Yes, Your Majesty," Gog responded.

"Ghidorah will assist you. I expect to see Jerusalem in flames," the Anubis said.

"Yes, Your Majesty," Gog assured the Demon Lord.

This was the first Gog heard of setting Jerusalem on fire. Were the flames the Anubis mentioned meant to be figurative or literal? He'd have to listen more closely next time. Gog decided Jerusalem's fate would be in his hands alone. He would control Jerusalem, not burn it down. And he would never, regardless of Ghidorah's favored position with the Demon Lord, take orders from anyone regarding Jerusalem, especially her. He had fought for Jerusalem for too many centuries to relinquish control of it now.

*****

"He appeared to me twice," Harold told David. "The first time, he gave me my boys' names. He said names were important. The second time, he told me to come to Jerusalem and wait for a 'God thing' to happen."

"What kind of 'God thing'?" David asked.

"I don't know." Harold thought for a moment and said, "So I intend to continue with my assignment as vice president and wait to see what happens. One thing I've learned through all of this is that when God wants me to do something special, He is fully capable of letting me know."

"What can I do to help you, my friend?" David's offer was genuine and sincere.

Harold looked at David and said, "Wait with me."

David and Harold finished lunch. They made plans to get together the next morning at the Temple Mount. After David left, Harold pulled up the list he made on his flight. He looked at item number one, "Meet with David."

"Check," Harold said to himself. "Next, item number two 'Call Hakim.'"

Harold found Hakim's number in his contacts and texted him. "I'm in Jerusalem. Can we talk?"

*****

"Your Majesty, I thought you should know that the pastor is planning to be at the Temple Mount tomorrow morning." Crusher was a mid-level demon who was stationed in Jerusalem to keep Gog apprised of any new developments. He had just flown into Brussels from Jerusalem to report to Gog personally.

"Do not engage him. Observe only. Let me know of anyone he comes in contact with. Try and identify who his main guards are and how many are assigned to him," Gog said. "And do not lose track of him. Take any additional troops you may need."

"Yes, sire." Crusher bowed low and headed back to Jerusalem with additional help.

*****

"What's the plan?" Blue asked Angel.

"I'm not sure. I don't think the enemy will stage a second attack so soon. But the pastor is planning to go to the Temple Mount tomorrow. It is rife with demons and danger. I will be on guard. I'd like you to stay hidden. The enemy still hasn't identified you. We may still be able to use it to our advantage," Angel said.

"Look at you, so strategic and everything," Blue teased.

"You're rubbing off on me," Angel said, only half kidding.

PART 9

Angel and the Abdel-Massih

"Hakim, how are you, my friend?" Harold asked.

"Not as good as you, Mr. Vice President," Hakim said.

Hakim responded to Harold's text as soon as he received it. He was asked to join Harold as soon as possible.

"Bigger title, double the responsibility," Harold quipped.

"Speaking of titles, you are now known as Abdel-Massih," Hakim said.

"Do I want to know what that means?" Harold was both concerned and skeptical.

"Oh, yes. It means Servant of Christ. You are definitely held in high esteem. You are a holy man," Hakim clarified.

"That is an honor I will truly embrace, thank you."

Harold was taken aback. To be known for one's faithfulness to the Lord and by unbelievers was humbling.

"Then maybe my request will be honored."

"What is it, Pastor?" Hakim asked.

"I would like you to set up a meeting with me and the leader of the protest." Harold prayed this request would be properly received.

"Oh, Pastor, that would be difficult. There are many leaders, but there is no one leader," Hakim explained. "In Jerusalem, protest just happen. The more momentum the protest gains, the more people get involved. And right now, there is a lot of momentum."

"Surely someone is in charge or more in charge than the others," Harold tried to reason.

"Oh, you see, there are political leaders, social leaders, religious leaders, local leaders, foreign leaders. It's organized chaos." Hakim was trying his best to explain the situation.

"Hakim, I get it. Do you think I can meet with all of them?" Harold wondered.

Hakim thought of a moment.

"Yes. I was just thinking. If I get one person to agree to a meeting with the vice president of the United States, no one will want to be left out. It might work. Allah willing," Hakim thought out loud.

"Good, do your best. Let's set up the meeting here at the hotel. It's far enough away from the Temple Mount. It's a neutral location, and they have a beautiful outdoor garden and seating area. We can relax and discuss the situation in peace. Say, Wednesday morning. Okay?" Harold thought this would be the best place all around.

"I'll try Abdel-Massih. I'll call you tomorrow. Allah, bless you." Hakim got up to leave.

"And may our heavenly Father bless you too, my friend," Harold said.

*****

Gog stationed demons at the Temple Mount. He sent guards to surround the Dome of the Rock and the Al Aqsa Mosque. He spread an army of agitators in the Old City. They perpetuated thoughts of violence and hostel conversations among the people. His demons propagated an anti-Israeli conspiracy theory that the Jews were planning to destroy the two Muslim holy sites and the Church of the Holy Sepulcher. And then they would restrict access to the city entirely.

So as not to raise the ire of the Demon Lord, Gog asked Ghidorah to incite as much crime in the main city itself, placing a strain on the Israeli police force.

On a rare occasion, Gog would disguise himself and walk the streets of man seeking death and destruction. He decided to walk the Temple Mount to find out for himself if any of the enemy was anywhere present. There wasn't an angel in sight.

He instructed his captains to take control of the Mount. "If one angel enters, attack him with ten demons. If ten angels enter, chase them away with one hundred. This is our time. We will not fail," he ordered.

Gog wasn't the only one in disguise that day. Blue followed Gog as he toured the Old City. She heard him growl orders to his captains. This "mass murderer of Jews" was planning to bathe the city in blood, Jewish blood. His arrogance and wickedness appalled her. She would do everything in her power to stop him. She could easily cut Gog down now but waited for Angel to call the play.

Gog got word that the pastor from America, Mr. Vice President, had called a meeting with the Muslim leaders in the city to discuss the current situation. He had to decide how to handle it. He could send his demons to disrupt the meeting. He could send spies to listen to the enemy's plan. He could go himself in his disguised form and see this pastor for himself. "Know thy enemy and know yourself. In a hundred battles, you will never be defeated." In the end, he decided to take matters into his own hands and attend the meeting, in disguise and in person.

*****

Harold's last item was to contact Sarah Kauffman to find out if he could get access the people of Jerusalem through a live TV broadcast.

"I'm sure we can get an interview approved with the station," Sarah said. "How do you want me to present your request?"

"Good question, I'd like to speak to the people of Jerusalem not as vice president or as a pastor but as a one person to another," Harold answered. "And, Sarah, I want you to do the interview."

"That sound serious, Pastor," Sarah said. "But you know I haven't been on the air since I was shot."

"I know, Sarah, but this is important. I have a message to convey to the people that can't wait," Harold urged. "I would like us to do this at noon on Wednesday."

"Consider it done," Sarah said.

*****

Early the next morning, Harold went to the Old City to meet David. He tried to look as inconspicuous as possible. His secret service agents gave him as much space as safety would allow. David was waiting for Harold at a small outdoor café. The agents sat at the other end of the open space. David and Harold ordered a pot of tea and toast for themselves. A few minutes later, the server brought yogurt, figs, dates, fried dough, biscuits, toast, dipping sauces, butter, jams, honey, nuts, olives, and two pots of tea.

The server looked at the pastor and smiled. He said, "It's on the house," and walked away.

Harold was stunned. By the time he thought to say "thank you," the server had gone. He gestured to his secret service guards for them to come and make a plate for themselves. They did.

Harold's intent to walk the Old City with David to get a feel for the city. He was also hoping to find some inspiration before he spoke to the people publicly. The protestors hadn't showed up yet. It appeared to be a quite morning with a "business as usual" vibe. He relaxed a while and enjoyed his breakfast. Then he and David began their walk.

Harold felt uneasy when they approached the Temple Mount. There was a malaise in the air. A palpable evil that beset him. He would have fell to his knees if David weren't with him. Instead, he found a place to sit and asked David if he could have a private moment. David obliged and indicated he wanted to take some measurements between the various structures in the courtyard. David pulled out a laser ruler and began to record distances.

Harold began to pray. He prayed thanksgiving for a safe trip so far. He prayed for Annie and the boys in his absence. He prayed for successful meetings with the Muslim leaders and Sarah Kaufman.

He prayed God would build a hedge of protection around the entire Temple Mount. He prayed that God would send His angels to encircle and protect the people and the buildings there in the same way He did for Elisha at Dothan.

Angel was standing next to the pastor. He heard bits and pieces of the pastor's prayer. He had kept his attention on dozens of demons moving throughout the Mount. He knew trouble was brewing. He just didn't know when things would erupt. He didn't want to be or couldn't be the one to start an encounter.

As the pastor prayed, a full army of angels descended upon the area. Horses, chariots, archers, spearmen, all shielded and armored. Angel recognized a few of the angel warriors from his time spent in the throne room of the Lord. He nodded at a line captain who saluted him in return. Angel reasoned that this army had been sent by the Almighty in response to the pastor's prayer.

When Harold had finished his prayer, he began to feel a positive energy in the air, like static electricity right before lightning strikes. He looked over at his security guards. They were unaware and unsuspecting of anything that had just transpired. The hair on his arms stood up. He got goose bumps all over his body.

"This is the city the Lord gave me to watch over, many years ago," a man said who was seated behind him.

Harold didn't need to turn around to know who that voice belonged to.

"And me?" Harold asked Melchizedek.

"And you. I've got a message for you. He would like you to deliver it to His city," Melchizedek said.

"What's the message?" Harold asked. His mind was spinning. This was the most unbelievable conversation he ever had.

"Prayer is more important than power," his mentor said.

Harold repeated the message to himself, "Prayer is more important than power." Harold took a minute and asked, "Are we talking about a 2 Chronicles 7:14 prayer or some other type of prayer?"

There was no answer. Harold wondered if he asked his question loud enough. So he slowly turned around to ask it again. There was no one there. Melchizedek was gone.

*****

By the time Harold got back to the hotel, Hakim had already brought a number of Muslim leaders to the outdoor "Hospitality Garden" at the hotel. Chairs had been set up in groups of four and placed around the garden. In all, there were twenty-four men, including Hakim and one disguised demon.

Angel already spotted Gog. He kept his eye on Gog. Angel was trying to discern what Gog had in mind. Angel was known for his hair trigger. Now was no exception. Blue was in disguise and lingered in the shadows of the garden. She, too, was poised to strike.

The pastor greeted his guests. Tea was served. The mood was congenial but cautious. The Muslim leaders did not know what to expect from this miracle-working preacher known as Abdel-Massih, but they all wanted to see him with their own eyes. It was a clear, sunny afternoon, the outdoor garden was bright but shaded by the various tree and plants located around the garden. There was a fountain in the center of the garden that lent a cooling mist to the mild breeze passing through the place.

Harold approached the podium that was positioned in front of a number of beautiful shade trees.

"Gentlemen, today, I wanted to speak to as many esteemed Muslim leaders as possible. I am asking you and the protestors you influence to stand down. I am aware of the rumors circulating that there are plans by the Israelis to remove the holy Muslim buildings from the Haram al-Sharif. This is just not true, and I give you my word that the US would not support such aggression.

"I did not come to this beautiful city to discuss who rightly belongs where or how all this..." Harold gestured around the area, "how all this came to be. You know the history of this city as well as I, possibly better. I did come, however, to ask you all to allow the spirit of peace to prevail. We all have a choice. We can choose to obey the Almighty's command to be still and experience his presence and peace. Or we can stiffen our necks against His command, bringing hostility and disorder and experience His judgment.

"Ultimately, everything belongs to God. He owns the cattle on a thousand hills. He holds the waters of the earth in the hollow of His hand. He is the sustainer of every living soul, yours, mine. We are all in his hands, and the breath of every human being is determined by His mercy and grace.

"If what I am saying is not true, then let every man on earth be a liar."

Harold looked around the room. He tried to read his audience. As far as he could tell, his words were being received well.

Gog started to move over to a group of imams to speak to them and influence their thoughts. But he was stopped in his tracks by a powerful force he could not explain or resist. It was as if a mountain had just landed on him. He was held in place. He could not speak, he could not move. Angel saw Gog's initial movement, and then for no apparent reason, he abruptly stopped. He had an excruciating paralyzed expression on his face. Angel looked over to Blue to see if she had done something to Gog. She had not. In fact, Blue was looking at Angel for some sort of explanation. Gog had no choice but to submit to the force that held him down.

Harold felt an urge to pray. He closed his eyes and bowed his head and said, "Lord, may you bless all of us here. For you've said, 'Blessed are the peacemakers for they shall be called the children of God.' May you guide us all to bare the fruit of your Spirit, love, joy, and peace. Amen."

The Muslims could not find fault in what Abdel-Massih said or prayed. As they looked up at the Abdel-Massih, they saw an amazing thing happen. The fig trees around the pastor began to sprout blossoms and grow fruit. The palm date trees followed suit. Within two minutes, the garden trees were filled with fruit. Then the flowering plants blossomed, and a shimmering light filled the garden. A rainbow of color shone through the fountain mist.

The men there had a difficult time processing what was happening. Some of them got up and touched what their minds could not process and eyes could not believe. A few braver souls picked the fruit and tasted it for themselves.

Hakim just stared. He shook his head in wonder. He sat down and soaked it all in. He thought, *This is the most amazing experience of my life.*

Gog realized he had just barely survived the presence of the Restrainer. As soon as he was released, he fled the scene. He found the Temple Mount deserted and surrounded by an overwhelming enemy army. His plans had been foiled on all fronts.

*****

Harold went to his room exhausted. He felt if he didn't lay down immediately, he would pass out. As he was about to change into shorts and a tee shirt when a knock came to the door. He dragged himself to the foyer and asked, "Who is it?"

"Mr. Vice President, it's me, Sarah. Could you tell your security we have a noon appointment?" Sarah asked through the door.

Harold opened the door to his suite and saw Sarah, a camera crew, her assistants, makeup artists, lighting people, sound engineers. Basically, the entire i24 News team and then some. His security guards were overwhelmed by their sudden appearance.

"Yes, yes, of course." Harold signaled his guards to let them in.

This time, Angel brushed by each person looking them in the eyes, checking for any weapons or evil intent. He found none. *Fool me once...* Angel thought.

"Pastor, can we set up in the drawing room opposite the picture window? The lighting would be perfect in there." Sarah didn't wait for a response. She turned to her crew and motioned to them to set up. "We've got twenty minutes and we air live. Are you okay with that?"

The makeup people didn't wait for a response and guided Vice President Washington to a large armchair opposite the picture window in the drawing room. They draped a sheet around the pastor's body and started to apply their wares. Sarah set up opposite Harold. Three cameramen stationed themselves around the room.

Before Harold could grab hold of the situation, the director was counting down, "Three, two, and," he pointed to Sarah.

Sarah smiled and said to the camera, "Good afternoon, Jerusalem, I'm Sarah Kauffman and we are broadcasting live from the American Colonial Hotel, and it is my distinct honor and pleasure to introduce my friend, Vice President Harold T. Washington." Sarah turned to Harold and addressed him.

"Vice President, welcome, again, to Jerusalem. You asked me to set up an interview with you so that you could speak to the people of Jerusalem directly. So here we are, what would you like to say to the people of Jerusalem?" She took a breath and leaned back in her chair.

Harold took a moment to compose himself and looked straight into the camera. "Thank you, Sarah. Hello, my friends. I'd first like to say, we have made some headway toward halting the protests at the Temple Mount. I've explained to the Muslim leaders that there is no need for immediate concern regarding the safety of the Dome of the Rock and the Al Aqsa Mosque. And I asked them to look into their hearts and take the path to peace for themselves, their people, and the region."

Sarah asked, "And how did they respond?"

"I believe it was received well. Time will tell," Harold answered.

"That sounds positive, Pastor," Sarah observed.

Some of the people in the room were shocked. Sarah just called the vice president of the United States her "pastor." They wondered how he would respond and, beyond that, how would the people of Jerusalem respond.

"It was," Harold continued. "Now, I would like to ask the people of Jerusalem to do something."

"Please, what is it.?" Sarah moved to the edge of her seat and leaned forward.

"I would like to ask the people to pray," Harold said. "Or I should say the Lord Almighty is telling the people of Jerusalem to pray. You see, Sarah, prayer is more important than power. And there isn't a force more powerful in the world than prayer.

"Let me explain, when Solomon and the people of Israel dedicated the original temple to the Lord, the Lord was pleased. He made a promise to them. I believe this conditional promise extends to us today, to you, to me, to all believers.

"God said, 'If My people, which are called by My name, shall humble themselves, and pray, and seek My face, and turn from their wicked ways, then will I hear from heaven, and will forgive their sin, and will heal their land.'

"Now, Sarah, here's my favorite part. The Lord then said, 'Now Mine eyes shall be open, and Mine ears attentive unto the prayer that is made in this place.'"

The camera caught Sarah's expression. She was at the point of tears. Not sad tears, but tears of wonder as Harold spoke.

"He's listening, Sarah. He's listening to His people when they pray. And since we have His ear, let's pray for peace." Harold paused for a moment to collect his thoughts.

Sarah said, "'Prayer is more important than power.' Didn't you also say, 'People are more important than places' and 'Peace is more important than politics'?"

"I believe I did," Harold said.

"This is amazing. You make it all so understandable. Could it all be just that simple, a purpose, a prayer, a promise? You are amazing," Sarah said.

"Whoa, I'm not taking credit for the things the Lord promises. And besides, a friend actually suggests to me what to say." Harold didn't realize he had just opened a can of worms.

"A friend suggested?" Sarah said. "Who's this friend of yours?"

"Well, actually, he's not a friend. More of an acquaintance. He drops in every now and then and advises me." Harold tried to walk his statement back.

"Pastor, please. Who could advise you? Who's this acquaintance of yours? We'd like to meet him." Sarah tried to coax Harold into divulging his mystery advisor.

"Really, I don't know that much about him," Harold explained.

"Surely you know his name, don't you?" Sarah followed up.

Harold stalled a little and silently prayed, "What should I say?"

He heard a clear answer to his prayer, two words, "The truth."

Harold smiled at the voice in his head. Sarah smiled back and waited. Harold continued looking at Sarah. He shifted his weight forward in his overstuffed armchair, as if he were only telling her. All of Jerusalem leaned into to listen for his answer. "He told me his name was Melchizedek."

*****

"All in all, it was a pretty successful trip," Chip said.

"It certainly got a lot of press. Any of it true?" Joe asked.

"That's the thing. All of it, all of it is true," Chip answered. "There's video of Pastor Harold's speech and then the fruit growing and flowers blossoming. It was as if it were some time-lapsed photography thing. The protests have ceased. Only a handful of people are walking around the Temple Mount with signs warning of imminent doom. But there are hundreds of regular people, Muslims and Jews and Christians, holding prayer meeting at the Temple Mount. They are gatherings separately and together to pray," Chip explained.

"What are they praying?" the president asked.

"They're playing for peace in Jerusalem." Chip looked down at his notes.

"And did we find out who this Melchizedek is?" Joe asked.

"No, secret service has no record of anyone meeting with Harold personally, secretly or otherwise. I can tell you this, there was a Melchizedek in the Bible whom Abraham paid a tithe to. That Melchizedek was the King of Salem, aka Jerusalem and a Priest of the Almighty. The Muslims and the Jews and Christians believe he was also a prophet of God who blessed Abraham to become the father of nations," Chip said.

"So Harold has increased his creditability at home and abroad. I don't see how any of this could be seen as a bad thing," Joe said.

"Not unless you're Satan," Chip said.

*****

Things have settled down, somewhat. The church and its property, occupants, and treasures are under close guard, my close guard. The cellar's contents are still secreted away and protected. The Ghibbore are in place and actively performing their duties. The pastor is still going strong. His ministry has doubled, again. He has planted churches in North Korea, Sudan, England, Italy, and of all places, Jerusalem.

He is the most sought-after diplomat and peacemaker in the world. Leaders of countries all over the globe want to spend time with him and ask him for his opinion and advice. There is talk that he will run for president after Joseph Kennedy's second term.

I've been promoted to general along with Blue. Blue and I are the next in line to sit on the Council together. Nothing will ever come between us again.

I believe the enemy is losing his grip on the world. He's going to have to make a major move soon or lose everything. We will be ready.

No one has seen Melchizedek since the Mount. But none of us believe we've seen the last of him.

Rabbi David Levin discovered that the location of the second temple was off by quite a bit. He is still working on new measurements.

This has been the greatest adventure of my life. I know we've got plenty left to accomplish. But in the end, goodness will prevail.

Praise be to the Almighty.

*****

Some nights after his return from Jerusalem, Harold had a dream, or was it a vision? He didn't know. He was taken up into heaven to meet his guardian angel.

"Hello, Pastor, I'm Angel," his guardian said.

"Oh my, do you mean you're an angel or your name is Angel?" the pastor asked.

"Yes." Angel smiled. "I have something to show you."

Harold recognized Angel as the golden angel he saw on the plane. In the blink of an eye, Harold was brought to Jerusalem. He was floating above the Temple Mount. In the distance, a dark cloud began to form. Others were on the Temple Mount, demons of all sorts. As the dark cloud advanced toward the Mount, it became larger until it filled the sky. The demons began to kick and scream. Angels moved into the area to take control. The demons fought for a day and a night. But when the night was over, the demons were gone.

The cloud moved to the Temple Mount. It became a whirlwind and began to descend as it rotated around the Mount. Lightning began to strike from within the cloud. Lightning struck for a day and a night. The Dome of the Rock was obliterated, and the rubble was swept up into the tornadic wind and thrown into the desert. Then, in the same way, the Al Aqsa Mosque was destroyed.

After the one horrendous night, the Temple Mount was scraped clean. The unearthly storm cloud evaporated. Not an errant speck of dust was left on the Mount. Then a cleansing rain began to fall. It rained for a day and a night.

Harold recalled the words he said to Hakim months ago, "If God Almighty wants the Dome down, no power in heaven or on earth can keep it standing."

Harold looked over to Angel and asked, "Is this real, or is it my imagination?"

"It's as you see it," Angel said.

"Is this happening now, or will it happen in the future?" Harold asked.

"Pastor, one day, you are to lead the building of the Temple of the Lord. It will be built in the place Rabbi David Levin tells you to build it. And you will return the Ark of the Covenant and its treasures to its rightful place," Angel said.

"Oh my, how can I accomplish such a thing? This land doesn't belong to me," Harold asked.

"Oh, but it does, Son of Melchizedek," Angel answered.

"What am I supposed to do? I mean, how am I supposed to accomplish such a thing?" Harold was dumbfounded.

"Pray," Angel told the pastor as he was returned to his bed.

"Pray?" Harold asked.

"Yes, Pastor, remember, God is listening."

To be continued...

About the Author

Anthony Scola has been a Christ follower for over fifty years. He and his wife of forty-three years have four children and fifteen grand-children. They have served as marriage counselors and Divorce Care leaders in their local church.

They served in AWANA for over twenty-eight years, bringing devotions to children in amazing and fun ways.

He loves the Word of God, but more importantly, he loves the God of the Word.

Anthony Scola can be reached at "mynameisangel.net".

CPSIA information can be obtained
at www.ICGtesting.com
Printed in the USA
LVHW111723170922
728625LV00017B/153